In Midnight's Shadow

Tales of Isyr

C M Debell

Copyright © 2024 C M Debell

All rights reserved.

No part of this book may be reproduced, or stored in a retrieval system, or transmitted in any form by any means, electronic, mechanical, photocopying, recording, or otherwise, without the express written permission of the publisher.
The characters and events portrayed in this book are fictitious. Any similarity to real persons, living or dead, is coincidental and not intended by the author.

ISBN-13: 9798323148929

Beta read by: Rowena Andrews

Edited by: Sarah Chorn

Proofread by: Isabelle Wagner

Cover by: Mibl Art

Author's note

This is a book of seven short stories that accompanies and hopefully deepens the characters from *The Many Shades of Midnight*. It was written because I finished that book and wasn't ready to let go. It's not a sequel and it's not a prequel, even though several of the stories take place in the fifteen years before the book starts (and if you haven't yet read *The Many Shades of Midnight*, be warned that this does contain major spoilers). Nor is it a collection of discrete, standalone stories. They all fit together to tell a bigger story, and they are meant to be read in the order in which they appear, even if that order might appear a little unconventional. But mostly they're just meant to be read, so I hope you enjoy reading them as much as I enjoyed writing them.

CONTENTS

1
AILUIN'S PEACE
First meetings and an ill-fated treaty.

55
CASSANA
The first time Cassana Gaemo met Alyas Raine-Sera, he was still reeling from the death of his father and she had just buried her husband; and she hated him.

101
SCARS
Why did Alondo send Brivar as the temple's representative to Alyas.

137
THE AUNT
Hailene and her busy spies.

151
THE FIRST TEMPLE
Avarel's temple of Ithol wasn't the only temple Alyas broke into. First, there was Lessing.

205
MIDNIGHT IN FLAERES
Rumours of monsters plague the northern borders of Flaeres.

241
THE LAST TIME
The last time Cassana Gaemo saw Alyas-Raine Sera.

255
CHARACTERS & GLOSSARY

AILUIN'S PEACE

ESAR

The Lathai came at dawn. There were six of them, appearing from the mist like wraiths, their painted bodies melting into the grey light, spears held loosely by their sides.

Their appearance sent a ripple of unease through the waiting Lankarans. They knew the stories. Every soldier in Lankara's army had heard tales of the Lathai, the silent mountain killers who struck without warning and showed no mercy.

They were bloodthirsty stories, but Esar wasn't sure there was much truth to them. For a start, the Lathai were known to avoid conflict when they could. It was their misfortune that conflict often came to them. He didn't doubt they could be killers if forced to it—*anyone* could be a killer—but this was just one more war they hadn't sought or started, so it was not that he was unsympathetic to Alyas's point of view, it was just that they had their orders, and they didn't include *this*.

Esar looked over at his foster brother, who was watching the approaching figures with nerveless intensity. "Remind me again what you think you're doing?"

Alyas never took his eyes off the Lathai. "Talking."

"Why?"

"Because that's what I was sent here to do."

"Not strictly speaking it's not," Esar pointed out. They stood a little apart from the rest of their party so he could speak freely. In case a reminder was required, he added, "By your king."

Alyas frowned. "If we're being specific, he didn't specifically order me not to."

"Are you being deliberately difficult?"

The Lathai had stopped at the far side of the clearing and were now subjecting them to a similarly intense scrutiny.

"Are you so anxious to start a war?"

"Start one?" Esar's eyebrows climbed into his hair. "We were sent here to finish one."

"I see no sign of a war, nor an enemy," Alyas declared. "If Raffa wants these mountains, he can have them peacefully or he can come here himself and do whatever it is he thinks is necessary."

"Which he sent you to do for him. You're going to push Raffa too far one of these days." He paused. "Why is Melar Gaemo here?"

Alyas glanced at him. "He is?"

"Yes, he arrived as we were leaving." When no more information was forthcoming, Esar pressed the point. "Why is he here? Why is the man with the ear of Diago of Flaeres in our camp when we are here to consolidate Lankara's hold on this territory? And don't pretend you don't know."

"Officially," replied Alyas, "he is here as a neutral observer for Flaeres."

"You know damn well that Diago claims this whole area, so he is *not* neutral."

"But we're not currently at war with Flaeres, so I can't just throw him out."

That was also not strictly true, since Alyas could very well throw Gaemo out, convention be damned, especially given the decades-long dispute over ownership of these bloody mountains. It was unlikely that there would be any real consequences. He just didn't want to.

"Unofficially?"

"I am going to tell you," his brother promised, "but not now, because it would take too long."

"And what am I supposed to do with him in the meantime?"

"Make his life difficult. You won't be the only one who thinks he shouldn't be here, so run him in circles, enjoy yourself at his expense, and make sure everyone sees you doing it. He won't mind. He'll be expecting it."

"That," said Esar, "does not reassure me. Send him packing and forget whatever scheme you have cooking. It won't end well."

Alyas pretended not to hear.

Esar sighed. There was no point arguing about it now. And while this was not ideally how he would have preferred Alyas to reengage with the business of living, it was a welcome change from the closed-off, silent existence of the months since his father's very messy, public death. So he let it go—for now—and instead directed his brother's attention to the thick fringe of pines curling round the left side of the clearing. "They'll have warriors in those trees."

Alyas's invitation to the Lathai chieftain had specified certain conditions, but they both knew neither would adhere precisely to the stipulations. 'Just in case' was always a good policy as far as Esar was concerned.

"I know," Alyas agreed. "That's why we don't."

"That's why… We don't? I sent—"

"And I called them back."

"You called them back." Esar wanted to throttle him, but he was conscious of the watchful gaze of the Lathai chief and his men. "What the fuck are you playing at? Next you'll tell me I'm not going with you."

Alyas took a quick step to the side, out of arm's reach. "You're not. And before you do something you'll regret—"

"You're assuming I'd regret it."

"—you're not coming for the same reason I don't want any of our men in those trees. There isn't a war *yet*. But there have been plenty. Those men back there know why we've been sent here and they're spoiling for a fight, though Yholis knows why. And those men out there"—he canted his head towards the Lathai—"will be expecting us to start a fight, because that's what every other Lankaran army has done. If they encounter each other in those trees, where neither of us is supposed to be, what do you think will happen?"

He had a point, but not enough of one. "Even more reason for me to go with you. If this doesn't go the way you want, you'll be on your own."

But Alyas was adamant. "And if this doesn't go the way I want, who'll be in charge if you're with me?"

Ah. There was the rest of the point.

"Exactly," Alyas agreed, seeing that he understood. "And Corado doesn't need an excuse to turn this into a bloodbath. Nor would he have any great objection to both of us being taken out in the confusion, so I'm going alone and you're staying here to keep things under control if I'm wrong. Which I'm not. Then perhaps we'll all get to go home alive."

AILUIN

Ailuin watched the Lankaran come. Alone. Arms held up and out, away from his body, away from the bright blades that hung at his hips, the hilts catching the first rays of the dawn sun in a blaze of light.

Isyr.

Only one man wore blades of Isyr steel. Even Ailuin, who had never travelled beyond his beloved mountains, knew that. Only one man, and he was dead. Travellers had carried the news from Avarel earlier in the year, just one more snippet of gossip out of Lankara's great capital, another small tragedy in a world that wrought them on itself as though it did not know how to live without suffering.

Gerrin-Raine Sera was dead. By his own hand, according to rumour. Now his son was here, wearing the blades that had made his father famous the length of Ellasia. And he said he wanted peace.

Peace. These Lankarans didn't know what it was. The Lathai knew. They lived in peace, always. Peace with themselves, with each other, with the world that nurtured them and gave them life. Yes, they took life—if they had to. They could make war to defend what was theirs. But peace was not something they lost, nor was it something others could give them.

When Lankarans said they wanted peace, what they wanted was the right to plunder Lathai territory without fear of reprisal. Their peace was a lie, a mirage, not to be trusted.

And yet, here he was.

Gerrin-Raine Sera's son had called and Ailuin had come, because that was a name that still meant something. Because while the man standing before him now could not give the Lathai peace, maybe he could stop the killing. And for that, Ailuin was prepared to listen.

The son stopped when he was still some metres away. The men at Ailuin's back had their spears poised, because though he was alone, he was not unarmed, even if his hands were empty. Beyond him, the Lankarans watched, tense with the expectation of violence. Had they learned nothing about the Lathai? The only violence they need fear was the violence they brought with them.

There was no such tension on the face of the dark-haired man before him, only fierce concentration, as though he could force the world into the shape he desired by his will alone.

Ailuin made a gesture and his men lowered their spears. He made another and those spears dropped to the ground. Sometimes you had to take the chance in front of you.

And if the son was anything like the father, he would not have lied about his intentions.

Very slowly, the man unbuckled his sword belt and removed those Isyr blades, holding them out before him. He did not drop them—who would drop such things?—but Ailuin was satisfied.

"Come," he said, beckoning. "Sit."

The Lankaran gave him a curious look—there was nowhere to sit but the hard ground—but they would do this the Lathai way. They would sit and know one another, and only then would they talk of peace.

Ailuin arranged his ageing bones cross-legged on the grass and his warriors backed away. He beckoned again, and the man came, pausing before mirroring his pose, the blades held across his knees.

He was younger than he seemed, and older. Rumour said he had watched his father die, and it was there on his face and in his eyes. A thin, agile face, framed by dark hair and brows, eyes that recalled the father though the face itself must owe its sharp lines to his mother. Gerrin had been a broad, solid man. His son was lean and restless.

"You asked for me by name," Ailuin said. It was one of the reasons he had come. A request, not a demand, and carried by a man from the plains who traded with the Lathai for furs and leather. An invitation framed with careful courtesy by someone who knew enough to care about such things. "May I know yours?" He knew it, of course. It was why he was here. But he also knew how much stock Lankarans put in names, in how they used them, and he was curious.

"Alyas." One name. Nothing else.

"Al-eye-as." Ailuin rolled the name on his tongue as he considered the offer of friendship contained within that choice. Lankarans measured their worth by the length of their names. Only friends and family called each other by only one name.

"You knew my father," said Alyas, as if he felt some explanation was required. His eyes were very dark.

"I met him, twice." Once on his way to Qido, the second time on his return. "I was sorry to hear of his death."

Gerrin's son looked away, and his hands gripped tight around his father's blades.

Ailuin had seen them only once before, when Gerrin-Raine Sera brought them back across the mountains from Qido—twenty years ago? No, more. Before this son was born. Gerrin had been as pleased as a child with a new toy, dazzled by their beauty and with no conception of what he had been given.

None of these outsiders understood. They looked at Isyr and saw only a thing to be possessed. A metal like any other. They did not see the life it contained. Or the death from which that life was inseparable, in an endless cycle as old as time. When they looked at Isyr, they saw none of that, and they had made of it these weapons of war.

This Isyr, though—it was different to the Isyr of his mountains. Darker, more restless. Even thirty years ago, Ailuin had felt a vague unease in the presence of these blades. Now it was an assault.

"May I?" he asked, holding out his hand. Then, when the man flinched, hand going to his hilts—not to draw them, but to protect them—he said, "Your father showed them to me once, long ago. I only wish to hold them."

Still, Alyas hesitated, and his hesitation had nothing to do with the fear of being disarmed among enemies. It was instinctive, possessive, a compulsive *need*. And Ailuin liked it not at all.

He waited, watchful, half expecting his request to be refused. There was a moment when Ailuin was certain it would be. Then Alyas laid the blades on the ground between them, lifting his gaze to meet Ailuin's. "My father spoke of you sometimes. He would be honoured that you remember him."

"It is I who am honoured," Ailuin said gravely, accepting this gift of trust and taking the blades onto his lap. He drew the slender sword from its sheath, careful to avoid its cutting edges.

Bared to the clear light of a mountain dawn, the Isyr sang with brightness and beauty, but as he touched his fingertips to the cool metal, the wrongness intensified—a keening of pain, of grief, swamping his senses with its mournful refrain. It was distant, yet such was its power that it dragged at him, reached out to him, and he knew that if he let it, if he but gave an inch, it would sweep him away.

Ailuin withdrew his hand, his fingers still burning from the brief contact, and looked into the wide, wary eyes of the man opposite.

Now he knew why Gerrin-Raine Sera had died. Did his son?

Ailuin shuttered the Isyr back inside its sheath and replaced the blades on the ground. "You must put these aside," he said as Alyas reached out to take them. He did not understand what he had felt, but he understood its danger, and it would overwhelm the son as it had overwhelmed the father.

Alyas froze. "I cannot."

"Why not?"

Gerrin's son averted his gaze, his father's blades cradled once more across his knees. "I cannot," he said again. "Don't ask me."

"Yet you have come to ask something of me," Ailuin pointed out. There was no doubt in his mind that what he felt, this man felt also.

"I have," Alyas agreed. "But I have something to offer in exchange. I—"

Ailuin held up his hand. "You cannot speak to me of peace and bring those weapons to my home." The blades sang of death, of desolation. They had killed, many times, of that he was certain. They hungered for death, no longer safe to be handled. The least he could do for Gerrin's memory was save his son from that. "When we meet again, you will leave them behind."

The struggle was evident. A spasm of pain crossed that lean face, but Alyas mastered it. "When we meet again?"

Ailuin smiled. "Today is to know the man who would make peace. In three days, we will talk. And this time, you will come to us."

Alyas glanced behind him to where the Lankarans were waiting. "I do not think my people will allow that."

"They will," Ailuin said with calm certainty, "because I will send my son to stand as surety for your safe return."

Surprise flashed across Alyas's face, followed by something else. He had not expected that, hadn't planned for it, and was instinctively wary. "It would be better—"

"This is how it will be," Ailuin said. "If our peoples remain strangers, we can never be friends. Only friends can make a lasting peace. You will come to us. My son will come to you. We will talk, we will know each other, and then we will decide if we can be friends."

Alyas frowned. He did not want to agree, Ailuin saw. It told him much, that hesitation.

"You do not trust us?" He knew it was not that.

Alyas shook his head. "I trust you."

"Then you do not trust your men."

"They are soldiers. They see enemies first."

"And that," said Ailuin, rising to his feet, "is why we cannot remain strangers."

It was a risk, but so many things in life were. His people either embraced this chance or they resigned themselves to another hundred years of wars, and the sincerity of *this* request he did not doubt. Even so, any treaty they made could not be just between the two of them. It had to go deeper or it would never hold. So this was the way it had to be.

As Ailuin rose, his *xhidan* swung free from his tunic, the Isyr carving catching the light as the blades had done. Alyas saw it at once and his eyes widened. He looked from Ailuin to the warriors at his back, clever eyes noting the cords around their necks from which hung their own *xhidan*, half hidden but visible if you looked carefully. At least one of them was also Isyr. It was another risk, but this was the one on which everything turned.

Alyas's troubled gaze shifted from Ailuin to the blades in his hands. He said, "It would be best if no one else saw those. I only have so much power."

And Isyr was Isyr. He might not covet it—why would he?—but others did, and for now the Lathai were still the enemy, still strangers. Perhaps because of it, they could never be friends.

Ailuin turned and beckoned Eldruin forward. His son came, distrustful and hostile. They were of an age, these two, yet the gulf that yawned between them was wide and deep. One was young enough still to want to fight against the injustice his people had suffered; the other was old enough to see the tragedy in perpetuating it. And, like Alyas, Ailuin only had so much power. He could make peace, but it was the young who must make it work. They had to *believe*.

Eldruin stood beside his father, offering a grudging greeting. Also on his feet, Alyas returned it, his eyes studying the young man's face. Did he see the similarities or the differences? Ailuin curled his hand around his son's *xhidan*, the warmth of bronze rather than the cool blue of Isyr. If the Lankarans would make peace, they must make peace with this, too—the *xhiden* contained the spirits of the Lathai, each one fashioned to represent the unique gifts of the child, a guide to their past and to their future. They could not set them aside. They could not pretend to be other than they were.

But Ailuin also could not push too far too soon, and for now, it was this man's reaction he had wanted to see.

Holding the *xhidan* so Alyas could see it, he said, "Eldruin will come to your camp, and you will come to mine."

Alyas looked from the bronze carving to Ailuin's Isyr, tucked away now, his hesitation clear. He had not known—Gerrin had not told him—and it changed things. A complication. What would he do?

Lathai scouts had been shadowing the Lankarans for days, ever since they had first set foot in the mountains. They knew everything about them, from the number of soldiers to the placements of every sentry. Should it become necessary, his people were more than capable of dealing with these invaders of their territory. Ailuin hoped very much that it would not become necessary.

Eventually, Alyas said, "When?"

Ailuin smiled. "In three days. We will meet here once more and begin our journey to friendship."

ESAR

"Sayari Gaemo," Alyas called, arriving back in the camp. "For what purpose are you here?"

Melar Gaemo, looking relieved, rose to his feet. He was surrounded by the guards he had brought with him—and those Esar had set—who now moved back so Alyas could get through. "I am here on the orders of my king, Your Grace." He handed over said orders for inspection.

Alyas dismissed the guards, the packet of papers unopened in his hand. "Come with me." And strode away, leaving the king of Flaeres's observer to follow at an undignified pace.

As they entered his tent, Alyas tossed the orders on his desk. "I thought we agreed you would wait."

"*We* did," Gaemo confirmed. "Diago is less convinced. He would like an observer for the duration."

"He might," Alyas retorted, unbuckling his sword belt. His armour followed. "But there's a reason I wanted you to wait, and you just put it at risk."

"Perhaps one of you could explain it to me," Esar said. He could guess at the general shape of it, but this was clearly a conspiracy of some depth, which surprised him, because as far as he was aware Alyas had done no talking of any kind in the last few months. But Gaemo had been in Avarel, and now that he thought about it, circumstances had thrown them together on more than one occasion.

Alyas perched on the edge of his desk, waving Gaemo irritably to the tent's only chair. Esar stayed planted by the entrance to ensure they were not disturbed while Alyas leafed through the papers Gaemo had brought with him. Probably checking they would pass inspection by more hostile eyes. When he handed them back, he said to Esar, "We both know there's no reason for us to be here. Raffa dreamt this whole thing up on a whim. He's not serious, but this is."

Not exactly on a whim, but Esar was prepared to grant that this was not the culmination of some long-held ambition on the part of Lankara's king. The whole expedition was little more than an excuse to get Alyas doing something—*anything*—after his father's death. Raffa, who was as worried as anyone, had grasped the first idea to come along and sent them out here in the hopes that it would distract Alyas for long enough for him to drag himself out of wherever he had retreated to. Esar couldn't fault the impulse, even if the idea was a terrible one. Did Raffa really think the best way to help Alyas deal with one pointless death was by making him responsible for getting more people killed for no point or purpose? So he should not have been surprised that his brother had found some way to subvert that intention, but did it have to involve *Flaeres*?

"He might not be serious," Esar hedged, "but that doesn't mean he's happy for you to conspire with a potentially hostile nation." He fixed Gaemo with a suitably hostile look. "How do you know we can trust him?"

"Esar," Gaemo said, offended, "how long have you known me?"

"I don't know, and it's irrelevant. What's *relevant*, as you both know, is that you are not on the same side, therefore this comes dangerously close to treason."

"Only if our intention is to cause harm to our respective nations," Alyas argued. "And that is precisely the opposite of what we're trying to do."

Esar shook his head in despair. "Good luck convincing Raffa of that when this goes wrong."

"Is he always so pessimistic?" Gaemo asked Alyas.

"Since when are you so fucking idealistic?" Esar snapped. "This isn't a game. Lives are at stake. Ours, if you want to get right down to it. And have you forgotten," he demanded of Alyas, "the enormous bloody obstacle to any kind of peaceful outcome that's *right here* in this camp?"

"What's he talking about?" Gaemo asked. "What obstacle?"

Alyas sighed. He hadn't forgotten. He had, after all, taken pains to ensure that Esar would remain behind during the negotiations today because he was all too aware of the potential trouble from that quarter. "The obstacle," he admitted to Gaemo, "is who he sent with me."

That was where Raffa's judgement had catastrophically failed him. There was no doubt that Corado was an effective officer, if by effective you meant vicious and bullying, whose men obeyed him through pure fear. The man was angry, bitter, and determined to prove himself the equal of the younger brothers who could name eighteen generations, with all the wealth and privilege that afforded them, when he had only one name, with everything that meant. The eldest son of a Lankaran lord and a Flaeresian serving girl, he had never been formally named by his father and thus was condemned to live life on the fringes of a society where possession of only a single name was the ultimate shame.

Corado, who had entered the King's Guard with the sponsorship of his father—who thereafter had washed his hands of his embarrassing indiscretion—and had beaten a bloody path nearly to the top. Along the way—quite how, Esar did not know—he had wormed his way into the king's favour and persuaded Raffa to put him in charge of the Guard contingent that accompanied the regular kingdom troops. And though, like everyone else, he was technically under Alyas's command, there was sufficient ambiguity around that point to enable Corado to make trouble at every turn.

Corado, who hated Alyas and everything he stood for and would do whatever he could to undermine him.

Gaemo didn't appear unduly concerned when Esar explained this. "Get rid of him," he said with a careless shrug. There was no doubt he meant permanently. For all his amusing flourishes, Melar Gaemo was ruthlessly practical. "Sounds like we'd all be better off without him."

"Get out, Melar," Esar growled. Appealing though the suggestion was, the murder of a crown officer was inadvisable for any number of reasons. As was this whole enterprise, and he had things he wanted to say to Alyas about that. In private, and before Gaemo had any more bright ideas.

Gaemo looked to Alyas, who gave him no encouragement to stay. Whatever agreement they had struck, Gaemo's presence clearly breached it, and Alyas wasn't happy. He was also likely worrying over the Lathai chief's decision to send his own son as a hostage for the negotiations. As a show of good faith, it was breathtaking. As a practical matter, it was already giving Esar a headache.

Giving up, Gaemo stood. "Fine. But those orders are genuine. Diago wants me here and he wants reassurance, so you"—he pointed his gloves at Alyas—"will have to talk to me."

"And you have to let me do this my way," Alyas shot back. "And that includes how I deal with you. Which is for your own safety," he added.

"And it would help if I flounced out of here, tattered and bleeding from all the strips you've torn off me?"

"Yes," agreed Alyas. "Yes, it would."

※

Gaemo went, complaining loudly all the way as Esar reunited him with his guards, both Lankaran and Flaeresian. But he didn't go far. He didn't have a chance.

Esar had barely made it back to Alyas's tent when they heard Flaeresian accents raised in challenge and the unmistakable sounds of an armed scuffle.

Alyas didn't pause to collect a weapon. He ducked outside, almost colliding with a breathless kingdom soldier who gestured unnecessarily behind him. There was no missing the confrontation just yards from his tent or the audience it had gathered.

Melar, who Esar knew to be handy with a knife in dark corners, was wholly unprepared to deal with Corado's brute savagery. Corado had his fist twisted in Gaemo's short cape, King Diago's representative half-strangled and struggling to free himself as Corado's men held back his guards.

"Corado!"

Silence fell. Heads turned. Every soldier recognised the tone.

Corado looked towards Alyas, but he didn't release Gaemo, who was starting to choke in earnest now.

"Let him go."

Corado's face twisted into a furious snarl and his grip tightened. Gaemo's face took on a panicked, purple shade.

Alyas snapped, "*Now!*"

Corado released his victim with a shove, sending him staggering back. Esar caught him, one hand under Gaemo's elbow keeping him on his feet. His eyes were wild, his usually perfect hair in disarray, and one hand explored a throat that was already showing the marks of Corado's attempt to strangle him.

Gaemo flinched as Corado thrust a meaty hand in his direction. "He's a fucking Flaeresian spy! You should have killed him the moment he stepped foot in the camp!"

It was a powerful accusation, and he flung it at Alyas like a weapon—who ignored it and advanced on Corado, forcing him away from where Esar was still propping up Gaemo. "Which is why he is *under guard* and has been since the moment he arrived. But he's also an officially sanctioned representative of a nation with which *we are not at war*, therefore he stays until he does something for which I can throw him out. And if you touch him again, you'll be the one thrown out. In disgrace. Do you understand?"

Corado, breathing hard, snarled, "Flaeres is an enemy. I should—"

"*Do you understand?*"

The words cracked like a whip. Corado lurched back as he finally registered the threat to the precious rank that lifted him above the shame of his birth. His fists clenched, his face flushing with fury. "You can't do that."

There was killing rage in those words, barely leashed. Alyas ignored that, too. "I can."

"Gods, he's going to kill him," Gaemo murmured, pulling himself from Esar's grip.

Esar, glad to have his hands free, moved closer to Alyas, who was unarmed—both blades and armour were back in his tent. Corado was not only armed, but with his extra height and the bulk of his armour he looked twice Alyas's size. He certainly looked twice as nasty, though Esar wouldn't have put money on it.

"Do you understand?" Alyas asked again, the words like chips of ice. "Back off, now."

Violence boiled between them. If Corado came for him, Alyas wouldn't hesitate to put him down, Esar was certain. But it would enrage Corado to the point of murder and might well lose Alyas some of the sympathy of the watching Guards, who needed to see their captain back down.

Corado was not beyond calculations of his own, despite the clenched fists and the breath that came in short, sharp gasps. "I know what you're doing," he hissed, the threat too low for the ears of the gathered soldiers. "I'm watching you. Talking to our enemy. Our *enemies*. You can't touch me. Try, and you'll regret it."

Alyas was unmoved. "I assure you, I will not. And if you do not leave *right now*, you'll see how little I'll regret it."

Corado backed off, but only a step. "I'm watching," he said again, the threat accompanied by a sneer that Esar really did not like. "*You can't touch me.*"

Alyas looked away first, his shoulders dropping, and Corado's face transformed with savage delight. But as he turned to his men, Alyas's foot snapped out, delivering a vicious kick to the back of Corado's ankle that swept the man's legs from under him, landing him on his arse in the mud.

"Can't I?" Alyas asked, standing over him. He snapped his fingers at the hovering Guard troops.

"Oh fuck," Gaemo muttered.

Oh fuck, indeed.

Corado roared with rage, but before he could regain his feet and rip Alyas's head from his shoulders, his men were there, pulling him up. Holding him back. Alyas just stood there and watched.

Corado struggled wildly, but his men hung onto him, dragging him away, and after a few steps, he let them. But his face was a portrait of hatred; Alyas was going to pay for that small victory.

If that concerned Alyas, it didn't show. He turned his back on Corado, who made an obscene gesture at Gaemo. Esar's hand snapped out and caught Gaemo's before he could return it.

The crowd scattered, disappearing as fast as they had gathered. Alyas watched them for a moment before turning to where Gaemo was straightening his rumpled clothing. "Do you see now why I wanted you to wait?"

※

Gaemo apologised and said he would leave. Alyas, lack of patience grating through every word, explained why that was no longer possible. And it was left to Esar to deal with the practicalities of ensuring the Flaeresian representative wouldn't be murdered in his sleep.

"Really, Esar, I think Alyas is exaggerating. I could just—"

"Shut up, Melar. He just risked everything for you. If he backs down now, it was all for nothing, and there's your precious plan gone up in smoke. So you're fucking staying until we can find a way to get rid of you that doesn't make it look like Corado won."

Gaemo, voice raspy and face rather pale, glanced fearfully across the camp to where the Guard troops were quartered. "And what's to stop him killing me while you do that?"

Very little, as far as Esar could see, but he kept that to himself. "Only the fact that Alyas still has the authority to take away the thing that matters to him most, but only bloody just, thanks to you."

"I could get caught spying?" Gaemo offered.

"Yes, good idea. Then Alyas will have to choose between killing you or losing the last shreds of his authority protecting an enemy. And I'll make it easy for him, do you understand?"

The blood drained from Gaemo's face, leaving his throat a stark line of red. He swallowed his objection and nodded.

"He needs to leave," Esar said, when he returned to Alyas's tent.

Alyas looked up at him, his chin in his hands. "I know. Soon as we can manage it."

"He's right, you know."

"Who is?"

"Melar. Better for everyone if Corado's dead. He'll never stop making trouble." Especially after today, but Alyas hadn't had a whole lot of choice about that.

The look on his brother's face told Esar the idea had crossed his mind, but it was even less advisable now than it had been before. Unfortunately.

"I can handle Corado," Alyas insisted.

Esar dropped into the chair Gaemo had vacated. There wouldn't be much sleep in either of their futures if they were going to keep Gaemo alive until he could be sent home. "Not while it looks like you're talking to Flaeres."

For a man who was half-Flaeresian, Corado's hatred for Lankara's neighbour had never made sense to Esar. It was his Lankaran father who was responsible for all the things Corado resented—his single name, the disdain of men who should have been his equals. All his mother had done was give birth to him. But that hatred was dangerous.

"You don't need Flaeres for this," he argued. "Make peace with the Lathai if that's what you're set on. Yholis knows, it's better than starting a war no one needs or wants. Raffa might even thank you. But send Gaemo home and forget about Flaeres."

Alyas shook his head. "Without Flaeres, nothing I do here will matter. This land we're standing on might belong to Lankara today, but one year or ten years from now it will be Flaeresian again. The Lathai know that as well as anyone. It's what they've been dying for all these years. What use is peace with Raffa today if next year it is Diago they must contend with?"

"Then negotiate your peace between Lankara and Flaeres and leave the Lathai out of it! Why do it this way?"

"Because Raffa didn't send me to Flaeres, he sent me here! And if I can't find a peaceful way out of this, we'll have to fight and too many people will die. And for what?"

That was the real problem. He would never admit it, but Alyas knew perfectly well why Raffa had sent him here. It had succeeded in shaking him out of that closed-down silence, but now he was trapped by the king's orders. And he had never dealt well with being backed into a corner.

"These mountains don't belong to Lankara or Flaeres. They belong to the Lathai. They always have. Fighting over them only makes us all poorer. I intend to persuade both Raffa and Diago to acknowledge it, but neither of them can take that step alone. They would be torn down by their own. But if they do it together and in doing so can offer the rewards of trade to those who would otherwise pounce on any sign of weakness, it will be seen in an entirely different light."

"Ithol's blood, Alyas." Esar stared at him in disbelief. It wasn't that it didn't make sense, it was that it made *too much* sense. Alyas wanted a rational solution to a conflict too deeply tangled with a complicated history and the emotional weight of national pride, and both those things were as far from rational as you could get. "This is madness. They'll never agree."

But Alyas was also not going to listen to reason. "Diago already has. All we need is a treaty with the Lathai that guarantees the trade corridor, and he will make his agreement official. Then Raffa has nothing to lose and everything to gain by going along with it. Both want a new start. *This* is a new start."

"Both also want to prove themselves," Esar pointed out. Diago had been king for less than a year, Raffa for a little more than twice as long. "And usually kings do that through war, not peace."

"Not this time," Alyas said firmly. "This time they will make peace."

And that was that.

ESAR

Two days before Alyas was due to meet with the Lathai chief, a new complication arrived. Esar watched him come, thick-headed from a night spent ensuring no one murdered their inconvenient Flaeresian, and tried to decide whether he was happy to see him.

"Esar Cantrell!" Nicor-Heryd Zand called as he dismounted with his small Guard escort. "You don't look like you're having as much fun as I expected."

"I'm not," Esar groused. "Why are you here, Nicor?"

"There's a welcome," laughed Nicor. "Messages from the king to Alyas. Avarel's as quiet as the grave, so I offered to bring them."

Esar regarded him with suspicion. "What messages?" They hadn't been gone that long. Not long enough for Raffa to start interfering.

Nicor retrieved the king's correspondence and handed it to Esar. "I haven't read them. They're for Alyas. Where is he?"

Esar contemplated the packet of letters as he thought about his answer. What Alyas was doing at that moment was what Esar had been doing all night, and the presence of Nicor-Heryd could either take that problem off their hands or turn it into an even bigger disaster than it already was. He was the senior Guard captain under the king's commander. If Corado was prepared to flaunt Alyas's authority, he wouldn't dare disobey Nicor. At least Esar hoped he wouldn't. But it depended on which side Nicor decided to take. On the one hand, Corado was his own worst enemy. On the other, Nicor was a career-driven younger son who had his eye on the top position and would play by the rules, which meant his loyalty would be with his own men first.

Fingers snapped under his nose. "Esar!"

He looked up. Nicor was still waiting for an answer. Well, there was only one way to find out how this would go. He handed back the letters. "I'll get him. Come with me."

It took a while to round up Alyas and find some men he trusted to take over guarding Melar, though now it was daylight there was less immediate danger from that quarter. By the time they returned to Alyas's tent, Nicor-Heryd had made himself at home. Someone had made him tea and he had his boots off and was reclining on Alyas's cot, the steaming mug in one hand, one of their maps in the other.

Alyas took this invasion of his privacy with bad grace. He snatched the map from Nicor's hand and kicked him off the cot. "What are you doing here, Nicor?"

Unrepentant, Nicor wiped tea from his leathers. "That's more words than I've heard from you in months. Things must be going well."

Esar winced. Nicor had always been blunt, but that was too blunt. Alyas reacted with stony silence, and Nicor, who seemed to realise he had gone too far, held up his hands. "I'm sorry. I didn't mean to make light. The king wants to know how you're getting on."

Which could mean anything.

"Then he could have sent anyone," Alyas pointed out. "Why are *you* here?"

Not because he was bored of Avarel, that was for sure. A decade older, Nicor-Heryd was comfortable in his position and prospects. He wouldn't risk it by coming out here if he didn't have to.

Nicor's rueful smile acknowledged that. "Came to see if Corado's behaving himself. Fin told the king not to send him. Don't know what he was thinking. That man hates us."

Fin-Barin Mais being Raffa's current Guard commander; 'us' being Lankara's named elite.

"He's behaving exactly the way you'd expect," Alyas replied. He didn't look at Esar. Nicor-Heryd Zand was not the man to appreciate the good-intentioned nuance in unsanctioned diplomatic endeavours. "Take him away with you if you like."

Nicor laughed, handing Alyas the packet of messages. "Like that, is it? Give him some enemies to kill and get him out from under your feet. One of them might even do us all a favour. Where is the enemy, by the way? It's awfully quiet round here. And why did I see a man in Melar Gaemo's livery?"

"There isn't an enemy yet," Alyas said, leafing through the letters. He pulled one out and handed it to Esar. "From Mari. And you saw Melar Gaemo's livery because he's here. Diago of Flaeres sent him once he heard what Raffa intended."

"So throw him out," said practical Nicor. "And what do you mean, there isn't an enemy? These mountains are crawling with Lathai."

"They are, and I can't," Alyas replied, scanning the letter from Raffa. He looked up into Nicor's frown. "We're not at war with Flaeres, though Corado very nearly changed that yesterday."

Nicor pulled a face. He didn't need anyone to draw him a picture. "All the more reason to throw Gaemo out. And don't tell me you can't. Who's going to stop you?"

"I will," agreed Alyas, his attention back on the letters. "When I'm ready. What's this about Hantara? Raffa's not seriously going to marry Sofia off to the Selysians? To *Kael Ito*?"

"He's thinking about it," Nicor replied, neatly distracted. "Makes sense, doesn't it? They've wealth enough to pay all our debts and it never hurts to have powerful friends."

"Syndicate money," Alyas said in disgust. "Lankara isn't in debt to them enough? And Kael Ito? You know his brother's reputation. Raffa would marry his own sister into that family?"

"Maybe if you'd been paying more attention the last few months you could have talked him out of it," Nicor said. "And if you care so much, finish what you were sent here to do and go home and stop him. It's not agreed yet. Besides, don't you have a wedding of your own to prepare for?"

Esar glanced up from the letter he had been pretending to read. His impending marriage to Mari was one of the few things about which Esar didn't know how Alyas actually felt. It had been the accepted future for so long that they had never really talked about it. Since he had shown no inclination to avoid it, Esar assumed he was happy enough, even if he knew Alyas held Mari in rather more sisterly regard than a new wife might prefer. It had been a distant prospect for many years, but Mari had turned twenty-one a month after Gerrin's death. Alyas would have to marry her soon or people would start to talk. Clearly, they already had.

"Don't you have business of your own to mind?" Alyas shot back. "You didn't need to come all this way for Corado. But now you're here, are you staying?"

"Depends," Nicor replied, absorbing this flash of temper without offence since he'd asked for it. "Do you need me to?"

"Not really."

"Then I'll—"

But whatever he intended to do was lost by raised voices outside.

Esar swore. "Not again." He tossed Mari's letter on the cot and ducked out to find an argument in full swing between one of the men he had left to watch Corado and one of Corado's Guards.

"Alyas!"

His brother appeared, Nicor on his heels. "What is it?"

"Trouble," said Esar.

Alyas didn't need to be told. "Find Gaemo," he said. "I'll deal with this."

Gaemo was nowhere to be found. Esar was still looking, trying not to panic, when Alyas joined him. He was furious.

"What?" demanded Esar, his imagination conjuring images of Melar in various stages of being murdered.

"Not that," Alyas replied. "Corado's left the camp. He's taken some men with him."

"Shit."

"Yes."

Thwarted in his attempt to start one war, Corado would do what he could to start another. And since it was the war they had been sent here to fight, Alyas's hands would be well and truly tied. And his hopes for a peaceful resolution in the grave.

"When?"

"Long enough ago to have done something irretrievable. Nicor's organising a search. He's not happy."

He wouldn't be, for different reasons.

"What are we doing?" Esar asked.

"What we have to," Alyas replied bleakly.

Assuming Corado managed to provoke the Lathai into attacking their camp, they had to be ready to defend it. Which explained the frantic activity.

"I need you. Someone else can find Gaemo."

One of Nicor's men was running towards them. Alyas saw him and stopped. "Did you find him?"

Face pale, the man shook his head. "Not yet. But there's something you need to see."

It was, Esar decided later, something that no one needed to see. Ever.

Nicor was waiting for them with a handful of men at the edge of a small grove not far outside the camp's northern perimeter. His expression was warning enough, even without the smell of blood. Someone had died here, and badly.

They slowed. Esar had to fight the urge to turn around—there was something here he didn't want to see, he could feel it—but Alyas walked straight up to Nicor, who held out an arm, blocking the way. "It's bad," he warned. "Worse than bad."

"Let me through," Alyas said, voice quiet. His face was pale, white lines of anger around his eyes and mouth.

Nausea swirled in Esar's gut. "Alyas…"

His brother ignored him. "Let me through," he said again, and Nicor, with an unhappy glance at Esar, dropped his arm.

A handful of paces took them through the screen of trees and into a bloody hell. In its centre, in a loose line, lay the bodies.

After the first glance, Esar looked away. The air was thick with death. It was in his throat and stinging his eyes. He couldn't think; he couldn't breathe.

Moments passed, his heart thudding painfully against his ribs. Nicor, white-faced, said something he didn't catch, then again more urgently, and he forced himself to turn back as Alyas took a step forward. Before Esar could stop him, Alyas reached the first body and dropped to his knees. He knelt by each of them in turn, removing the bloody rags around their eyes and the ropes at their wrists, pausing to straighten the necks of their strange tunics.

"What's he doing?" Nicor murmured, his voice shaky.

Esar said nothing. If he spoke, he'd be sick. The Lathai hadn't been gagged. They had no tongues.

Alyas lurched back to his feet. "I'll kill him."

"Corado," Esar growled. Fucking Corado. Fuck him. No one else would have done this. But he hadn't done it alone. There were five bodies here.

"Hang on," Nicor protested, hurrying after Alyas. "You don't know this was him."

"It was him," Esar said, grateful to be away from that horror. Anxious to avoid another.

Alyas jerked away from Nicor. He was heading straight for the camp, fury eclipsing reason.

"You can't kill a man with no proof!" Nicor shouted after him. When Alyas didn't slow, he spun around. "Stop him, Esar!"

Esar, who would have liked nothing better than to murder Corado, was already moving. And it wasn't lack of proof he was concerned about.

"Alyas!"

His brother turned. "Don't try to stop me, Esar. You know this was him."

"I know," Esar agreed, catching up, Nicor at his heels. "And if you think about it for a moment, you know *why*."

This wasn't a random act of brutality, though Yholis knew, Corado was more than capable of it. This was a deliberate, calculated attempt to sabotage Alyas's peace talks with the Lathai and undermine his entire command in the process. And if he wasn't careful, it would succeed.

"I don't care. He dies. Did you see them?"

"I saw them." Esar kept his voice calm. "I saw them. But you need to slow down, think about this. Otherwise, you're just giving him exactly what he wants."

Nicor, catching up, asked, "What are you talking about? How do you know—"

Esar thrust out a hand to shut the man up, his eyes locked on Alyas. "It was Corado. No doubt. It's why that matters. Alyas—"

But Nicor was like a dog with a bone. "You have no proof! We're at war—"

Alyas dragged his gaze from Esar. "We're not at war!"

Nicor ignored that. "Tempers run high. I'm not saying it's justifiable—"

"What are you saying?" Alyas demanded, and if his voice was cold before, it was molten rage now. "That these things happen? We should just, what? Accept it? Put it down to stress and high spirits? We start treating our prisoners like that, what do you suppose the Lathai will do to our men when they take them? Which they will.

If those were your men back there, would you still say *these things happen?*"

Nicor stepped back before his anger, his face paling. "Of course not. Ithol's blood, Alyas. What was done—it was wrong, an abomination. I'm not arguing about that. But you can't kill a man without proof."

"Then I'll find proof. Out of my way, both of you."

They found Corado waiting for them outside his tent, surrounded by his men, brutal triumph on his face. Just sitting there, having done *that* to five other living, breathing human beings. And for no better reason than to force Alyas's hand.

He surged to his feet in surprise when he saw Nicor. "Captain—"

"*Shut up*," Nicor barked. He might not be prepared to accept the charge without evidence, but he was no fool, and he knew Corado. "Where have you been?"

"I'll tell you where he's been," Alyas said, too angry to let Nicor handle this. "He left here, disobeying a direct order, and he found himself some Lathai prisoners. Didn't you?" he snarled at Corado. "Prisoners you tortured before you killed them. Give me one good reason why I shouldn't do to you what you did to them!"

Corado's men were on their feet now, looking nervously between Alyas and Nicor. Others had joined them, drawn by the shouting. Rumour spread, whispers passed from man to man. Emotions swelled as the crowd grew, the atmosphere volatile.

"Some Lathai are dead, are they?" Corado mocked him, playing to the mood. "Some of the enemy. You can't kill them so you'll kill me, is that it?"

Yholis, this was bad.

"They were people! For what you did to them, you deserve nothing less."

Alyas was furious, beyond furious. Esar couldn't blame him; he felt the same. But the dead were Lathai. The enemy. And most of the army had not seen the bodies. They knew only that Corado had violated the terms of the truce to take prisoners and that those prisoners were dead.

And, as Nicor had pointed out, they had another problem.

"You can't prove shit," Corado sneered. "Show me a witness who saw me take them."

That problem.

"I saw," said a quiet voice.

Esar turned; he swore.

Melar Gaemo stepped through the ranks of soldiers and said to Alyas, "I saw him. I was on the north side of the camp. I saw him bring them in. He tied their hands and he… he did things to them." His face was white and shaken; he was telling the truth. He was also the worst possible witness.

Only Esar, who knew him best, saw the flicker of hesitation as Alyas grasped the weapon Gaemo had handed him. If he wasn't careful, it would wound him more deeply than Corado. But he couldn't leave it lying there unclaimed either.

"A witness," he said, voice harsh. "Not just to their capture, but to what you did to them."

Corado, his face split by a savage smile, raised his hands to his audience. "You'll take the word of an enemy over me?"

"He's the representative of a foreign power!"

"He's the representative of shit-all," Corado sneered with the confidence of a man who knew he was winning. He was accused of murdering one enemy by another, and the army would not stand for it. "He's the king's bed mate, and this is a set up."

Esar met Nicor's gaze and saw the same realisation; Alyas would lose this, and there was nothing they could do. If they intervened, he would just lose faster.

"I'm the official representative of the government of Flaeres, here with the permission of your commander," Gaemo said, and Esar wanted to throttle the man. He was trying to help, but his help would bury them.

"We're at war with Flaeres!" Corado shot back. "I would be serving my country by killing you."

Alyas grabbed Gaemo by the arm and shoved him back towards Esar. "We are not at war with Flaeres, but we will be if you kill him, and do you think you will be some kind of hero? That the king will thank you for starting a war *he does not want*?"

"The king's orders—"

"Are mine to follow. You follow mine. But you didn't, you disobeyed, so now you're done."

A murmur ran through the crowd. "Fuck you," Corado roared. "Touch me and you'll regret it. You're the one who's done—talking when you should fight. *Coward.*"

"And what do you call a man who kills unarmed prisoners?" Alyas snarled, oblivious to the shocked stares. "Who tortures and mutilates men with their hands tied and blindfolds on their eyes?"

There was a shift in the mood of the crowd at that. A small one, but it was there. Killing Lathai was one thing, but torturing unarmed prisoners… Every man here would fear falling into enemy hands and having the same fate visited on them.

Alyas played on that fear. "A man who cut out their tongues so they couldn't scream. Who took his pleasure of them while they were helpless."

That last was not true, judging by Corado's face, but to deny one charge was to admit the rest. He was white with rage. He tried to speak, but Alyas didn't let him, his hand lashing out to grab the leather cords Corado had strung around his neck. He dragged them free, and Esar caught a glimpse of metal in his hand. "A man who steals trophies from the dead?"

Alyas ripped the cords loose, the force of it scoring a friction burn on Corado's skin. Corado clapped a hand to his neck, hissing in pain.

"Shall we fetch the bodies?" Alyas asked, whatever he had taken from Corado held in a white-knuckled grip. "Let everyone see what kind of monster you are."

Nicor's eyes flickered to Esar, who shook his head. If Alyas wanted the bodies brought out, he would have ordered it directly. And he wouldn't, because if he survived this confrontation, he would have to account to the Lathai for the murders, and he would not treat their dead with such disrespect.

But without them, words wouldn't be enough, *and Alyas had to know that*. Which was when Esar finally realised what he was doing.

A spasm of fury crossed Corado's face, his fists tightening. It was coming. Yholis, he hoped Alyas hadn't misjudged this.

Esar shot Nicor a meaningful look. He needed to be ready.

Against all precedent and expectation, Corado controlled his rage, keeping his fists by his sides. He was no fool; he knew what was happening.

Alyas, who was right up in hitting distance now—Esar forced himself not to look away—said something that was too quiet for anyone but Corado to hear.

The blow came out of nowhere—and Esar had been expecting it. Corado's fist hit Alyas as he was turning, crashing into his temple and spilling him to the ground, where he lay, *not moving*.

The violence of the assault froze the assembled soldiers for a critical second. Esar shoved through the shocked men separating him from his brother. "Take him," he ordered Nicor-Heryd, who was standing by Corado with one hand hovering by his arm. What the fuck was he waiting for?

Esar knelt next to Alyas, who had rolled onto his side and was trying without success to rise, blood pouring from a cut above his eye. He had dropped the trophies he had taken from Corado and Esar scooped them up without looking at them, sliding them inside his armour as he got one arm under Alyas's shoulder, supporting him to sit. If he got up now, there was a good chance he would pass out. He had invited the attack—had *needed* Corado to strike him—and now he needed just as much to see this through. But the blow had been a bad one. Esar wasn't sure he could.

Around them, the shock was fading. Corado shook off Nicor's restraining hand, the milling soldiers waking up. Whoever moved first would sway them. Alyas had to *get up* and finish this.

His brother gripped his arm, bracing against his strength. "Help me."

Esat tightened his hold, levering Alyas upright so he could get his feet under him. He did not let go. Letting him fall on his face at this point would not be helpful.

Alyas turned his bloody face to Corado. "Put him under guard," he said to Nicor-Heryd, the words slurred but clear. "Tomorrow, you're taking him back to Avarel for trial."

"Fuck you," Corado spat. "You're not putting me on trial. I'm not the one who's plotting with the enemy."

But he had been goaded into going too far, and he knew it. He had struck his commander in front of a hundred witnesses. And not just any commander. Everything that Corado hated most about him was what made Alyas-Raine Sera untouchable. For what Corado had just done, Alyas could kill him where he stood, and every man here knew it.

"You took and murdered prisoners under a flag of truce, you threatened to a kill an official representative of a foreign power, and all these men saw you assault me," Alyas snarled. "Be grateful I don't string you up right here. Take him away."

Finally, *finally*, Nicor recalled what was expected of him and took charge. Corado struggled and cursed them, but Nicor's men held him firm and dragged him roughly through the crowd. Sentiment that had been tilting in his favour was now hardening against him, and even among those who shared his feelings about the Lathai, he was feared, not popular. They all knew Alyas could have had him killed for any one of the charges he'd laid against him; Alyas knew that if he'd tried, he'd have had a mutiny on his hands—until Corado had obliged by trying to kill *him*. Esar wondered what he'd said to provoke that blow, then decided he didn't want to know. If he put his mind to it, Alyas could make anyone want to hit him.

He wasn't done yet. Pulling himself as upright as he could, Alyas rounded on the gathered soldiers. "Those of you who helped him, give yourselves up now and you'll return to Avarel with your former captain. Take your chances at a trial. Fail to do so, hide here, and when I find you, which I will, I'll execute you. No trial. No mercy. I won't care if he made you do it. I won't care what your excuses are. You'll die."

Absolute silence. Men looked at each other, kingdom troops edging away from the scattering of men who had come with Corado. No one came forward.

"Last chance," Alyas said. He was starting to sag and Esar tightened his grip. It was too soon to collapse.

There was a shuffling of feet. A man pushed his way to the front in the scale coat of a King's Guard, his face pale but set, eyes darting between his feet and Alyas's furious, battered face.

"You meant it? We go to Avarel, for trial?"

Too fucking late if he didn't. There was no going back now.

Alyas said nothing, just stared at the man in silence. He was trembling, whether from anger or Corado's assault, Esar couldn't tell. "To Avarel," he said at last.

The man nodded, still unable to commit to looking at him, and half-turned, a tilt of his head calling others forward. Esar glared at them as they emerged, six of them, all younger than their spokesman, all terrified. Boys. No older than the Lathai they had killed. That they had tortured.

As if he could hear the thought, the spokesman said, "We didn't do those things to them. Corado—"

"I don't care," Alyas snarled. "Nicor, more prisoners for you." Then, to the cowed, shamefaced knot of men, "Get out of my sight before I change my mind and finish this right now."

They moved, almost running towards Nicor's men, desperate to get away from Alyas's lethal fury. Esar braced him as they went, taking more of his weight. That display had cost him, but he had done it. Bruised, bleeding, barely able to stand, he had faced down an army ready to turn and held them. Now he just had to keep them.

The crowd began to break up, officers recovering their sense of duty and yelling orders at their men to stop fucking around and get back to work. The threat of a Lathai attack hadn't lessened; it was more likely than ever. If they weren't careful, they would be caught completely unprepared.

Nicor planted himself in front of Alyas. He winced at the blood. "I'll send a surgeon," he said to Esar. They had several representatives from the Temple of Yholis with the army. He looked at Alyas with a mix of respect and frustration. "He could have killed you. I thought he had for a moment. I hope you know what you're doing."

He made no more protests about proof. The trophies had answered that point, as had the men who'd given themselves up.

Alyas tried to smile, but his swelling face mangled the expression. Just how close Corado had come to a killing blow was frighteningly apparent. If Esar wasn't holding onto him, he would be on his knees.

"Just get him out of here, Nicor," he said, the words as much a mess as his face. "Leave the rest to me."

Nicor-Heryd hesitated. Esar could see he wanted to argue, but Alyas was rapidly moving beyond coherent response. Corado had put every ounce of his anger and hatred behind his blow and it had very nearly undone Alyas's stratagem to contain him. If he couldn't function again, and soon, it might still do that.

"You leave first thing," Esar told Nicor. "No one sees him between now and then, understood?"

They had to keep Corado isolated until they could get him away from the army, and they had to deal with the bodies and what came next.

With a last worried look at Alyas, Nicor went. Esar, seeing the colour drain from his brother's face, said unsympathetically, "If you're going to be sick, for the love of Yholis, wait until we're out of sight."

"Move then," Alyas mumbled and Esar carted him away. He was going to collapse and it couldn't happen out here. His authority had taken enough hits for one day.

※

Melar Gaemo stuck his head inside the tent while the surgeon was there. "How is he?"

"Get the fuck out of here, Melar," Esar snarled. "Don't make this worse than it is."

Gaemo went.

"Well?" Esar asked, turning back to the surgeon.

"Well," the man said, rising and looking down at Alyas, who was well and truly out of it now. "He's still alive, so he'll probably stay that way. Try to keep him from getting into any more fights for the next few days." This wasn't his first duty with the army. His bedside manner was as rough as the men he tended.

If Alyas had to get in any more fights, Esar reflected, they had a serious problem on their hands, but he didn't say that out loud.

The surgeon asked, "What do you want us to do with the bodies?"

Esar rested his head in his hands, trying not to think about what he had seen. The bodies of Corado's prisoners. The mutilated, brutalised Lathai prisoners.

When he looked up, the surgeon was watching him with anger in the lines around his eyes.

Esar glanced at Alyas's sleeping form. "He wants them treated with respect. We're going to have to give them back, so do what you can." To make it look less horrific—if that was even possible.

"That man…" the surgeon began, words failing him. He had been to the grove. He'd seen what had been done to those men, barely more than boys. "Your brother should have killed him."

"I know," Esar agreed. He was as anxious as anyone to see Corado dead. "He couldn't, not then."

The surgeon sighed, packing away his things. "Keep him still as long as you can," he said in parting. "And if he gets dizzy, make him sit down before he falls down. Someone needs to keep control of this pack of bloody butchers. The last thing we need is another incident like today's."

Then he was gone and Esar was left to worry on his own.

※

Nicor joined him in the morning while it was still dark. He would be leaving with Corado at first light, but he didn't like it and he came to share his dislike.

Alyas was awake. He'd come round an hour before, groaning as he rolled over, hands cradling his aching head. "Yholis, just cut it off," he said in response to Esar's redundant question.

"Don't tempt me. You've done enough bleeding for one day. Surgeon said to stay down and you'll probably live. And if you get up, I might just hit you myself."

Alyas peered at him between his fingers. "What for?"

"What for? For nearly getting yourself killed, that's what for. Do you have any idea how close you came to losing control of this whole thing? And to Corado of all people?"

"I have some idea," Alyas replied. "You don't have to rub it in. Where's Melar? He needs to leave. He's not safe here."

"Oh, really?" Esar retorted. "He shouldn't even be here. I know what you're doing, the two of you. And I understand why. And Yholis, Alyas, you're right. Corado did as much to prove that yesterday as anyone, but just because you're right, doesn't mean you're in the right. This isn't something you can solve by waving your hand and making a hundred years of history disappear. And you're assuming anyone else wants to solve it. Half the courts of Lankara and Flaeres made their names and their fortunes fighting in these wars. Maybe it's only you who wants peace."

"Who said anything about peace?" Nicor's voice asked from the entrance, arriving at perhaps the worst moment. "That's not why the king sent you here, Alyas, and you know it. Corado's an animal, but he's not wrong about that."

Alyas tried to sit up. Esar kicked him and he stayed down. "Nicor. Is he ready to leave?"

"He is but I'm not," Nicor-Heryd said. "Not until I know what's going on."

"What's going on is Corado murdered five unarmed Lathai while I was negotiating with their chieftain," Alyas shot back, wincing at the force of the words. "And you're taking him out of here before he can do anything else *to start a bloody war*."

"You mean the war you were sent here to fight? I have eyes, Alyas, and a brain, which I'm starting to think you don't. The king didn't ask you to negotiate, so what do you think you're doing?"

"Trying to keep you alive!" Alyas snapped, then buried his face in his hands. It was a long moment before he spoke again, and Esar could tell he was suffering for that show of temper.

"Do you know what the casualty ratio is when we go up against the Lathai? Do you? I do. They kill three of us for every one of them, because they know these mountains and we don't. Work it out for yourself, Nicor. We don't have enough men. If we start a war, we'll lose."

"And that's why, is it?" Nicor asked. "That's why you're doing this?"

Alyas looked at him wearily. "Why is everyone so eager for war? We've been fighting over these mountains for a hundred years and what have we gained? Generations of grieving mothers and *nothing* else. There's nothing in it for us. Our own people don't even want to live here. There's no wealth to claim. It's land for land's sake, and you know it."

"And Flaeres?" Nicor asked.

"Flaeres will see sense if Lankara does," Alyas asserted. Exactly what he'd done to ensure that was true, Esar preferred not to dwell on. Melar Gaemo had plenty to do it with, and Yholis, his presence here had nearly sunk Alyas already. Which was why Esar was sending him back to Sarenza as soon as it was light, and if that made a mess of Alyas's plans, so be it.

"Think about it, Nicor," Alyas said. He'd managed to get himself halfway upright, leaning on one elbow. "If we end these wars, we can open the border with Flaeres permanently. Instead of sending your men here to die, they can be craftsmen or traders or farmers. Do you have any idea how much the country's tax revenues go up from trade when we're not killing each other? Do you know how deep in debt we get when we are? Just think what we could do with that money instead. It could lift the crown out of reliance on syndicate loans, for one thing, and if we're no longer taking their money, we get Raffa out from under their thumb. Think what it would mean!"

So, that was it. Not just peace and an end to all this pointless death, but freedom from the syndicates' influence. It was a tempting vision. Even hard-headed Nicor, who had his eyes firmly fixed on his own career, was in danger of being moved by it. Esar could see it in his face.

"So, I need you," Alyas said, "to get Corado out of my way and pray we can still salvage something from this mess. Because I have to take the bodies of those men back to the Lathai and if they decide they'd rather kill me than talk to me, I can't say I'd blame them."

Nicor, who had also seen the bodies, looked sick at the thought. "You still think you've got any chance?" he asked. "I'll support it if you can pull it off, but Esar's right. You're assuming anyone else shares your ambition."

Alyas was silent for a beat. Then he said, quietly, "Diago does."

Nicor stared at him, his expression pained. "So that's why Gaemo's sniffing around? Ithol's blood, Alyas. Just shut up, all right? I don't want to know anything else."

Esar knew how he felt.

"Nicor—"

"No," Nicor snapped. "Just no. I'll take Corado back for you. I'll make sure the king knows what he did. But that's it, understand? Don't involve me in this. Make him see sense, Esar."

"I'm trying. Stay down," he growled at Alyas, who was trying to get up again. He'd have to get up soon. He couldn't re-establish his authority lying on his back, but soon wasn't yet.

"Take a courier with you," Esar told Nicor, his warning look keeping Alyas pinned in place. "Send word when you make it to Avarel."

Nicor-Heryd nodded. With a last look at Alyas, he ducked out of the tent and into the pre-dawn dark.

"See?" Esar said to his brother.

Alyas draped an arm over his eyes. "Shut up, Esar."

ESAR

Alyas was sitting down when Esar returned the trophies he had taken from Corado, which was a good thing, judging by the way his face paled when he counted them and realised there were only four.

"Are you sure?" he asked for the third time.

Esar, who wasn't at all sure, said, "I had my hands full with you, if you remember. Which you probably don't. I didn't see any others. Why?"

The leather cords with their strange pendants were draped across Alyas's knee, two made of copper and another two of silver. They were carved with designs similar to the painted whorls the Lathai wore on their skin, each one unique. Personal.

"I can look," he offered. Had he missed one? But if he had, someone would have picked it up by now and they'd never see it again. Alyas could hardly order its return. Matters were too delicate for that to be tolerated. And if Corado still had it, it was too late. Nicor had left with him hours ago.

Alyas shook his head, his expression bleak. "It'll be long gone."

"Why?" Esar asked again. "Why does it matter so much?" He could understand that Alyas wanted to return them with the bodies, but the torture and death of the prisoners was a far greater impediment to his hope of salvaging the negotiations than one missing amulet.

Alyas raked a hand through his hair, wincing as his fingers

brushed the ugly bruise. He'd spent the morning dealing with one thing after another, making sure the whole camp saw he was upright and capable, and now his ragged edges were showing. "It matters," he said, "because I don't know what it was made from."

That was not terribly informative. "Silver?" Esar offered, looking at the others. "Copper?"

His brother picked up the four remaining pendants and laid them on the cot beside him. "Or Isyr."

Esar stared at him in silence for a long time. "Since when," he asked at length, "do the Lathai have Isyr?"

Alyas gave a helpless shrug. "I don't know, but they do. And if anyone finds out, if Corado has an Isyr pendant and he takes it back to Avarel…"

He didn't need to finish that thought. If a suspicion of this reached the wrong ears—and as far as Esar was concerned, that included the king's—Alyas's hopes weren't just dashed, they would be crushed under a syndicate-backed takeover that would make this half-hearted expedition Raffa had dreamt up look like a country stroll.

It was precisely because Alyas knew Raffa wasn't serious that he felt justified in subverting his original orders to deliver what he thought was a greater prize. But that would change the moment the king or his blood-sucking syndicate creditors thought there was Isyr in these mountains. There had been rumours for years of Isyrium deposits in Lathai territory, but no one had ever found them and neither Lankara nor Flaeres were sufficiently convinced to authorise the vast expenditure required to launch a full military conquest of the region to find out. Which was why they were here with an army of only four hundred. Alyas had spoken only truth when he'd told Nicor they didn't have enough men.

"Send someone after Nicor?" But even as he said it, Esar knew they couldn't. If Corado had Lathai Isyr, whoever they sent to retrieve it would know it too, and that was already too many people for a secret.

"It's too late," Alysa said. "We'll have to cross that bridge when we come to it—if we come to it. One pendant is proof of nothing on its own. First, I must convince Ailuin he can still trust me."

Esar clasped his hands to stop himself from doing something that would not have improved his brother's current state. "You can't think you're continuing with this. The best you can hope for is that we don't end up in a war *today*. After what Corado did, they'll never make peace, and if he has Isyr, that peace is doomed anyway."

Alyas's face tightened. He wasn't going to be reasonable. "If Corado has Isyr, all the more reason to make this work. I'll convince Raffa somehow. If I don't, these people will die—all of them. Our father would not have wanted that. Not because of…"

Not because of what he'd done, and what it had done to his son.

"Our father," Esar began, then stopped, one look at Alyas's face warning him it would do no good. He wouldn't hear it.

Esar had loved his foster father. Gerrin-Raine Sera was the only father he'd ever known. His death hurt in ways he could not put into words. But he was also furious with the man for the manner of his death and the damage he had caused. That he had taken his own life was bad enough, but that he should have done it in such a place and in such a way, while Alyas watched… Esar would never forgive him for that.

And if, in trying to prevent another tragedy that was a direct result of the first, Alyas caused himself more harm, Esar didn't know what he would do.

"Diago is willing," Alyas insisted. "Melar is certain that if we can deliver a peace treaty, Diago will support it, and then Raffa will have no reason not to. He wants an end to these border wars as much as anyone—we've talked about it for years—he just doesn't know how to go about it." At Esar's sceptical look, he added, "I know you don't like him, but he is trying."

"I don't dislike him," Esar said carefully. "I just have less faith in his consistency. You're not the only one with influence and the syndicates are a lot more annoying. And Raffa's never been good at taking a stand."

"He'll take one this time," Alyas said, "because I'll make sure there's no reason not to."

"And Corado?"

"Leave Corado to me," Alyas replied. "I won't let him stop this."

AILUIN

The heartache began when five of their scouts did not return on time. It deepened, later, when it was certain they never would. Ailuin listened to the reports, his hand raised to silence the shouting, the wailing, the cries for vengeance. Inside he was weeping.

It was, praise the spirits, an elder among the tribe's warriors who had led the party that found the Lankarans with the bodies, and Ailuin was thankful that calmer heads had prevailed. That they had watched and listened and not done as his son would have done, or any of the younger men and women. As he might have done once, long ago.

Five of their tribe had been brutally murdered. They had not been killed in battle. They had been taken. Tortured. They had died in fear and pain far away from their kin. Their *xhiden* had been taken.

It was a desecration, a violation so terrible it stopped thought. Without their *xhiden*, their spirits would be lost to the tribe forever. Gone as if they had never been. The pain of it ached to the core of him, pulsed in time with his grief for an opportunity lost and a future that would be written in blood when it could have been so much more.

Because Gerrin-Raine Sera's son had sat before him and held out the promise of peace. Then he had snatched it back; then the Lankarans had done what they always did.

And Ailuin had nearly sent his own son among them.

"If he doesn't come," Ailuin told Eldruin, "you may do as you wish."

"And if he comes?" Eldruin demanded. His anger had the scorching heat of youth and the raw bitterness of grief. He had lost friends.

Surely, he would not come. What hope was there now of peace between them? Of friendship? The Lankarans had shown who they were. What they were. It wounded, that knowledge, but not as deeply as what they had done. Not as deeply as what was to come.

They had taken the *xhiden*. The Lankarans had stolen their people from them forever.

Gerrin would have come.

The thought hurt, striking to the heart of his pain. For a brief moment, he had dared to hope. But Gerrin-Raine Sera was dead, and his son Ailuin did not know at all. What was a name, in the end, but the thing you called yourself? Alone, it meant nothing. He would not come.

"If he comes," he told Eldruin, "then I will decide."

※

He came. He did not come alone, but he came.

He came as he had come before, with his hands out, and this time they were not empty.

Ailuin raised an arm, a signal to those behind. A signal to wait. His heart thudded with painful, dreadful hope.

He allowed Alyas-Raine Sera to approach, the man at his side nervous and watchful, his eyes flitting between the warriors ahead and Ailuin on his own in the centre of the meadow.

As before, Alyas stopped when he was still some paces away. He was afraid, not of the warriors with their spears raised and bows drawn. He did not even look at them. His fear was Ailuin's.

As before, Ailuin beckoned him forward. He was unarmed, the blades that sang of death nowhere on his person, and his face was swollen and bruised, one eye ringed with black and crusted with blood. His head was tilted to one side as though it hurt him to hold it upright. One of his own had done that.

Something deep inside Ailuin unclenched when he saw it. Come what may from this point on, at least he had not been mistaken when he had chosen to trust Gerrin's son.

Alyas took a step forward. The man at his side stopped him. Tall and broad, his bluff features were creased in a worried frown that looked like it had taken root there too long ago for a man who could not be more than thirty. Something passed between them, too low for Ailuin to hear, and the man dropped his hand. His frown stayed.

Alyas came on alone. His heart aching with the weight of his people's grief, Ailuin said, "You have come to tell me that some of the children of our tribe will not be returning home."

Alyas held out his hands, the hands that held the lost *xhiden*, and offered them to Ailuin. "I'm sorry." His voice cracked and broke on the words.

Ailuin looked at the *xhiden* on his palms, reading the names and the lives of his tribe's lost sons in the sacred carvings, and felt his heart quicken with anger and regret. With fear. "One is missing."

Those wary, dark eyes met his. "I know." Alyas hesitated on the question he did not want to ask. Or perhaps that he did not want answered. "Is it Isyr?"

Of course it was Isyr. That was why it was missing. A child of the tribe lost forever to Lankaran greed. "Where is it?" The words were harder, fiercer, than he intended.

Gerrin's son made a helpless gesture. "The man who did this... I took them from him. I thought I had them all. When I realised..." He took a breath. "He's taken it. But I promise, I will find it and I will return it."

If he comes, then I will decide.

But the decision had never been his. It had been this man's, and with that promise, he'd just made it.

Alyas was still holding out the *xhiden*. Ailuin took them, feeling the spirits of his people return to him as his fingers traced their names. "You will return their bodies?" he asked.

Alyas nodded. "We have cared for them. We do not know your ways. If we have done wrong, I apologise, but know that we have treated them with respect."

It was Ailuin's turn to nod, slow and deep. "Respect is never wrong." The flesh no longer contained the living spirit; only their xhiden held their essence now.

"What was done to them…"

Ailuin stopped him. "I have been told. My people saw you find them." It was the only reason the Lankarans were not already dead, because someone with the wisdom to *wait* had seen what he'd done and heard what he'd said. He looked into that guarded face. "What is it you want from us?"

It mattered so much, that question. So much that the asking of it almost undid Alyas's careful control. He drew in a breath. "I do not ask you to forgive us. I know that is not possible. I want what has happened here between our peoples to never happen again. I want you to help me ensure it never does."

Ailuin looked past him to where the Lankaran army was arrayed in neat, nervous ranks. Such a small force, but they were led by a clever man and that made them dangerous. His own warriors were all around them; the ones they could see in the meadow were but a fraction of the Lathai's strength, in sight only because it was expected.

If Eldruin and the other young men and women of the tribe had their way, this crime would be punished with more death. But tragedy need not always beget tragedy. Alyas was trying to salvage something from the wreckage of his hopes. The Lathai could do the same, or they could pursue vengeance for their tribe's deaths and escalate a decades-long tragedy that would never see another chance like this.

Alyas saw the direction of his gaze. He said, "I know you have us surrounded. I know you have since we arrived. These men don't deserve to die for what another did. He will be punished, I swear it. But he was my responsibility, as these men are. It is my failing, not theirs, that allowed this to happen."

"So it is from you that we must take the price of our people's deaths?" Ailuin asked him, and saw the man behind Alyas tense.

Alyas felt it, too, one hand flashing a warning. "Yes, if you must."

Ailuin nodded again as he thought about that. "Very well. Tell me of your peace and I will tell you my price."

As before, they sat. As before, Ailuin summoned Eldruin, who crouched by his side, hatred in every taut line of his body. Beside Alyas sat his brother, Esar, whose watchful gaze never left Eldruin. Ailuin had heard of him. One of Gerrin's fosterlings. He nodded gravely and extended his welcome. Behind them, frozen in anticipation, both armies waited.

Alyas talked, and as the afternoon sun began to fall, he spoke the words of Ailuin's dream. A future in which the Lathai no longer needed to fear the avaricious impulses of their powerful neighbours. A future that was all theirs, to fill with their stories, with their peace and the peace of the land.

It was a powerful dream, and like all such dreams, it was tenuous, uncertain.

When he fell silent, it was Eldruin who spoke first. Eldruin who, despite his anger, had *listened*. "You cannot make this promise. Not for Lankara or Flaeres."

"No," Alyas said, "but I am as close as you will come to someone who can, because I am prepared to try."

And he would not be here, with this promise on his lips, if he did not believe he could make it real.

Eldruin looked at his father, seeking his guidance, but Ailuin did not give it to him. It was the young who had to make this work, the young who had to believe in it. His son frowned, turning back to

Alyas. "The one who is responsible—you will not give him to us?"

"I can't. He's gone."

"Because you sent him away!"

"Yes, I sent him away. I sent him back to Avarel, where he will be tried for what he did, and punished."

"And we are supposed to trust Lankaran justice?" Eldruin demanded. "You should have given him to us."

"If I had done that," Alyas told him, "I would have squandered this chance. If I had given him to you, I would be dead and we would be at war."

Eldruin stared at him, disgust on his face. "This is what you ask us to embrace? Peace with a people who would kill to protect a murderer?"

Alyas met his hostile stare without flinching. "Would you hand over one of your own to an enemy, knowing the fate that might await them?"

"We are not like you! We don't torture our prisoners!"

"But my people don't know that, just as you do not know us. That is what I want to change! *Help me.*"

Because they were strangers, and strangers cannot make peace. Only friends could do that. Would Eldruin understand? Could he look past the hurt and see the healing that was there for the taking?

Silence stretched out between them. There was an agony of indecision on Eldruin's face. He wanted the comfort of that healing, Ailuin could see it, but he feared betraying the friends he had lost if he allowed their killers to go unpunished.

It was Alyas who broke the silence. "We don't have to be enemies," he told Eldruin, pleaded with him. "Don't let one man's evil dictate all our futures. We are more than that."

Eldruin, fists clenched, gave a strangled sob. "Ranul's *xhidan*—"

"I will return it."

It was too much. Thrusting to his feet, Eldruin walked away. There were tears in his eyes.

Alyas dropped his head, shoulders slumping. He had tried so hard, and he was very tired. Ailuin's heart ached for both of them, for the needless tragedy of it.

Then Eldruin was back, standing over them, and his anger vibrated from him in waves. "Do you swear it?" he demanded. "You will bring it back to us?"

Alyas, fierce hope in his eyes, promised, as he had before, "I swear it. I will find it and I will return it to you."

Eldruin gave a short, sharp nod. "Then do as you wish."

He did not stay. Where the anger had been, now there was only grief and loss, and he would not let these others see that. But he left behind something more precious than words.

Ailuin reached across the space between them, held out his hands. Alyas took one. With a hesitant glance at his brother, Esar took the other.

"Strangers cannot make peace," Ailuin said with tears in his eyes. "So we must be friends."

AILUIN

Of course, such things were not as simple to do as they were to say. Ailuin knew that. You could not, as Esar protested, just wave your hands and turn enemies into friends, but perhaps if you waved them enough, someone might respond. And from unpromising beginnings it is possible to build great things. It is also possible they will fail.

The Lankarans stayed in the mountains for several weeks. And cautiously, slowly, they came to know one another. It started with little things, trinkets traded here and there, drinks exchanged by those bored on watch. Then little things became bigger things, snippets of language shared, stories told, names learned. Strangers became people, and people could, in time, become friends.

But there was still one thing left to do.

On the eve of the Lankarans' return to Avarel, Ailuin went to extract his price.

As he usually was, Alyas was with Esar. Or perhaps it was more accurate to say that Esar was with Alyas, because Ailuin had the measure of these two now and the complicated ties that bound them.

"When this is over," he said to Alyas, "whatever happens"— because like all dreams, this one was uncertain— "you will return here with the Isyr that was your father's, and you will leave it with me for a time." Not forever, he could not ask that, just for a time.

Alyas flinched, something close to panic in his eyes. One hand gripped tight to the sword hilt. "I don't—"

"This is *my* price," Ailuin said firmly, "for forgoing the blood you owe us."

Alyas looked away; Ailuin could see the pulse flickering at his throat. Esar, startled and wary, met his eyes over Alyas's shoulder, caught between concern and gratitude. He had lost a father too. He might not understand why, but he would feel the wrongness of it.

Alyas was silent so long Ailuin thought he would refuse, and if he refused, that meant it was already too late. But Ailuin didn't think so. The strength of will that could impose this treaty on two peoples so determined to make war would not be overcome so easily.

"When this is over," Alyas agreed at last, though his hand still gripped the hilt, the knuckles white with tension. And then, as though he needed to convince himself, he said, "I will succeed. I will bring you your peace."

"You already have," Ailuin told him. "Because of you, our peoples are no longer strangers. Because of you, these men will go home and they will tell different stories about the Lathai, stories of people, not enemies, stories of friendship, not war. In time, those stories will do more to break down the walls between us than any words in a treaty."

But Alyas was very young, and that was not enough. He wanted to hammer the world to fit his vision, and he had not yet learned that the world does not like to be forced into shape. Kings liked it even less.

"I will do more than that," he promised, as Esar watched with an uneasy frown. "I will make this real."

❧

He was wrong, of course. Catastrophically so. Because greed poisons everything, and Lankara's king had caught the scent of riches. And for that he sacrificed not only a friend and four hundred lives who could have told the truth of those weeks, but the future of his nation as well. The Lathai, neither their lives nor their deaths, ever entered into it. Only Isyr mattered in the minds of kings.

But Alyas kept his promise, both of them. Though it was perhaps Esar who kept the first. Months after word came that Lankara's king had torn that peace to shreds, that he had done worse to the man who negotiated it, Esar brought his brother to the Lathai because he did not know what else to do or where else to go. And Ailuin took from Alyas his father's blades, with their endless, nerve-searing song of grief, and for a while he moved, he talked, and he slept, sometimes, unhaunted by dreams.

But it did not last.

There was too much anger in them for peace or rest. Too much guilt for the promises they had made that others had broken. And one yet unfulfilled.

So they left, and it was two years before they returned, arriving one day with the dawn. They were going back to Avarel, Alyas said, and he handed Ailuin the Isyr blades. "I can't take them. Keep them safe for me."

He did not say why, but Ailuin knew. He knew what they had been doing, what they had been looking for, the syndicate probes they had turned back, the mining convoys they had searched. They were returning to Avarel to retrieve the *xhidan* that had been taken, and that night Ailuin spoke to the spirits of his tribe, and he promised them their lost one would return. Then he waited.

CASSANA

THE FIRST TIME

The first time Cassana Gaemo met Alyas Raine-Sera, he was still reeling from the death of his father and she had just buried her husband; and she *hated* him.

It was at an event in Avarel—she no longer remembered what or where. Melar had taken her, trying to distract her, and Alyas had been dragged there by Esar, she learned later, for the same reason. They were thrown together by well-meaning brothers as though their pain was something in which they might find common ground, but the only connection they found was one of mutual irritation. He was cold and distant, uninterested not just in her, but in life in general, and she was too easily hurt. It was a time in her life when she'd needed kindness, and he'd had none to give, not for himself or for her.

"Don't do that to me again," she told her brother as their carriage pulled away at the end of the night. "What an awful man. I pity that poor girl who has to marry him. Did you see her? So young and pretty and bright, and he's so…"

"You mean the young lady who spent all night making eyes at the king?" Melar was stretched out against the cushions, one leg propped up on the bench and eyelids drooping. He at least had enjoyed himself, taking full advantage of their host's hospitality.

It was true. She *had* noticed that, but it was hardly surprising if the girl was so ignored, a fact she pointed out to her brother.

"She is not ignored. He is, in fact, very fond of her. Maybe not in all the ways a wife might wish, but there are worse bases for a marriage, wouldn't you say?"

She would, but she was in no mood to admit it. It was how her own marriage had begun, and she had been happy enough until the wasting sickness took Gaden from her. But that wasn't the point. "It didn't look that way to me. He paid her not the slightest bit of attention the whole evening."

Melar opened one eye and surveyed her with an amused expression. "He paid no one the slightest bit of attention, and you know why, so don't take it so personally."

"I am not taking it personally! I have no interest in that man at all."

"Don't you, Cass?" her brother asked, enjoying her outrage. "Then why have we spent this entire journey talking about him? Oh, don't worry," he grinned, fending off her furious blow. "He's leaving for Orleas in a few days and you won't ever have to see him again."

"Good." She sat back, leaning into the cushioned seats. "I don't want to."

Melar just smiled and went to sleep.

THE SECOND TIME

The second time she met him was in Sarenza little more than five months later, both him and Esar the worse for drink and flushed with the success of their peace-making with the Lathai. It was a glimpse of another life, of what might have been if Raffa had chosen a less destructive way to lay claim to Mari-Geled, if Alyas had not been so badly hurt by it that he had been unable to see that Cassana could have given it all back—the life and status he had lost—here in Sarenza. Or perhaps he'd never wanted it. Perhaps what they'd had was enough.

Not that she had any desire to give him anything that night, but she couldn't hate him either. He had every reason to celebrate what could have been a historic achievement, even if, as she had believed at first, it was at the expense of her nation. Rumour had flown ahead of them of Lankara's new treaty with the Lathai and, like the rest, Cassana wondered why they had come to Sarenza—to flaunt their victory?

Melar, who was not an ambassador then (though he already had the king's ear and a lot else besides), laughed at her suspicion and asked her why she thought constant border wars with Lankara were a good thing.

"I don't," she protested. They were wasteful and pointless, killing young men for no purpose. Whatever the outcome, they would be back at it in a few years—or months, if things got really tense—and those young men would be joined by yet more casualties of national pride. And, she supposed, by the Lathai, too.

"Then perhaps you should not be so quick to jump to conclusions," Melar chided, tapping his gloves against his leg as he waited for her by the door. "Now hurry up. I don't want to be late."

Cassana paused, giving her brother a searching look. He was not late, far from it. "Why? You've never been on time to anything in your life."

Melar looked affronted, though he could not deny it. He considered lateness a virtue; it allowed him to make a dramatic entrance. "Because, dear Cass, you will not be the only one to jump to conclusions, and I would very much like this not to go wrong. It would be a waste of an awful lot of effort."

She frowned at him. He had been gone for weeks and he had not said where. "What have you done, Melar?"

"Conspired with the enemy, of course," he said airily. "Now, *come on*! If this is a success, I shall be a hero. If you make me late and it all goes wrong, I shall not."

There was an urgency to him that suggested there was truth behind his flippant words. It was hard to remember, sometimes, that beneath the amusing façade he liked to affect, Melar had a core of Isyr steel. *His* nerves made *her* heart flutter, but she stopped stalling, finishing up the stitching to repair the ripped seam of his cape—he hadn't said how that had happened either—and it was only when she was straightening it over his shoulders that she said, "Conspired with *him*?"

"Well, it certainly wasn't with his king," Melar said, amused by her dislike. "Yes, with *him*. Because neither of us wishes to see these expensive, futile wars continue, and sometimes, when you are handed an opportunity, you have to act."

"And Diago?" It was one thing for men like Melar and Alyas-Raine Sera to have an opinion on foreign policy, but kings had other considerations, and ensuring they didn't look weak in front of their rival rulers was usually chief among them.

"Diago," her brother said, picking his words with care, "does not disapprove in principle, and that is why we must pull this off tonight."

Cassana thought about that. "And Raffa-Herun?" The man who had initiated this latest military expedition.

"That is less certain," Melar admitted. "But Alyas believes he can persuade him."

It was, she decided, an awful risk. Especially to come here rather than take whatever treaty they had negotiated to their own king first. But there was some logic in it. If Alyas could bring his king not only peace with the Lathai but the agreement of Flaeres—as long as it was advantageous to Lankara—it would be that much harder for Raffa-Herun to refuse to honour it. Assuming he could keep his pride in check.

Melar inspected her repair in the mirror—it was one of his favourite capes, deep Isyrium blue on the outer face, a garish jewel red on the inside—and grinned. "Come along and spectate if you like. There are bound to be sparks."

"No, thank you." She avoided such occasions since Gaden had died. He had been her shield, his warmth and good humour swallowing up the attention she hated, allowing her to shelter in his shadow. Now that he was gone, her shield was gone too. It had been less than a year and still sometimes his absence took her breath.

"Are you sure?" Melar pressed. "This is a matter that would benefit from a woman's perspective, and you are the most sensible woman I know."

"No," she said, more firmly. "Tell me about it tomorrow."

※

It was very late when they woke her, the sound of laughter drifting up from her garden and pulling her out of a dream of Gaden. There was a cruel moment when, half-awake, she thought she heard his voice, then her brother laughed and she remembered. Gaden was dead. She was alone.

It's a bitter thing, memory. Forever reminding you of what you've lost, yet without it, what was lost was gone forever. And there were so many memories from that night, of Alyas and of Melar. Memories that made her smile even as they brought tears to her eyes. It was the start of so much, though none of them knew it at the time. And she held those memories tight for all that they hurt.

It was anger, that night, that rescued her from painful memories. Lankaran accents filtered up through the laughter, and it was with outrage that she realised who was in her garden. Melar had brought them *here*?

It was a warm night, the heart of Sarenza's summer, and she didn't bother dressing, merely wrapped a robe over her nightgown and marched into the garden. She didn't need to be dressed to throw them out.

She found them perched on the low wall that surrounded the small shrine to Yholis, down by the spring, and well on their way to being very drunk. Melar held out his arms as he saw her. "Cassie! Come, join us. We're celebrating."

The other two grinned at her, indistinct shapes in the darkness. Melar had found a handful of Isyrium bulbs from somewhere, but they were nearly burned out and the tired blue glow did little more than illuminate the ground between them, which was littered with empty bottles.

She snatched them up—they were from *her* cellars. In this state, they would probably fall on them and do themselves an injury. "Celebrate somewhere else," she told Melar. How dare he bring them to her house?

"But, Cass," he protested, without a trace of shame for raiding Gaden's wine cellar. "It's tomorrow. Let me tell you about it!"

"It's tonight," she said. "Go away, Melar."

One of the shadows stood. "Sayora Gaemo," he said with a wobbly bow. "We apologise for intruding. We will leave at once."

"Sit down, Esar," Melar said. "She doesn't mean it. Oh, come on, Cass," he pleaded. "Where else can we go?"

Not to his home, which was little more than a couple of rooms that he occasionally graced with his presence when it was time to pay his rent. Since the age of seventeen, Melar had spent his nights with Diago when he was in Sarenza. Or at her house, if that were not possible.

"I don't care," she said. The Lankarans had to be staying somewhere. They could go there. Anywhere but her garden.

"Cassie," her brother wheedled, trying to stand. She corrected her assessment; he was already very drunk. "Don't throw us out. We did it. Diago signed."

"Yes, and you're a hero," she said with a sigh. There was a good chance they weren't capable of going anywhere at this point. "Except you haven't done anything yet, have you? You're one signature short. So maybe you should save your celebrating until Lankara's king puts his name to your precious treaty. *If* he even does." And she was far from convinced that would happen.

"He'll sign," said a quiet voice. *His* voice.

"Why? Because you'll tell him to?" Her tone was sharp with impatience. She couldn't see his face, but she could see the bright outline of the Isyr blades he had placed on the wall by his side. It had struck her, even then, how they were never far from him, even in her garden at midnight.

"No." He sounded amused. He sounded rather more sober than her brother or his. "Because he stands to win more than he stands to lose."

He was so sure. They all were. Three young men, delighted with their own cleverness and believing they had wrapped the world around their little fingers. How wrong they were. And it changed them all.

At the time, his confidence only irritated her further. "Oh, carry on then. Since it isn't in doubt. Good night."

"Stay, Sayora," he said as she turned to leave. "Since we're already keeping you awake."

Melar leant towards Alyas-Raine Sera and said in a whisper the Lathai in their far-off mountains could have heard, "She doesn't like you."

Esar choked. Alyas leant forward into the fading light of the bulbs and looked at her. "But she loves you," he said to Melar, a casual hand propping her brother up as he overbalanced. "And she thinks I'm wrong." He said it like a challenge, and it sparked her anger. He saw it and gave her an infuriating smile. In the blue glow, his face showed the fading marks of bad bruising. Someone had saved her the trouble of hitting him.

But he had, nevertheless, identified the source of her irritation. He could scheme however he wanted, she didn't care, but he had involved Melar, and her brother's involvement put him at risk. And, potentially, Diago too.

"Tell me, Sayora, is not friendship between us worth a little risk?"

"Of course it is," she snapped. He was being deliberately ambiguous and it annoyed her. He had no claim on *her* friendship. He was also not as sober as she'd thought. "But just because you think this is a good idea, it doesn't mean your king will agree. And then what happens to my brother and Diago?"

"What happens to us you mean," Esar muttered. "If Raffa doesn't agree, we're all fucked."

That won him a glare from his brother and from her. Melar was giggling to himself in the background. She hadn't seen him this drunk in years. It was indication of just how nervous he had been that he had drunk himself into this state so quickly.

Alyas-Raine Sera, on the other hand, appeared not to be possessed of nerves, which was all very well, but he was playing with people's lives.

"What reason does he have not to?" he asked her now, though why he cared what she thought, she didn't know. He had given no indication he even remembered her. "Nothing changes. This treaty merely formalises the reality that already exists. Flaeres claims the mountains. So does Lankara. Over and over." He made a spiralling motion with his hand. "What have we gained from them other than debt and death?"

"Very eloquent," she retorted. "But you know it's not about that. As far as Lankara is concerned, those mountains are Lankaran, so why should your king give them up? And don't tell me to save lives."

"Why? Isn't that a good enough reason?"

"It's a very good reason, don't twist my words. But it is not, generally speaking, a reason that moves kings."

"Maybe not," he agreed, taking the flask that Melar thrust at him. "But money is." And Raffa-Herun, she would discover, needed money more than most. Lankara was nearly buried under syndicate debt, debt from which Alyas badly wanted to free him. Badly enough to have engineered this treaty; badly enough to want to convince a woman he barely knew. She was less clear on why *she* was bothering to argue with him.

He held out the flask. She shook her head, lifting Melar's legs from the wall and dropping them to the ground so she could sit beside him. Once again, Alyas caught her brother before he could fall.

"The Lathai's territory is so small," he said, as Melar struggled to stay upright. "It extends no further than the foothills on either side of the spine. It's a ridge of rock. It means nothing to us and everything to them. If we give it to them, Lankara and Flaeres lose nothing."

"Not true," she replied. He wasn't naïve. She shouldn't have to tell him this. But he seemed so very young in that moment, though she was thirty-three and he was just five years younger. "They lose face."

"Or," he said, fixing her with an intent look, "they create an opportunity that offers much greater rewards than what they're giving up."

"And what's that?"

"Trade. Wealth. We create a trade corridor between us through Lathai territory. If we respect the Lathai's claim, they have agreed to guard it. If we are no longer rivals for the land, if we are at peace with the Lathai, trade can flow freely across the mountains as it never has in the past. And when merchants grow rich, so does the crown. And that is why Raffa will sign, because one thing kings always need is money."

He thought he was so clever. He was, handing two young kings a huge win if only they had the vision to accept it. Peace and prosperity, a chance to turn their attention to those domestic matters so often ignored when complications arose outside a nation's borders. That Diago wanted it was obvious. It might even have been Diago, through Melar, who had planted the seed of this plan, because Yholis knew, Flaeres had its hands full dealing with its more powerful neighbour to the north. If Diago could settle matters with Lankara, it would allow him to concentrate on the problem that was Qido.

But it all meant nothing without Lankara and surely Raffa-Herun would not appreciate the order in which they had approached this.

Alyas remembered the flask in his hand and passed it to Esar. "Raffa has a stiffer neck and too many complications," he said when she pointed this out. "He can't make the first move. It would be a concession."

"But he *can* accept Diago's concession? If you make it look like it is Flaeres that is backing down, Lankara can do likewise?"

He grinned. "Exactly."

"But why make a spectacle of it?" That part didn't make sense, especially if Diago was always going to agree.

"Because if this happened behind closed doors, neither your lords nor mine would accept it," Alyas replied. "It had to be a public spectacle. Your court had to see that Diago had no part in it, and Raffa must never know any different."

"No, indeed," she said in despair. "Can you imagine the consequences should it be discovered that the King of Flaeres had conspired directly with subjects of a rival nation to undermine that king's authority?"

He laughed, damn him. He was enjoying this. "Don't forget the outrage here if your lords thought they had been deliberately bypassed. That's why everything went through your brother."

Melar waved a lazy hand at her; he was practically horizontal now.

Esar held out the flask and she snatched it from him. If she had to debate with a drunkard, she may as well join him. "Then why are you here?"

Alyas grimaced. "Because even the best plans sometimes fall apart."

Esar snorted. "Sometimes? What he means, Sayora, is that he fucked up and we had to ensure that fuck up didn't fuck the whole thing up."

"Esar," Melar murmured. "Language."

Cassana took another drink. "So your perfect plan wasn't perfect after all?"

"There are no perfect plans," Alyas said with a flash of irritation, and she had to hide her smile because at long last she had gotten under his skin. "What Esar means is that we never intended to come here at all. Melar was supposed to bring the proposal to Diago, but Diago didn't hold his nerve and sent him too early. Things got a little out of hand."

Which was certainly an understatement for her benefit. "Out of hand how?"

Her brother rubbed at his throat, which was hidden that night by his collar, and said with high drama, "I was nearly *killed*."

"I warned you," Alyas said without a hint of contrition. "If you'd waited, I could have dealt with Corado, then I wouldn't have had to throw you out and we wouldn't have had to come here and do your job for you."

"Should have killed him," Melar muttered.

"That's what I said," Esar agreed. "He's not done causing trouble, whatever you think. Don't say I didn't warn you."

Alyas put his hand out for the flask with an expression that suggested he had heard all this before. "And killing him, of course, would have been entirely free from consequences."

"Can't make trouble if he's dead," Esar opined with the wisdom that came from the bottom of a bottle.

"Gentlemen," said Melar, waving an arm above his head. "Although I approve of the general sentiment, please refrain from plotting murder in front of my sister. You're making her uncomfortable. And!" He lurched upright, too quickly, requiring Alyas to catch him for the third time. "And," he said, "you've left out the best bit. How I saved the day."

Alyas, caught with the flask at his lips, choked and coughed. Esar slapped him on the back so hard he nearly fell off the wall. "I don't think—"

Melar waved away his objection. "He said we needed the women there," he told her, pointing at Alyas. "If you remember, I tried to persuade you to come."

Not terribly hard, though. He knew she hated court functions.

"You were missed," Alyas murmured. He was looking at Melar like a hunter might watch a rabbit about to trip a snare.

"You were," Melar confirmed. "I said you're the most sensible woman I know."

They had wanted the cooler heads of women, she guessed, because men were too often ruled by pride in such matters. How many wars had been fought because a man didn't know how to back down? And many of those women had lost sons, brothers, husbands to the border wars; many had sons still to lose. An appeal to end that pointless death would find a receptive audience with the wives and mothers of the court, and of course Alyas would have thought of that, because he would do whatever it took to get his own way.

But even as she thought it, she felt ashamed. Why should he not do whatever it took if peace was the outcome? *Isn't that a good enough reason?*

Cassana had no sons to send to war. Gaden's illness had stolen that chance from her, and at thirty-three and a widow, she was unlikely now to have children. But there had been a time when, newly married, a house full of children was all she'd wanted. Even now, the silence in her hallways was a sharp pain. How much sharper the pain of children silenced?

"Anyway, Aunt Gennia nearly sank the whole thing," her brother confided. Aunt Gennia, the queen mother and not their aunt at all, who adored and disapproved of Melar in equal measure. Aunt Gennia, who clearly had not been let in on the plotting. "She decided it was men's talk and tried to herd all the women from the room."

Cassana almost smiled. "Go on then, what did you do?" Melar and Diago's mother had an ongoing battle of wills over so many things—most recently who Diago should marry—and the last thing you did with Aunt Gennia was take her on directly.

He cast her a sidelong look. "Don't be angry, Cass. I told Maria Gorlani you were sick in bed, but you had asked for her to tell you everything that happened. So, of course she had to stay, and the others wouldn't be left out."

She couldn't speak, she was so angry. Alyas and Esar exchanged looks and leant back, disappearing into the shadows. "Melar!" But even through her outrage, she had to admit it was a clever choice. Maria was both a friend and the wife of a man who, left to his own direction, would have opposed the treaty through sheer lack of imagination. A man, moreover, who would have carried a lot of the others with him. But he also adored his pretty young wife and would do anything to please her.

Which was not the point. Melar had no right to involve her in this. "So now I have to lie for you, too?" And to her best friend.

"I know, I know," Melar said, too quickly. "But it worked, didn't it? We won, Cass." The flask had made it back into his hand and he raised it to Alyas. "We won."

That was almost the last coherent thing she heard from any of them, and she left them shortly afterwards to continue drinking to their victory, or what seemed like a victory that summer night. It hurt her heart even now to think of the way it was twisted away from them, how Raffa turned it into a tragedy with his rage and jealousy and greed. She found it hard to believe that Alyas had never seen it, that he had misjudged so badly and put such trust in friendship, because the man she came to know gave his trust so sparingly. But, like her and Melar with Diago, Alyas had grown up as a friend and companion of Lankara's heir. And, though there had been no sign of it the only time she had seen them together, he had adored the young woman he had thought of as his younger sister. That they should both betray him had simply never crossed his mind.

It changed him. And when Raffa laid the deaths of all those men at his feet, it very nearly broke him. It would have, she guessed, if not for Esar. If not for the one person he could count on without question, for anything, who had stayed loyal through the bad years that followed. Years of which she knew next to nothing. Because it would be three years before she saw him again, and it was absolutely nothing to do with him that in those three years she turned down two perfectly good offers of marriage. Indeed, she never thought of him at all.

THE THIRD TIME

The third time Cassana Gaemo met Alyas-Raine Sera, she nearly died, and it was entirely his fault. And when he laughed as he apologised, utterly unrepentant—that was when she realised she loved him.

The third time she met him, he broke down the door of her bedroom in the middle of the night and took her hostage. It was years before Melar stopped grumbling about how much that cost him.

It was, more accurately, the Gorlani guards who broke down her door. Alyas simply walked in because the latch was loose and she hadn't bothered to wedge it closed. It never occurred to her that she might need to. But it was certainly his fault that the guards smashed in the door since they were looking for him.

Either way, she came awake in the middle of the night with a man's hand over her mouth and a voice she recognised saying, "Don't scream. I won't hurt you."

She did scream, of course, or tried to. What did he expect? But it was muffled by his hand, and the room she had been given in the Gorlani's house was at the far end of the guest wing and all the other rooms were empty.

The lamp by her bedside flicked on as he lit the bulb and she looked into the startled eyes of Alyas-Raine Sera, disgraced former duke of Agrathon, last seen drunk in her garden three years previously, arguing with her over a peace treaty that would see his life destroyed within weeks.

"Sayora Gaemo?" He withdrew his hand as if she had bitten it. "What are you doing here?"

On another occasion she might have enjoyed having shocked him, but she was too shocked herself to do more than stare. "What am I doing here? What are *you* doing here?" She had never expected to see him again. She had certainly never expected to wake up and find him *in her bedroom*. It was so surreal she couldn't think straight.

If he suffered the same affliction, he mastered it quickly, stepping back from the bed, his attention turning to the door. "I won't be here long."

Which was just the kind of infuriating non-answer she expected from him. Cassana threw back the blanket and got up, pulling on a robe. He was in her room uninvited—in her friend's house, uninvited, in the middle of night—and she was not going to lie in bed and wait for him to leave as though it were a matter hardly worthy of note.

He glanced at her as she lit the room's main bulb, flooding it with light. "What are you doing?"

"What are *you* doing?"

He was dressed in dark leather and light armour, and he had wound leather cord around the Isyr hilts of his weapons to disguise their brightness. He was very plainly up to no good and Maria was a friend. "Why are you here? Tell me or I'm calling for help."

He ignored her, one ear pressed to the door. "Does your brother know where you are?" The loose latch clicked shut as he fiddled with it, and he stood back in satisfaction.

"What? What does it have to do with him? Maria and her husband are friends. I'm staying with them."

"So Melar knows?" He took her by the elbow and pulled her with him across the room. She tried to shake him off, but he was insistent, fingers gripping tight into the muscle of her arm.

She slapped his hand and he let go as they reached the window. "No, he doesn't know. Why should he?"

Cool air rushed in as he threw open the shutters. "Well then, this is awkward. Because your brother paid me to come here and steal from your friends."

"What? Why?"

"You'd have to ask him."

She was incensed. "Why would you agree?"

"For money," he said with biting patience. "I am in need of it these days, you may have heard."

Footsteps pounded down the corridor outside. He was by her side in an instant, a hand on her arm, a finger to his lips.

The footsteps passed her door, continuing down the hallway. Alyas released his grip and reached out to douse the bulb. "It would be very bad if I were discovered here. You were asleep all night, understand? You heard and saw nothing."

Cassana nodded. She was shaking. He saw it, dragging the blanket from the bed and throwing it round her shoulders. Then he returned to the window, stepping out onto the balcony. Her room was on the first floor, just above the terrace that stretched out into the ornamental lake at the rear of the Gorlani's country house.

She followed him. "What are you doing?"

"I was going to leave the same way I got in, but I suspect that won't be possible now. So a swim it is." And he climbed onto the balcony railing.

Someone hammered at the bedroom door. "Sayora!" The latch rattled.

He was back by her side, close enough to feel the beat of his heart. "Answer. Ask them what they want."

"Sayora! Are you in there?" The door rattled again.

"Why should I?" she hissed.

"Because if they catch me, I shall tell them who sent me and why. And that would be Melar's career over, and possibly worse."

Gods, but she *hated* him.

"What do you want?" she called, trying to sound half asleep. She did sound angry. "It's the middle of the night!"

"Apologies, Sayora," called a gruff voice. "We're looking for an intruder. He was last seen in this corridor."

"I was asleep," she snapped. "My door is locked."

There was a short silence, punctuated by a further attempt on the door. Whatever Alyas had done to the faulty latch held it firmly closed. "I must ask you to open this door, Sayora."

"Whatever for?"

In her ear, Alyas said, "Can you swim?"

She flashed him an outraged look. "Of course I can swim!"

Alyas made a choked sound. He was *laughing!* Before she had time to react, he had the blanket off her shoulders and was using it to mop up the blood from a shallow cut he had made on his arm with his knife. Then he threw the blood-stained blanket onto the bed, which was already in considerable disarray, and was dragging her back out onto the balcony.

The attempts at her door progressed to thuds as bodies threw their weight against it. "Sayora, please! Open this door!"

"Now would be the time to scream," Alyas observed as he climbed back onto the railing. He meant to take her with him!

She took a step back but he was faster, his hand whipping out to grasp her arm. "I can't leave you here. It will look like you helped me escape, and then suspicion will certainly fall on your brother."

"But if I escape with you, he looks entirely innocent?"

"You're not escaping with me. I'm taking you hostage. Didn't you see the blood from our struggle?"

She did scream then, in pure, spitting rage.

"Very good," he said. "It's much easier to take a willing hostage and we don't have a lot of time." A loud, splintering crash underscored his point and Cassana looked back to see that the Gorlani guards had broken through the central plank of the door.

Alyas didn't give her time to decide. He dropped down on the other side of the railing, his feet wedged into the gaps to keep himself from falling, and hauled her towards him. "It's too late now. They know I'm in here."

She called him the worst name she could think of, which only made him grin, and let him help her over the balcony.

"Hold on," he murmured by her ear. "I won't let you fall." Because she was trembling again, and it had nothing to do with the cold.

Then he disappeared and she nearly screamed, until his voice came from a few feet below. "It's not far. I'll catch you."

The door to her room disintegrated with a final crash and Cassana let go.

Strong hands caught her round the waist as she fell, then his hand found hers and he ran along the stone balustrade of the Gorlani's terrace towards the dark water of the lake.

There were shouts from her balcony, which was suddenly crowded with guards. Alyas turned, pulling her close and clamping a hand over her face, covering her nose and mouth. Then he stepped back into nothing and freezing black water closed over her head.

❦

Cassana had learned to swim in the lake at the country estate where her parents had spent their summers, but she had never swum in that lake at night at the advent of winter. The icy water shocked all thought from her head, the cold a physical pain. She gasped, and only Alyas's hand over her mouth prevented her from filling her lungs with water.

Their heads broke the surface together and she sucked in a huge gulp of air as instinct took over and she kicked with her legs.

"Take a breath," Alyas said by her ear. Before she had time to do more than obey, her head was under again and he was swimming with her through the dark water, away from the terrace. She twisted in his grasp, turning over so she could better propel herself, and when they next surfaced, she hit him.

The drag of the water took most of the force from the blow, but it served its purpose. He released his grip, treading water beside her. But as she opened her mouth, he clamped his hand over it and cautiously turned her head.

They were not far from where they had entered the lake, just outside the glow of the lanterns in the hands of the guards lining the edge of the terrace. If she called out, they would find her. Alyas might evade them in the darkness, but he might not. The moon was full and bright. She did not doubt he would go through with his threat to tell them who'd sent him, and she couldn't risk Melar.

"Ready?" he murmured.

She nodded, taking a breath, and they were back under, his hand on her arm ensuring they did not lose each other. They swam like that, only surfacing to breathe when she thought her lungs would burst, until they were far enough away that the guards would not hear them. It can't have been more than a minute, and by then he was doing more than just keep hold of her. The cold was burrowing into her, a freezing burn that sapped the energy from her legs and constricted her chest.

She couldn't go any further; she didn't remember where they were going or why. Her head sank under the water. Panic took over. Her legs kicked out and her foot struck the soft mud of the bottom of the lake. Then he was dragging her out onto the bank and the cool night air cut through the wet fabric of her nightgown, shocking her anew.

Beside her, Alyas collapsed onto his hands and knees, then onto his back, his breath coming in short, harsh gasps. He was dressed in heavy leather, weighed down by weapons and armour, and he had done most of the work getting her to shore, but he could not lie there in the mud, not even to catch his breath. He was shivering as badly as she was. If they stopped, they'd freeze. Even through her exhausted haze, she retained enough sense to know that.

"Get up!" she snarled, shaking his shoulder, and he rolled over again, back onto his knees. "Up!"

He put an arm round her waist, heaving himself upright, and they each leant on the other for those first few steps. Then he withdrew his arm, tugging at the shoulder straps that secured the plated vest he was wearing, but his hands were too numb and he gave up. She reached out to try; he shook his head, teeth chattering. "Keep moving. Find Esar."

Which meant, thank Yholis, that someone was looking for them. The late autumn night wasn't bitterly cold, but soaked and badly chilled, it was cold enough to be deadly. If they didn't warm up soon… But it was hard, so hard, to force her frozen legs to walk when all she wanted to do was lie down and sleep.

His cold fingers found hers and he tugged at her hand. They stumbled together until her muscles started to work and she pulled free, staggering along in his wake, movement coming more easily now, coherent thought reforming.

She swore at him, furious. He managed a shaky laugh, which only angered her more.

Esar found them a few minutes later as they straggled through the undergrowth, her sodden dress tangling around her ankles and catching on briars, the silence between them brittle with her outrage and his choked amusement.

He saw Alyas first; she was several metres back, tugging her filthy hem free from a snag. "What in Ithol's name happened to you? You're freezing." Then, a few seconds later. "Why are you wet?"

She heard Alyas say, "We had to swim." At least his teeth were chattering as badly as hers.

"We?" Esar looked past him and his eyes widened. "Sayora Gaemo?"

"She helped me."

Esar pinched the bridge of his nose. "So you threw her in the lake?"

"Either that or… implicate her in the theft. Melar didn't know… she was there."

"Melar," Esar snapped, "is going to have your head for this." His eyes sharpened on the blood dripping from Alyas's wrist. "Is that yours?"

Alyas glanced at his arm. Water had mixed with the blood, marking pink trails down his fingers. He wiped them on his leg, fingers trembling with cold. "It's nothing."

Esar grabbed his arm and pushed back the cuff. "You'll live." He turned his attention to Cassana. "And you, Sayora? Are you hurt?"

She shook her head and nearly fell. The world wobbled. Someone steadied it. Esar was by her side, wrapping his jacket around her shoulders, which was still warm from his body. "It's not far." His voice rumbled in her ear, deep and reassuring. "We'll get a fire going, warm you up."

She nodded, clenching her jaw to stop her teeth cracking from the force of her shivering. Esar said something to Alyas over her head, then he was urging them both to move, one under each arm, carrying on a largely one-sided conversation with his brother as they went. Sometime later, she let him bundle her onto a horse. Then he was sitting behind her, solid and warm, and she could finally give in to the urge to sleep.

Cassana had no idea how long they rode, but when she woke, it was daylight. She was wrapped in blankets beside a fire and she was *warm*. It was so glorious that she just lay there and enjoyed it, until the quiet murmur of voices intruded on her comfort and reminded her where she was and why.

"If I'd been with you—"

"We've been over that. Then you wouldn't have been here to find us."

Cautiously, Cassana opened her eyes. Alyas was on the other side of the fire, in a similar state to herself, Esar by his side. They were in the throes of a muted disagreement.

"You couldn't have found some other way?"

"They were right outside the door! I could hardly leave her there. This way, she's an unfortunate victim. Melar pays us a nice ransom—"

That was too much. "He will not!"

Alyas's eyes snapped to her in surprise. He grinned across the fire. "Of course not, but the world will think he has and both of you remain above suspicion."

Cassana wrestled with the blankets, trying to free her arms. She could not argue with him swaddled like an infant. "There would be no suspicion if you hadn't burst into my room in the middle of the night and thrown me out of the window!"

"And if you hadn't been there," he retorted, "I wouldn't have had to."

As if it were her fault! If he'd been closer, if she hadn't been wrapped up so tight in several layers of blankets that she could hardly move, she would have hit him. Then, to make matters worse, he laughed—*laughed*—at her outrage.

Esar, who was staring at Alyas as if he had never seen him before, said, "Sayora, allow me to apologise since my brother has no manners. We'll get you back to Melar as soon as we can, I promise."

Get her back to Melar? What was she? His poor widowed sister who relied on his charity and could do nothing for herself? Was she not an independent woman with her own means and her own life? "You can take me to my home," she snapped. "My brother can do as he pleases. *As I do*."

Esar held up his hands in apology. Alyas smothered his amusement in the blanket that hung round his shoulders. He must still be delirious from cold, she decided, as she got her arms free and saw the deplorable state of her nightgown. She sighed. "Can I please have some clothes?"

※

They gave her dry clothes, oversized leathers that were made for a much larger man and hung off her small frame. She didn't care. They were clean and warm and she changed into them gratefully, discarding her filthy, tattered nightgown.

She was attempting to comb out the tangles in her hair with her fingers when Alyas found her, holding a bowl of hot soup as a peace offering. She was tempted to turn her back, but the chill had not entirely left her, and she wanted the soup more than she wanted to hurt him. He saw it too, damn him, his eyes brimming with laughter.

"Would you believe me if I said I was sorry?" he asked, placing the bowl on the ground and sitting opposite her.

She glanced at his face, at the amusement he wasn't even trying to hide. "No."

He had also changed, scrubbed clean of the mud and debris from the lake, though he was barefoot. Clearly, he had not thought to bring spare boots. Or maybe he didn't have any. The thought was a sharp reminder that this was no longer the same man she had met in Sarenza.

For money, he had said in her bedroom when she'd asked him why he was there. *I am in need of it these days, you may have heard.*

She looked away and her gaze snagged on the edge of a bandage peeking out from the cuff of his jacket. "Are you badly hurt?"

He frowned, then shook his head. "No. It's barely a scratch. But Esar is… Esar. How is your pride faring? I can see your modesty has been well tended."

"No thanks to you."

He put a hand on his heart. "I beg to differ. Those are my clothes you're wearing."

"Liar." They wouldn't fit him any better than they fit her. They must be Esar's.

He didn't deny it, picking up the soup and holding it out. "The point is to eat it while it's warm."

She snatched it from him, hot broth spilling over to scald her fingers. "You're not having some?"

"Oh, I've been force-fed already. Esar is Esar, but he does make good soup."

He watched her eat and she watched him, trying to reconcile her memories of the man who had argued so fervently for that peace treaty with one who was now apparently a thief for hire for anyone who would pay. But his whole life had been taken from him, even his names. Who was she to judge, or presume she knew how that should change him?

It had changed him physically. Hardship would do that, she supposed, though she doubted it was merely physical hardship that had put the shadows on his face. His dark hair was longer than it had been, brushing the top of his collar, and the shirt itself was plain, undyed linen. It had been repaired more than once with neat, practised stitches, not a skill a duke would have expected to need but one he had obviously mastered, along with some other less respectable skills. Like burglary. Only the blades at his hips remained the same. He had unwound the leather cord that hid the glow of Isyr, and she found it hard to believe, seeing them, that his king had not taken them, too. Perhaps he'd tried. Perhaps she did not want to know what Alyas might have done to keep them. There was so much she didn't know.

"I owe you an apology," he said, breaking the silence that was becoming awkward.

"What makes you think I'll accept it? You broke into my friends' home, you stole from them, and you took me hostage by threatening my brother."

"Oh, not for that," he said with that infuriating laugh in his voice. "It's possible I was less than courteous to you once."

Cassana contemplated the half-empty bowl in her hands and thought about throwing it in his face, but he would probably laugh at that, too. "Once?" she asked, her voice admirably calm. "Which occasion in particular are you thinking of?"

"In Avarel," he said, surprising her. "I was… cold. You didn't deserve it. You had suffered a loss and I should have been kinder."

He should have been, but he had suffered a loss of his own and she could, perhaps, have been more understanding. "I will accept that apology," she told him. "Especially since I was not aware you had noticed my presence."

It wasn't laughter, now, in those dark eyes. "How could I not notice you?"

A warmth spread out from her middle. She placed the bowl on the ground, grateful for the opportunity to hide her face. He might mistake the flush in her skin from the hot soup for something else. She was *not* blushing.

"When did you start stealing things for Melar?" she asked, because what was she supposed to say to that?

"When did you learn to swim?" he countered.

"At our summer estate as a child," she said, "and I asked first."

"You make it sound like a habit."

"Do you ever answer a question?"

"That's unfair," he protested. "I have answered several of your questions, and to answer this one, tonight was our first time stealing for your brother."

She pounced on the distinction. "But not the first time you've stolen something."

"Do you want me to apologise?" The words had bite.

"Why? Would you?"

There was a brittle pause, then Alyas sighed. "If you want to know what this is about, ask Melar. You may find it is not so simple as you suppose. And if I have sunk even lower in your estimation because of my apparent delinquency, then please remember that we have had few options these last few years, and we do still need to eat like everyone else."

He stood, the warmth between them cooled like the remains of the soup, and in sudden panic, she said, "You still haven't apologised for kidnapping me."

Alyas paused. She thought he would snap, that she had broken the fragile beginnings of understanding that had been growing between them. Then he said, "If I apologise, it would mean I wish I hadn't done it, and that would be a lie."

The warmth from the soup faded quickly after he left. Cassana resumed her attempt to comb out her hair and very definitely did not think about what he'd meant, because if she did, she would be in danger of forgetting what he had done and that she was *furious* about it.

Her fingers caught on a stubborn knot and she gave up. Her hair was too tangled and her fingers too cold, and why was she bothering anyway? Using a torn strip of her nightgown, Cassana tied her hair out of her face and went in search of warmth.

Esar was sitting alone by the fire, building it back up, a pile of kindling by his side. He looked over as she approached, noting the blanket pulled tight around her shoulders, and shifted so she could sit beside him on the log he was using as a seat.

As the fire licked at the fresh wood, she crouched gratefully in its warmth, holding frozen fingers as close to the flames as she dared. When her teeth stopped chattering, she asked, "Where's your brother?"

"Gone to meet yours," Esar replied, poking at the fire. "Did he apologise?"

"For throwing me in a lake? Not entirely."

Esar grunted. "Sounds about right. Are you hungry?"

She shook her head. "He gave me soup."

"Who needs an apology when you have soup?" He was smiling. "How much trouble will we be in with Melar?"

"For throwing me in a lake?" Melar would probably find it funny.

If Alyas was right, he might even be grateful. "Nothing you can't handle, I'm sure."

Esar looked like he could handle most things, the years since she had last seen him hardening his soft edges and putting the first greys in his hair, though he was younger than her. She had no idea what they had been doing or where they had been, and she had not thought to ask Alyas. She had been too focused on her own outrage. There had been rumours, of course, that had placed them everywhere from Qido to the Steppes. Such wild, outlandish rumours that she had dismissed most of them. Melar had shrugged his shoulders and pretended ignorance, and they would be having words about that, and a lot else, when she next saw him.

Once Esar had the fire going again to his satisfaction, he left her and busied himself with various small tasks while she dozed, still exhausted from the night's exertions. Some while later—Cassana had lost all track of time—he boiled water and made tea. It tasted old and gritty, but she didn't complain. It was hot and strong.

They didn't speak, but it wasn't an awkward silence. Esar was easy to be with, the complete opposite of his brother in so many ways. Yet the bond between them was stronger than ever. It was only Alyas who had been cast out of Lankara. Esar did not need to be here; he had chosen to be.

"What happened?" she asked as they drank the tea. "In Avarel?"

It had been a huge scandal, not just in Lankara. A stupid, cruel, pointless scandal and a tragic waste not just of an opportunity that would not come again, but of good men, loyal friends, who had negotiated a peace at great risk to themselves. And been punished for it.

It should have been an embarrassment for Diago, who had over-ruled the doubters at his court and put his trust in the treaty, but Raffa-Herun's response was so excessive, so unfair, that even in Flaeres, outrage had been directed at Lankara's king, their sympathy entirely with the man he had wronged, even when word spread of the loss of the army for which Alyas had been blamed.

She had wept when she heard, that night in her garden still vivid in her memory, when they had talked of the peace and all its possibilities with the future stretching out before them. That historic peace that could have freed two nations from their intractable, endless border wars and made them prosperous allies, even friends. That instead had ended in blood and betrayal and heartbreak.

Esar was still poking at the fire, but his shoulders were rigid with anger. "What happened? Raffa didn't want to know, that's what happened. I've never seen him so angry. You were right, he wouldn't listen. That treaty—it could have given him so much. And maybe Alyas should have done it another way, but he took the chance that was there." Esar gave the fire a particularly furious jab and Cassana coughed on a lungful of smoke, tears stinging her eyes. "All Raffa had to do was reach out and take it. He took everything else instead."

Everything else. His names, his title, his honour, his future, even the woman he was supposed to marry. Surely it hadn't all been for Mari-Geled?

"Was he very heartbroken?"

"Heartbroken? It nearly bloody killed him—" Esar caught sight of her face; his own went through a rapid readjustment. "Oh, you mean about Mari?"

"No, I…"

But Esar was grinning, and her face flushed with heat that had nothing to do with the fire.

Then his smile faded. "I have no idea. And I wouldn't ask him, not about any of it. Especially not about… well, any of it."

"About the army?" she guessed. That had to hurt the most.

Esar sighed, tossing the stick into the flames. "Not that. Please. Don't bring that up." He hesitated. "I haven't seen my brother laugh in three years. He laughs with you."

"At me, I think you mean."

"No, Sayora," he said quietly. "Not at you."

The words did more to warm her than the merrily burning fire, and she had to look away to hide her confusion. "My name's Cassana. I'm wearing your clothes. I think we can put formality aside." As if she didn't know what Lankarans were like with names.

But Esar just grinned. "Cassana, then. And I mean it. Whatever you're doing, keep doing it."

Now she was in danger of blushing again, as if she were a girl of twenty, not a woman of thirty-six, and she didn't want him to see it, so she asked, "Was it very bad?"

Esar's smile vanished. "Yes," he said, staring into the fire. "It was very bad."

"Because of the army?" His forehead creased into a frown, and she stopped him before he could warn her, again, not to ask. "You tell me, if you don't want me to ask him." Because she needed to understand what had happened. Because maybe she wanted to make Alyas laugh, every day, and so she had to know.

Esar gave her an assessing glance, weighing that. "I can't tell you what happened," he said at last. "We weren't there and we don't know."

It was the truth, she was sure. If Alyas was not above playing games with the truth—and was certainly not above using it as a weapon—Esar's honesty was of the plain, straightforward kind. A tightness in her chest released. She hadn't believed the accusation. She had seen them in Sarenza. There was no way the men she remembered from that night had just come from the kind of slaughter they had been accused of, but there had been times when she'd wondered whether there must have been some truth beneath the lies, if for no other reason than the harshness of the punishment.

"What do you think happened?" There was no world in which they hadn't tried to find out.

Esar leant forward to put another log on the fire. "Four hundred men don't just disappear. Someone killed them."

"How? Why?"

He shrugged, his shoulders tight with anger. "We left them at the barracks. We saw Raffa, he did what he did, we left."

Cassana felt an absurd desire to laugh. What Raffa did was destroy their lives and possibly worse besides. "And then what?"

"I don't know! That's what I'm trying to tell you. They were alive when we left them. It must have been a year later that we heard what happened. What Raffa said happened."

Which was that the army he had sent into the mountains with Alyas had been wiped out, destroyed by the Lathai he had been ordered to subdue. That, in response to this failure, this culpable tragedy, Lankara's king had stripped his friend of everything, including his homeland. But if that army really had made it back to Avarel, they would surely have been seen. People must know it wasn't true.

"The barracks are outside the walls," Esar said. "We were sent there because the city barracks were full. And yes, I've asked myself a hundred times whether that was a lie, whether the whole thing was planned. I've spent nights wondering what happened to them and why no one ever questioned it, but the truth is, I don't know. Maybe people wanted to believe it. Yholis knows, everyone loves a scandal. Raffa wanted Alyas gone and he gave them a scandal. Cowardice, incompetence, corruption, treason." He ticked them off on his fingers. "That peace became a plot to hand the whole bloody thing to Flaeres. And those men, they knew the truth. A handful of people who say they saw the army arrive at the barracks are easily ignored. Four hundred men who were right there for the peace talks, who knew what happened, who made friends with the Lathai who supposedly slaughtered them—not so easily ignored."

He scrubbed his hands over his face, leaving behind smears of soot. "And it was all so unnecessary. He could have just asked Alyas for what he wanted."

"Asked me for what?"

Cassana started, saved by Esar's quick reflexes from taking an undignified tumble off the log.

"Don't stop on my account," Alyas said from behind them, his voice frosty. "What could Raffa have asked me for?"

"Alyas," Esar warned.

His brother ignored him, picking his way to join them, neat as a cat with all his hackles up. "If you want to examine my crimes," he said to Cassana, "you could at least do it to my face."

"If I want to examine your crimes," she retorted, responding to his anger with her own, "I hardly need look to the past. Did you give my brother whatever it was you stole for him?"

"I did," he replied in the same tone. "And negotiated a nice little ransom for you while I was at it."

"You didn't," said Esar.

"I did," Alyas assured him. "A down payment on future services. It must look real, after all. But don't let that distract you. What is it you want to know? Whether I led my men into a trap? Or if I ran away and left them to die? Or perhaps whether, to protect myself, I allied with your country to betray my own? Take your pick. I have so many juicy crimes to choose from."

"Stop it," Esar snapped. "Why shouldn't she ask? You kidnapped her. She has every right to know what kind of man you are."

"Because I would have thought," said Alyas bitterly, "that Sayora Gaemo is one of the few people who might have seen it for the lie it is."

Because she had been there in Sarenza, because Melar was her brother and he had been with them in the mountains for at least part of the time. The viciousness of his barbs measured the depths of his hurt. She had hurt him.

"I never believed it," she said, meeting those angry, dark eyes. "How could I?"

He flinched and looked away. "So it's just gossip you're after? You want to entertain your friends, is that it?"

And just like that she was angry again. "My *friends,* like the people you robbed last night? Put your wounded pride away since you are relying on me not to entertain them with that detail."

"By all means, do so. It's your brother who will suffer for it. I have nothing left to lose."

Esar kicked at the fire in frustration. A cloud of sparks and ash exploded upwards just as she drew breath for a furious comeback.

"That's enough, both of you!"

Cassana's lungs filled with smoke. She coughed, tears streaming down her face. She coughed so hard, Esar thumped her on the back, her chest tearing. When the fit finally subsided and her eyes cleared, Alyas was gone.

※

He hadn't gone far. Ignoring Esar's well-meant advice to leave him to sulk, Cassana followed, finding him with his horse. He had removed the bridle and was lifting off the saddle when she joined him. She didn't speak, just picked up the comb he had left on a tree stump and started loosening the dried mud on the horse's flank. He watched her—probably checking she knew what she was doing, as if she hadn't grown up with horses—then he too picked up a brush, and they worked in silence as the horse snorted and stamped its feet, its breath misting in the chill air.

"I was being honest," she said, when that silence had stretched on too long to bear. "I never believed it."

Alyas froze, a tension in him that had nothing to do with anger. Then he sighed. "I'm—"

"Don't say you're sorry," Cassana cut in. "I know you're not, and why should you be? But I wasn't asking because I doubted you. I care enough to want the truth, so you can draw in your claws."

"I have claws?" he asked, amused.

"Savage ones," she confirmed. Wherever he had been, the roads had been bad, mud caked all up his horse's legs. If they didn't remove it, it could cause irritation or infection or worse.

"Did Esar satisfy you?" he asked after a time.

"He told me he doesn't know what happened. Is that what you'll tell me?" She was looking at him as she spoke, so she saw the way he stilled.

He didn't answer at once, his face turned away so she couldn't guess what he was thinking. The silence stretched on so long that she resigned herself to it, and the disappointment was sharper than she'd expected. Then he said, "He wasn't lying. We don't know."

"But?" It was inconceivable that he hadn't pursued the truth. His name had been ruined. It wasn't just his pride that was wounded, it was his entire being. She could feel it.

"Why?" Alyas rested his forehead on his horse's neck, his voice muffled by its mane. "Why did he do it? It never made sense."

'He' must be Raffa-Herun. His *friend*. The king for whom he had risked so much.

She didn't try to fill the silence that followed, letting him work out for himself how to navigate those treacherous waters.

"We've known each other since we were children. If he had been... I would have *known*." His pain *ached* through the words. "Four hundred lives snuffed out just so he could get what he wanted? How can a man hide his nature so completely? He can't. It doesn't make sense."

It had bothered her, too, that he could have misjudged his king to such a degree. He was not the kind of man, she guessed, who was prone to such errors. "So it wasn't Raffa?"

His hand paused its work; he flashed her a sharp look. When he spoke again, his voice was guarded, careful. "It must have been. His own army in his own city? That couldn't happen without his knowledge and say-so. It's why that matters. Why is everything."

"And you know why?"

"I don't," he said, attacking his task with rather more vigour than it required, "know anything. The answers to that question are in Avarel, but the one time we went back, I nearly got Esar killed." And he wouldn't risk that again, that was clear.

Again, she said nothing, merely swapped the comb for a brush and continued grooming the poor horse that didn't deserve to be in the middle of this.

Slowly, the anger faded. "Perhaps he did just want Mari. There were things he wanted… I knew that. I did not think he wanted them so much that he would take everything else because he couldn't have them. But I no longer trust my judgement where Raffa is concerned."

That surprised her. "What things?"

He didn't answer, but his eyes slid to the tree from which he had hung the Isyr blades that had been his father's.

The deadly lure of Isyr. It was a disturbing thought. "Would you have given them to him?"

"I would have killed him." The admission was stark, unadorned. Perhaps the most honest thing he had ever said to her. It was her first glimpse of the hold the blades had on him; it wouldn't be the last. She had no idea then what it was they did to him, or the strength of will it took to remain himself. She didn't understand all the ways they had already changed him or the price they would take.

I would have killed him.

If she had known, would she have let that go unchallenged as she did?

The undergrowth crunched behind her. Esar, no doubt, come to check that they weren't killing each other. The horse stamped and whinnied, shaking its head, and she murmured soothing noises, her hand rubbing its neck in long, gentle strokes.

He watched her. "You're good with horses."

"My father loved them. I spent half my childhood in stables. And you're changing the subject."

"Should I not?" he asked with sudden bitterness. "It's hardly my favourite. Raffa might have killed them, but they still died because of what I did. I wanted to keep them alive, so I made peace, and they died anyway. I won't ever forgive him for that, but I am also guilty."

No, no, no! She wanted to scream it at him. He looked so defeated, so tired, and she couldn't stand it. "So, that's it? The truth doesn't matter? You've given up?"

That made him angry. He glared at her over the horse's neck. "I don't give up."

I don't give up.

He would say those words to her years later, after the disaster at Orsena, and tear her heart out with them, because they would both know he was lying. But he wasn't lying now, and neither of them could know what lay ahead. She wouldn't have changed any of it even if she did. But oh, it hurt to remember. Because he did know why those men had died, or thought he did, and it was the pursuit of vengeance that drove his restless life, that would keep him from her side for months at a time, that in the end would set him on the path that would take him from her forever. That would also take her brother and so much else.

If she had known, what would she have done differently? What could she have done?

"I don't give up," he said again with quiet intensity. "And their deaths will be paid for. Every single one."

"You and Esar?" she asked. She didn't want him to give up, but that single-mindedness scared her.

To her surprise, he laughed, looking at something over her shoulder. "There's a few more of us now. See for yourself."

She turned. Behind her, on the tallest horse she had ever seen, sat an equally tall Steppelander, his brown face split into a grin, a woman perched on the saddle at his back. Behind them, more horsemen were emerging from the trees, all armed and armoured. Not Esar checking on them after all.

"Who are they?" she asked.

His smile was full of fierce pride. "My company."

They weren't many, that company. Just a handful of men and Keie, the Steppes woman. But it would grow, in size and reputation, and grow quickly. Alyas and Esar chose their contracts carefully, they did impossible things, or things that seemed impossible, and as the stories spread, the company grew.

But, back then, they were just twenty, all sleeping on top of each other around a single campfire, Cassana sandwiched between Keie on one side and Esar on the other. Keie had lent her a comb and insisted Cassana help her practise Flaeresian. In return, she'd offered to teach Cassana how to use the spear she wore strapped to her back, an offer Cassana politely declined.

Agazi, the tall Steppelander, had brought a message from Melar agreeing a place to meet the following day to relieve them of their 'hostage'. Melar had also sent a note to Cassana, in which he failed to conceal his amusement at her predicament. She'd screwed it up and thrown it on the fire, around which she was once more huddled, trying to fall asleep.

She learned one more thing about Alyas that night. That he avoided sleep, or at least, he did so when he wasn't alone. As she lay on the hard ground, listening to the snores of the men heaped around her, she watched him on the other side of the fire. He was sitting with his knees drawn up, one hand fiddling with a pebble, turning it over and over in his fingers. Every so often, the motion faltered as he drifted towards sleep, then he would recover it, and she realised he was keeping himself awake. He had no need to—others were standing the watch, Esar had been insistent on that point—and he was clearly tired. He hadn't slept the night before and had been riding half the day. But he persisted until it was painful to watch him jerk himself awake each time exhaustion pulled him under.

Eventually, when it was clear he would lose his fight against sleep, he climbed to his feet and walked away from the fire and into the night.

Before she could think about what she was doing, Cassana wriggled out from between Keie and Esar and followed. Esar rolled over as she stood, looking from her to where his brother had been, then rolled over again. She could have sworn he was smiling.

Once up, Cassana quickly realised her mistake. The moon that had been so bright the night before was now hidden behind thick clouds; away from the brightness of the fire, she could see nothing. She felt her way cautiously, hands out to either side, until she tripped on a root she couldn't see and nearly fell.

A hand caught her wrist. "Are you following me?"

She let him steady her; his grip hurt. "Yes." There was no point denying it.

"Why?" His tone was not welcoming.

There were many things she could have said to that, none of which would have sounded any better than the truth. And she was too old, she decided, to play games. "Because I wanted to."

She couldn't see his face, but she could feel his surprise. His fingers released their vice on her wrist and she rubbed at the sore spots they left behind. "Thank you."

"What for?"

"For not letting me fall on my face. Now I'm here, can I stay? Esar snores."

He laughed softly. "He does not."

Her eyes were adjusting to the darkness now, enough for her to see the outline of his face. He was tucked against a hollow at the base of a tree. After a moment, he shifted to one side so she could fit in beside him.

"Why don't you want to sleep?"

She was close enough to feel him tense. "Do you always ask so many questions?" The bite was back.

"I don't usually need to."

He sighed. "Someone has to stay awake."

"Yes, but not you."

Through the silence she heard the faint scratch of the pebble, turning over and over in its merciless rhythm. She reached out and closed her hand over his, stilling it. "You don't need to do that."

He made a choked sound, snatching his hand away. Through fingers pressed tight against his face, he said, "You have no idea…"

How could she if he wouldn't tell her? "You make sure of that, don't you? But if you never let down your guard, how will you ever let any comfort in? Besides, you're poor enough company after one sleepless night. I've no wish to experience your claws after two. So let me stay awake for you, and I promise, if you need me to, I'll wake you."

It wasn't hard to imagine what he was afraid of. Or why, when he couldn't stay awake any longer, he had found a place to hide away. What must his dreams be like for him to fear them that much?

"Cassana." Barely more than a breath, it was the first time he had ever called her by her name, and it ached with exhaustion. His hand found hers and twined them together in the darkness.

"Sleep, Alyas," she murmured, using his name. She squeezed gently and felt him, finally, relax against her. She was so tired it hurt, but she could stay awake if it meant he would sleep. Which he did, almost as soon as he surrendered, and did not, as far as she could tell, suffer the nightmares he so obviously feared. And as his breathing evened out, her own eyelids slid closed.

※

Esar woke her in the morning with a gentle shake and a mug of hot tea. Alyas was asleep beside her, head pillowed on his bent knees. He didn't stir as she stretched stiff muscles, nor when she reached out to take the tea and brushed his arm with hers.

Esar looked from her to his brother, still sound asleep, and shook his head. "You do have the magic touch, don't you? Can I persuade you to stay? Keie thinks you'd be good with a spear."

"Keie is wrong."

Esar grinned. "I don't know about that. When he wakes, tell him Agazi's gone to collect your ransom."

He returned to the fire and Cassana drank the tea, which was too strong and unsweetened, and tried not to disturb the sleeping man by her side. But he roused eventually, woken by the sounds of the camp being dismantled, coming awake with a start, hands reaching on instinct towards the blades by his feet.

Then he turned his head and saw her and his expression changed, morphing from confusion to something close to panic that hurt her heart to watch.

"Did I—?"

She shook her head. "You didn't make a sound." Or if he had, it hadn't woken her, which was much the same thing.

He nodded, not meeting her eyes, and after a moment stood.

"Agazi's gone to meet Melar," she told him, because Esar had asked her to.

He nodded again, leaning down to gather up the blades. She sipped her tea and let him collect his thoughts.

Evidently, they were very scattered, because he stood there for some moments, one hand gripping a silver-blue hilt. And it was so very hard not to do or say anything to startle him, but Yholis, he was the most frustrating man she had ever met. Could he not just accept what was right in front of him?

Across the camp, Esar was watching them, his habitual frown creased deep across his forehead. She knew what *he* wanted, at least.

Someone called out a question.

Alyas unfroze. "Cassana."

He said her name like it hurt. It did hurt. Then he was walking away, over to the activity around the fire, and Esar shook his head in despair.

※

Agazi rode back into the camp at midday, his saddlebags bulging with her ransom. Melar being Melar, Agazi also brought her a clean dress, which Keie helped her change into, chattering all the time in broken Flaeresian, trying to tempt Cassana to stay.

"Are you sure?" Esar asked when she handed him back his spare clothes. He was smiling, but he was also serious. What was wrong with them all?

"I'm quite sure," she said, though that was not true. She didn't know what she wanted, only what she didn't want, which was for Alyas to disappear from her life and another three years pass before she saw him again.

As for what he wanted, it was impossible to know. They hadn't spoken again since he'd woken, and he'd found an endless succession of things that needed his attention throughout the morning, things that were elsewhere, away from her. She could have been hurt. Once, she would have been. But she hadn't known him then, and she was starting to suspect that it was not from his men that he had wanted to hide his nightmares.

All too soon it was time to meet Melar. He was waiting for them on a lonely stretch of the Sarenza road, looking like he couldn't decide whether to be entertained by the farce of her ransom or annoyed about the money he had handed over. His down payment on future services. Whatever that meant.

Esar cupped his hands to help her mount the horse Melar had sent, his face clouded with a frown, but he didn't say anything. He didn't try to interfere.

Now she was a little hurt. She was returning to her life that was so very different to his, and if they parted like this, would they ever see each other again?

Then, finally, Alyas appeared and took the lead line from Esar, who handed it to him with a smile of satisfaction twitching his mouth. Alyas ignored his brother, walking the horse slowly towards where Melar was waiting, tapping his gloves on his knee with impatience.

"I owe you another apology," Alyas said, looking at her, his face as open as she had ever seen it.

"No, you don't. Nor an explanation."

A flicker of relief crossed those sharp features. "Thank you," he said. "For last night. I needed that."

It was an admission, and he made those rarely. He had likely not slept so many hours together in a long time. She had given him that, at least.

"Perhaps you should sleep next to a woman more often." They were halfway to Melar now. They were running out of time.

He glanced up sharply. Her tone was light, her heart anything but. Dark eyes searched her face as each step took them closer to parting. To her life that would never be the same.

"Will I see you again?" she asked, because she couldn't bear it.

He stopped, stilling the horse with a practised hand. Over his shoulder, Melar made a 'what's going on?' gesture. She ignored him, because Alyas was looking at her in a way that made her feel things, deep inside, that she had not felt for many years.

"Cassana," he said with a wry smile. "Run away with me."

She laughed. "With you, or with *you*?"

He glanced behind at where his little company waited. "With me, but also with us."

"No." She leant down and kissed him, a mere brush of her lips on his. "But next time you are in Sarenza, you may call on me." And by Ithol, he'd better.

His smile was like the sun coming out. "I will, Sayora."

He had known she would not say yes. That this life was not for her. Her refusal had not hurt him. Her invitation delighted him.

He said nothing else. They were walking again, but the silence this time was full and beautiful.

Alyas stopped by Melar, who was staring at her with eyes like saucers. His mouth opened and closed without making a sound as Alyas untied the lead rein and handed it to her. Then he walked away.

Melar looked at her in astonishment. "Cass?"

She rode past him, a secret smile on her lips.

"Cassana!" her brother called. "What was that? Did you *kiss* him? Cassana, come back!"

SCARS

The following story takes place partly within the timeline of
The Many Shades of Midnight

BRIVAR

The journey to Avarel was, if not restful, then at least unexciting... Perhaps the most surprising thing about that week, other than the absence of catastrophe, was Alyas coming to Brivar, unprompted, on the evening of the first day and handing over the Isyr blades. "Only until Avarel."

– THE MANY SHADES OF MIDNIGHT

When Brivar had left Avarel to accompany his cousin Lord Sul on his mission to retrieve Alyas-Raine Sera from his fifteen-year exile, he'd known exactly who he was—an apprentice surgeon at the Temple of Yholis, two years from completing his training and attaining the goal he had worked towards for thirteen years. Now, returning, he was no longer sure where he fit into the future he had dreamed about. Because Alyas, without consulting him—although admittedly to protect him—had reordered Brivar's neat, predictable existence and appointed him his personal surgeon.

And Brivar was still grappling with everything that meant—and how, more importantly, he would explain it to Alondo, the master of the temple—when it finally occurred to him that this might not have been his first encounter with Alyas-Raine Sera. Though it was certainly the first time that either of them knew it.

They were almost back in Avarel before the suspicion began to form, and it was, of all things, a scar that jogged loose the stubborn childhood memory. Or rather, two scars.

Lankara's capital was two days distant still, though its huge walls were already a dark mass against the green of the valley, the sun sparkling off the tiled roofs of its towers. If Brivar squinted, he could just make out the Temple of Yholis, nestled below the palace in the temple district. His home. Or was it? It was all so confusing.

Shouts and laughter drew his attention back to the company. They had stopped for the day by a bend in the river as it curled towards the city, and many had stripped down to wash off the dust and sweat of the road. Brivar watched from the bank. It was hot for early spring, but not *that* hot, and he shivered in sympathy as warm bodies met freezing water, preferring to wait for the Isyrium-heated baths at the temple.

Alyas appeared beside him, hair still wet from his own swim and colour in his face at last. He crouched on the shingle, watching hardened soldiers splash each other like children, hands that would otherwise have been tangled in Isyr hilts instead playing restlessly with the flat river stones. The blades were still stowed carefully with Brivar's pack, and he intended for them to stay there until they reached Avarel. He was certain Alyas would recover faster removed from their influence.

The water was cold with mountain run-off, too cold to stay in for long. Esar emerged, shivering and laughing, to good-natured jeers from those hardier souls who stayed in. He turned as someone called his name and Brivar's eyes were drawn to the stark line of scar tissue low on his left side, the skin purpled with cold. The scar was old and long-healed, but it shocked him a little. He might only be an apprentice, but he was experienced enough to recognise a wound that should have killed. He had watched men die from wounds just like that. Esar must have been very lucky—or the person who tended it very skilled—to have survived such an injury.

Alyas saw the direction of his gaze and winced. "It was a long time ago."

"How did it happen?" It wasn't what Brivar had meant to say, but "he should be dead" seemed a tactless response in the face of what was clearly a painful memory.

There was a small silence. Then Alyas said, "We were near a temple," answering the question Brivar hadn't asked. Or, more likely, choosing not to answer the one he had.

"Which one?"

It was professional interest, because just taking Esar to the surgeons at a temple of Yholis was no guarantee of survival. It would have taken great skill and no small amount of luck to have tended such a wound. His master at Avarel's temple could have done it—had done it, in fact—but there weren't many surgeons as skilled as Alondo.

Alyas picked up a pebble, turning it over in his hands. "I don't recall."

Brivar glanced sideways at him. He recalled perfectly well—he wasn't likely to forget a detail like that—he just wasn't going to say, and Brivar had learned by now that there was no point pressing. Alyas would have his reasons for not wanting to talk about it and it wasn't hard to guess what they might be. He had lived a life of violence. Brivar had seen the marks it had left on his body, but there would be unseen scars too, and he had no right to poke them to satisfy his own curiosity.

That did not, however, stop him from being curious. He couldn't help it. He was a surgeon in training—*the company's* surgeon in training—and if Alyas truly meant to keep him, treating such injuries would be the story of his future, not just a map to their past. He had seen the physical scars when he'd tended the wound on Alyas's shoulder, and he had glimpsed the deeper, invisible ones during the na'quia poisoning, the cure that had nearly killed him. Brivar still found it difficult to think about that, or the things he had heard.

How much of that was the Isyr blades, carving their own indelible scars, year after year?

It was a discomforting thought. Those older scars were altogether safer territory. Brivar didn't share difficult memories about those; he didn't know their stories. Like the long, precise line that ran the length of Alyas's forearm, or the ugly white crescent on his upper arm, a cut from a blade that must have carved out a flap of skin. It would have bled badly and had been closed with a pattern of stitches Brivar would know anywhere. He set stitches just like that; he had learned how from his master.

That scar had been niggling away in the back of his mind since he'd first seen it, sparking a hazy memory of a man with blood running down his arm, pleading frantically with someone, Alondo perhaps. An old memory from his earliest days at the temple. But Alyas and Esar had been two years gone by then, exiled by the king and far away from Avarel. Or they should have been.

The city's walls rose high and forbidding in the distance, casting their long shadow over the company and its captain. How would it feel to be banished from your home, your family, for fifteen long years? How would it feel now, two days away from a return you never thought you would see?

"Did you ever come back?" Brivar asked, the words slipping out before he could think better of them.

Alyas went still. "Come back where?" His tone was guarded.

Brivar dropped his gaze, a flush creeping up his face. "I'm sorry." He should not have asked. If they had returned to Avarel during their exile, they certainly wouldn't tell anyone. It would have been punishable by, well, he wasn't sure, but something bad.

The awkward silence stretched out. Alyas stood. Brivar didn't look at him. There was a crunch of pebbles as he turned to leave, then he said, "Esar doesn't remember anything."

Brivar turned, but Alyas was already walking away. Was that a warning not to ask or an admission? He thought again about the memory, trying to tease out the details, but it had lain forgotten in the back of his mind for too many years and the edges wouldn't come into focus. Besides, there was no reason to think the man in that memory was Alyas.

It could have been anyone.

No reason at all, except Alondo's unmistakable signature on his arm.

※

Brivar didn't see Alyas again that day, or Esar. Their increasing preoccupation contrasted with the buoyant mood of the rest of the company, invigorated by their cold swim and prepared to make the most of their last few days on the road before they reached the city and whatever awaited them there.

Plagued by his own confused feelings about his return to temple life, Brivar was more than happy to allow the company to immerse him in their uncomplicated existence, determined to enjoy his final days of freedom. He pestered Della to teach him how to make flatbreads like the Lathai since he had developed a fondness for them, but she shrugged and told him to ask Storn. He asked Agazi instead, who was more approachable than the Qidan with his fierce warrior braids and too many scars.

Della and Keie laughed at his attempts to stretch out the sticky dough, hands that were so skilled at his profession made clumsy by the unfamiliar task. After several failed attempts, Keie took it from him and worked the dough into a flat sheet that he filled with the onions and herbs he had collected. Then Agazi showed him how to roll it into a spiral and flatten it before placing it on the hot coals.

Brivar sat back, sucking a singed finger, the aromatic smell of cooking bread wafting up in the smoke. Storn drifted over, making a show of inspecting his efforts, and Brivar was sure he saw him wink at Agazi before wandering off again.

He poked at the fire, wondering how to ask what he wanted to know, and eventually just came out with it. "Did they ever come back?" he asked Agazi. "Alyas and Esar? To Avarel?"

Agazi gave a one-shouldered shrug, his other arm tucked around Keie. "Not since I've known them."

"How long is that?"

"Ten years? Twelve? You want to turn it now," he added, nodding at the flatbread that had started to colour. "Ask them."

"I have," Brivar admitted, flushing, as he flipped the flatbread over, blistering another finger in the process.

Agazi laughed at his discomfort. "You mean you asked Alyas, and he gave you to understand that you should mind your own business? Haven't you learned yet that you're always better off asking Esar?"

Esar doesn't remember anything.

Had Alyas been talking about the wound or what had led to it? With that kind of trauma, it would not be surprising if Esar's memory was unreliable. Brivar wasn't sure why he wanted to know so badly. Was it just professional curiosity or that fragment of memory nudging him?

We were near a temple.

Could it have been the Avarel temple? Could the man he remembered have been Alyas? But if so, what were they doing there when they should have been far away? It was none of his business, but he couldn't let it go.

"Esar doesn't remember."

Agazi sat forward, extracting his arm from Keie's waist and plucking the forgotten flatbread from the fire before it burned. "You asked him?"

Brivar shook his head. He was half-certain those words were a warning not to ask. He wasn't sure why he wasn't heeding it, except for that niggling memory.

Help him, the man had said, talking about some unseen companion. No, not unseen. Brivar had glimpsed him carried in, just for a moment, limp in the other man's arms, both of them slick with blood. It had been his first sight of the consequences of violence, and he still remembered the shock and horror of it, the sense of the man's panic, vast and uncontrolled, and the contrasting blanket of Alondo's calm. He retained little more of the memory than the emotions, the details lost to time, as though he had deliberately set them aside. Now he was picking at them, like an irritating scab, and could not stop.

"I think I've been told not to."

Agazi frowned. Then he shook his head, ripping a piece off the cooling bread before passing it to Della. "In that case, don't ask me. Why do you want to know?"

Brivar took the bread Della handed him, warm and appetising. "Because I think I saw them at the temple once, when I was a child."

Della poked him in the side. "You never mentioned that. You met them?"

"Well, no," Brivar admitted. "I was hiding in a cupboard."

Thirteen years ago

Brivar hated the temple dormitory. He had slept alone at home, his brothers long grown and out of the nursery. Nights at home had been peaceful, quiet. A dozen sleeping ten-year-old boys were not quiet, the room a constant susurration of little sounds—blankets stirring, sleepy words, soft snores. Someone to his right was crying. He thought it must be Haylen. His eyes were always red in the mornings.

Brivar turned over and pulled his pillow over his ears, but it was a feeble, thin thing, not at all like the duck-down pillows he was used to, and it did nothing to stifle the sound of Haylen's misery. Brivar didn't need anyone else's misery; he had plenty of his own. Part of him wanted this so badly, the part that listened in rapt fascination to the Varistan's lessons, that watched quietly in the background as the temple's surgeons tended their patients. But another part of him missed his home so dreadfully that tears would come on him from nowhere at any time. Times like the dark of the night when he was surrounded by the other apprentices and yet so alone.

The sobs became a snore, dragged in through a clogged nose, and Brivar gave up. Throwing back the blanket, he stuck his feet into his shoes and crept quietly to the door. It squeaked as he slipped through, but he no longer worried that the noise would wake his dorm mates. It never had before. Or, if it had, no one had said anything.

He did this most nights. Not *every* night, just those when he couldn't sleep and the homesickness took hold hard.

The first night, Varistan Alondo had found him wandering the corridor outside his office. Brivar had been terrified. The temple's master was not unkind. Quite the opposite, in fact. He was gentle and patient with his young charges, but he could be stern and a little frightening if they did not listen. So Brivar had been shocked when instead of chasing him back to bed with a scolding, Alondo had invited him into his office, given him tea, and talked to him about his family until his eyelids started to droop, and he'd woken the next morning on a bed in one of the temple's surgical rooms.

It had become something of a ritual for him in the month since. If he couldn't sleep, he made his way to the peace of the surgery where the only sound was the music of the fountain outside the window. Sometimes Alondo would peer round the door and find him there, other times he would simply drift off in the silence to be woken by the clatter of the cooks preparing breakfast in the hall across the courtyard, his cue to return to the dormitory before the other apprentices woke.

In the few weeks he had been at the temple, the peace of its nights had been undisturbed, but he learned one night that just because the rest of the world was asleep, the services of the temple could still be called on.

As he muddled his way to wakefulness, Brivar's first thought was that it must be morning already, but the voices and footsteps were too close, too frantic. He heard a voice he didn't recognise call out a desperate plea for help, and the Varistan's quieter, calming tones.

Brivar rolled off the bed. *They were coming to this room!* As he darted towards the door, the footsteps stopped. Alondo's voice said clearly, "Bring him in here," and Brivar knew the Varistan had spoken to warn him. *Too late.*

In a panic, Brivar looked for somewhere to hide, but there was only the bed, a chair, and the linen cabinet beside the door on top of which the surgical equipment was stacked in neat boxes.

He flung open the cabinet, relieved to find it was only half full, and crawled inside just as the door to the room burst inward and chaos invaded his haven.

Peering through a crack in the cabinet door, the sound of his breathing loud and frantic in his ears, Brivar watched as a leather-clad man limped into the room, struggling under the weight of another man who had been stripped to the waist and was covered in blood. The remains of his shirt were tied around his middle and its red-soaked folds stood out with dreadful clarity against pale skin.

Brivar clapped a hand over his mouth and squeezed his eyes shut.

The door to his hiding place opened.

He froze, terrified, but no exclamation gave him away. He opened one eye. Alondo reached in and withdrew a pile of clean linen. He met Brivar's frightened gaze and put a finger to his lips, then closed him back in the reassuring darkness.

※

Della nudged him, passing him another flatbread, hot from the fire. Brivar looked up to see that Storn had joined them and had taken over the task he'd abandoned.

"Well," she demanded. "Did you see them or not?"

Brivar looked away, unsettled by the memory. "I'm not sure." In those first frantic seconds, he hadn't seen either man's face, not clearly, and his memory was indistinct and clouded by the years. "It was a long time ago."

"There could be trouble," Agazi observed, "if the king ever found out."

Exile had closed the borders of Lankara to Alyas for all time. That he had been recalled now had nothing to do with a change of heart on the king's part. Who knew how Raffa-Herun might choose to punish past transgressions if it suited him?

Storn flipped a flatbread, removing it from the fire to cool before putting another on the coals. "Lucky no one knows anything then."

There was pointed meaning behind his casual tone. The company was protective of its captain, as Brivar had reason to know. He took the flatbread Storn offered him, meeting the Qidan's direct blue gaze, and nodded. He would leave it alone. It was a long time ago and there were, Brivar reminded himself, more important mysteries to unravel. Like finding a way to stop this plague that had consumed whole towns and almost killed Alyas. Or understanding what the Isyr blades were doing to him and why. He would have his hands full; there would be no time for wondering about old scars.

The Varistan saw him and beckoned him over. Alyas turned at his approach. His face was shadowed by the portico, but Brivar thought he saw relief in his dark eyes.
"Your patron wishes to speak to you," Alondo told Brivar, his voice carefully neutral. "You may use my office."
The door closed and they stood there looking at each other in silence. Then Alyas unbuckled the blades and held them out to Brivar. "I need you to take these for a while."

– THE MANY SHADES OF MIDNIGHT

Brivar was right. The chaotic weeks that followed the company's return to Avarel left no space for fretting about events years in the past when what *might* happen scared Brivar more than he wanted to admit. And there was nothing he could do to help, nothing Alyas would allow him to do, except spend those weeks closeted in the temple library looking for something, anything, that might lead them to some answers.

Because Ilyon, the man who had guarded the temple's Isyr treasures, who had been alone in the vaults with them for years, had plunged a blade into his own neck after the Isyr whispered to him and drove him mad. Because Alyas's father had done the same and Brivar was desperate to prevent Isyr from killing him, too. Old scars faded into insignificance compared with the open wound of Isyr.

But not even the disastrous events in Cadria, when the Selysian Syndicate had stolen the blades and Alyas had taken them so violently back—events of which he had no memory—could persuade him to give them up. Until he had no choice.

So when the collapse came at last, when Alyas finally did what everyone had begged him to do and surrendered the blades once more into Brivar's care, it was almost too late. And only then did Brivar realise that he had been looking in the wrong place. He had been so focused on the threat of Isyr that he had forgotten there was a third scar, and it was the crisis that third scar precipitated that unlocked the mystery of the other two.

Not that he was thinking about any of that when Alondo closed the door of his office and left him alone with Alyas, who held out the blades and said, "I need you to take these for a while."

Nothing could have been further from his mind when he took the Isyr from Alyas and saw what it had done to him.

Brivar didn't think about the scars through all the long night that followed, as he waited for Alyas to return with Frey. Not until hours later when Alondo ushered him into the surgery where he had spent his homesick childhood nights, the newborn cries of Keie's baby still echoing in his ears, and this time he was the one confronted with a difficult surgery.

Dragged from one moment to the next from his joy at the birth to the sight of the king's conflicted Guard commander with his unconscious burden, there was no time to think at all. No time to do anything but cut the poison out of Alyas before it killed him. Then, when it was over, Brivar dropped the scalpel from nerveless fingers, empty of everything. His knees shook. He had been awake all night; exhaustion crashed down.

Alondo put a hand on his shoulder, pushing him towards the chair. "Sit. I will finish here."

Brivar hesitated, reluctant to leave any part of this to someone else, even if that someone was Alondo, but the shaking in his knees had progressed to his hands and he could do no more.

He sat, averting his eyes from the stillness that was so unnerving. Alyas was never still. From the moment Brivar had met him he had been in constant motion, possessed of a fraught energy that defied everyone and everything. Until it couldn't. Now Brivar's hands were coated in his blood and he was left wondering whether he had done enough.

But it was over now and such thoughts served no one.

Brivar looked up from the blood on his hands to where Alondo was closing the cut he had made. For a precious moment, there was nothing for him to do. He tipped his head back, resting it against the wall as fatigue hit him like a hammer, and his gaze slid away from Alyas towards the shadowed corner where the cabinet stood.

The memory slammed into him, fragments reforming with frightening clarity. The night his haven had been disturbed by blood and chaos; the last night he had slept outside the apprentices' dormitory. The night he had, in fact, spent huddled uncomfortably in the cupboard in this very room.

Brivar stood, walking to the old cabinet with the dents and scratches he knew so well. The cabinet he had used so many times over the years and never given more than a passing thought to the hours he had spent curled up amid its sheets and towels.

He crouched as he reached it, fingers tracing the crack in the door through which he had peered in fascinated terror at the man with the bleeding arm who had carried his friend into this room and begged Alondo to save his life.

If he turned to his right, he would see Alondo working on Alyas. But as a child, his view of that side of the room had been obstructed. He had not seen the frantic effort to save Esar's life. All he had been able to see was Alyas, who had watched it all from the chair where Elenia had left him, forbidding him to move.

Brivar had forgotten Elenia had been there. But of course she would have been. There was no one better at the really delicate work than the Varisten. He could see her now, as clearly as if she stood before him, younger but no less intimidating, forcing Alyas away from the bed so Alondo could work.

She had ordered him to take off his jacket then bundled a wad of cloth into his hand, holding it against his bleeding arm.

Alyas had looked up at her and that was when Brivar had first seen his face. Past and present collided as he saw it again, the memory vivid and clear. Dark hair, longer than it was now, angular features tempered by youth, still to be marked by the years, by illness and Isyr. That peculiar blend of restless energy, of movement never quite stilled, even in exhaustion.

Brivar blinked, dispelling the disturbing flash of memory, and returned his gaze to Alondo. He watched his master's careful, precise rhythm as he set each neat stitch and tied it off, the actions so familiar he could follow them in his sleep.

"It *was* you. You stitched the cut on his arm. You saved Esar's life. Here, in this room."

Alondo, his work finished, set aside his needle. "I wondered if you remembered that."

Brivar blinked again, fatigue blurring his vision. "I didn't." But he remembered now, all of it, and he looked at his master with new understanding.

Thirteen years ago

A sense of frantic movement just beyond his sight was Brivar's primary memory of the first hours hunched in his uncomfortable refuge, his eyes rivetted on the man in the chair whose attention was focused on the bed Brivar could not see.

He must have slept at some point, because when he woke, Elenia was gone and there was a quiet stillness to the room that suggested the emergency was past. The dark-haired man's head had lolled back as though he could no longer hold it upright. His eyes were still open, just, but the hand that had been holding the cloth to his arm had long since given up the task and his sleeve was red to his wrist.

Alondo moved into view, pulling up a stool and taking the man's arm in one hand. "Let me see this," he said gently, positioning an Isyrium bulb so its light fell on the ugly cut.

The man jerked, shaking his arm free. His whole body swayed with it. "Help Esar."

His friend. Esar.

"I have helped him," Alondo told him, recapturing his arm before he could pull away. "He's in Yholis's hands now. It is time to help you."

As the man glanced towards the bed where his friend lay, hidden from Brivar's sight, Alondo undid the fastenings on his shirt and helped him pull it over his head. The sword cut was the worst, but bruises were forming across his ribs and down his side, some of them dark and ugly. Alondo ran gentle fingers over the contusions. "Who did this to you?"

The man flinched from his touch, turning his head away. "It doesn't matter." Then, "They're dead."

The words were so quiet that Brivar had to strain to hear them. They frightened him. *This man* frightened him. He had *killed* people. But the Varistan seemed neither shocked nor scared. He merely reached for a soft cloth and began to clean the wound. As the flap of skin fell back, fresh blood welling up, Brivar let out an involuntary squeak.

The man's head snapped towards the sound, suddenly alert. He started to rise.

Alondo tugged at his arm, keeping him in place. "We have a mouse problem, that is all. Sit still."

"Alondo…"

Brivar watched his master press his cloth on the bleeding cut, pain and pressure holding his patient still. "There's nothing here to alarm you, Alyas."

"If anyone knows we're here—"

"No one will know," Alondo assured him, his words slow and soothing, the way he spoke to the new apprentices when they were scared and missed their families. It was clear now that they knew each other. There was more than familiarity in Alondo's voice, there was fondness there too. "No one will find you."

The man—Alyas—peered into the darkness where Brivar was hiding. "Your mouse—"

"My mouse has no one to tell but other mice. And what would you do? You cannot move Esar. Besides, he has every right to come and go in Lankara as he pleases. It is only you who may not."

The tone that worked so well on the apprentices did nothing to alleviate his patient's surge of anxiety. "You think that would stop Raffa? He'll hurt him to hurt me. I can't risk it."

He tried to stand again and this time Alondo put a firm hand on his shoulder and held him in place. "Sit down." His voice was no longer soft and soothing. Brivar knew that tone; he knew not to cross it. Alyas clearly did too, because he subsided, allowing the Varistan to continue his work.

"I need to stitch this," Alondo said after a tense silence. "Can I trust you to stay here while I fetch what I need?"

Brivar could not hear the response, but evidently it satisfied his master, who rose stiffly and left the room, all his supplies exhausted by the surgery on his first patient.

Left alone, Alyas did not stay put. Frightened, Brivar shrank back, but the cupboard doors were not thrown open, nor was he dragged out into the room. Instead, Alyas limped towards the bed where his friend lay, disappearing from view, and the silence was punctuated only by the thud of Brivar's heart.

The door snicked open. Alondo said in a resigned tone, "Sit back down before I have to pick you off the floor." When he was not immediately obeyed, the Varistan set down his bundle of equipment and retrieved his patient, depositing him back in the chair.

As he unrolled the silk pouch, Brivar's master offered what reassurance he could. "He's lucky. The blade was sharp but small. A different weapon would have done more damage. The wound is deep and has bled badly, but Yholis willing, it will not kill him." As Alyas's tired eyes left Esar to focus on him, Alondo said, "Will you tell me what happened?"

Brivar stifled a gasp. He was newly come into his training, but some things he had learned already. A surgeon should confine their questions to those that shed light on the nature of the complaint and its treatment, not to question the circumstances in which an injury occurred. As a child, he was not clear on why. It was only later that he would realise how inconvenient such knowledge could be. Yet here was the Varistan asking for information he did not require.

Alyas leant his head back. "It was my fault."

Alondo said, "When is it not?" But the words did not match his tone. "What did you do this time?"

If Alyas heard the gentle teasing, he gave no sign of it. "We came to find something. Something that was stolen. I promised to return it. Mari must have found out we wanted it. She wrote…" His head dropped. "Her letter told us where to find it. And I wanted to see her. I didn't think…" He looked away, towards the bed. "Esar did not want to come."

Alondo's hands continued their work. "You should listen to Esar more often," he admonished. "Your sister would not write to you."

Alyas frowned, still staring at Esar. "Why not? If she didn't want to marry him—"

Alondo put a hand on his shoulder. "Look at me. You do not need to worry about Mari. That is one burden you can safely set aside. She is happy. Raffa dotes on her. She would not risk that, not even for you. Better to ask yourself who would write in her name and why. Someone who knew what you wanted and that it would draw you back. And, it appears, with not very friendly intentions. Hold still." Nimble fingers retrieved the needle and set the first stitch to a hiss of pain. "So, think. Who might want you dead?"

"Apart from Raffa?" The words were sharp with bitterness.

Alondo shifted his stool, pulling the little table with his tools closer. "Hurt you, perhaps. But kill you? I do not believe so." He tapped Alyas's arm in warning then set the next stitch, saying, "I heard that someone waylaid one of Ithol's donation convoys between here and Orleas."

There was no response from his patient, who had his head tipped back and turned to the side, his body rigid with tension. Alondo sighed. "What Ithol's temple did to your father was wrong. They should not have taken his bequest for themselves. But it is not wise to cross the temple, and this is just the kind of revenge their inquisitors would take."

Alyas jerked away, pulling his arm from Alondo's grip. "My father did nothing!" he said fiercely. "He left that bequest so they would help people and they took it all because of what *I* did! Raffa erased his name and they used it as an excuse to take for themselves everything he left in their care. *They had no right.*"

There was so much anger, so much hurt in those words, but Alondo reacted to neither. He merely reclaimed Alyas's arm, stilling him so he could set the next stitch. "So you took it back?"

Silence again.

The Varistan did not look at him, nor did he press that silence. He merely observed, "Our temple has received several anonymous donations recently, large ones. We used them to establish a school for the miners' orphans."

Alyas didn't speak, but Brivar saw his head turn. He was listening.

Alondo kept his eyes averted. "Your father hated to see children left orphaned; he hated that you lost your mother so young. Hated that it stole so much of him from you, too. It's why he took in Esar and Mari. For you and for them." There was a measured pause. "We named the school after him."

Alyas's head dipped, dark hair falling across his face, but it couldn't hide the sob that caught in his throat. "You tried to help him."

"I did," Alondo agreed, tying off the stitch. "And he wouldn't let me." The words hung, full of meaning, and eventually Alondo sighed. "Let us say, for a moment, that it was you who stole the convoy. And the temple knew…"

"They could never prove it."

Alondo chuckled. "I doubt a little thing like proof would concern Ithol's agents."

"And reveal what *they* stole? Worse, they stole it from the king, since he now owns my father's estates."

The king.

The realisation hit Brivar hard, stealing his breath. *Raffa.* They were talking about *the king*. He had heard the name, but he had not thought… Who called the king by his birth name? A king who was clearly no friend. Fear curled its way through his bones.

It was Alondo's turn for silence as he once more picked up the needle. "Very well. Perhaps not Ithol then. Who else's nose have you tweaked recently?"

Alyas flinched as the stitch was pushed through, his face paling. Brivar had watched the Varistan set stitches before. He could do it in minutes. Alondo was taking his time, drawing this out. Drawing Alyas out, making him talk, and Brivar wished he would stop because their talk scared him.

"There's the syndicate venture that was sent packing from the mountains just three months ago, and that rumour at least was explicit in naming both of you, as I'm sure you intended. Nor was it the first. So, if not Ithol, perhaps the syndicates?"

The silence this time was of a different sort. Not reticence or denial, but the effort of a tired man to gather his thoughts. "They hated my father."

"He hated their influence and the way they did business," Alondo agreed, watching that pale face closely. "But that was his quarrel, not yours. Why are *you* making an enemy of them?"

Alyas's head turned determinedly away. He wasn't going to answer that. Alondo said, "Did you find it at least? The thing you were looking for? Or did you only find trouble?"

The question jerked Alyas upright, his panic almost knocking over Alondo's small table. "My jacket…"

"It's here," the Varistan said with deliberate calm. He picked up the discarded jacket and something fell out, hitting the ground with the ring of metal. His view obscured by his master's back, Brivar could not see what it was, but he saw Alyas catch Alondo's wrist as he bent to pick it up. He was fully, dangerously awake. "Too many people have died for that already."

"Yes," the Varistan said, freeing himself from Alyas's grasp to retrieve whatever it was. "I imagine they have." And he slipped it back inside the jacket, folding the leather carefully and handing it to Alyas, who gripped it tight with his good hand.

They sat like that, still and silent, for a long moment, then Alondo returned his attention to his task, straightening the little table. "What will you do with it?"

"Return it to the people it was stolen from." Alyas's voice was tight and strained. "I'm sorry, I can't—"

"Nor should you," Alondo assured him as he checked that his stitches had survived the sudden movement. "Not if that is the reason you are both here, like this."

Alyas looked back towards the bed where his friend lay, and his silence was weighted down by things Brivar did not understand. There was something dark and bitter and dreadful here, and he wanted very much to close his eyes and cover his ears, but he couldn't look away.

Alondo set the final stitch and started cleaning his tools as though that silence weighed on him, too. Then, as he stood, Alyas dragged his head round to look at him. "I made a mistake and a lot of people died. But I didn't kill them. I didn't do what he said I did."

And Alondo, the Varistan of Avarel's temple whom Brivar had never once seen lose his composure, took Alyas's head in his hands and said in a voice that cracked with emotion, "I never thought you did."

Brivar blinked back tears for a hurt that wasn't his and when he could see again, Alondo had gone and there was just Alyas, once more staring at the bed. The burst of energy had faded and he was slumped in the chair, head rolled to one side. Alondo reappeared with a cup in his hand. Brivar knew what it was, already able to pick out the scent of the herbs it contained after only a few short weeks of training. Blue star-violet for pain, cannavery for sleep.

Alondo offered it to Alyas, who shook his head. "I need—"

"No, you need to listen to me. You cannot do anything for Esar except worry. You cannot hide him better than he is already hidden. And if you do not rest, you will be joining him on that bed and then you won't even be able to help yourself."

Alondo's voice softened, once more holding the soothing tone

Brivar recognised so well. A hand brushed the dark head, the gesture so fond and familiar it made Brivar's heart ache. "Sleep, Alyas," he said, putting the cup to his lips. "Everything will be easier when you wake."

"I can't lose him."

"You won't. Not today. Drink."

He got his way, if for no other reason than that his patient lacked the energy to resist, and as Alondo took the empty cup, he said, "It seems to me that if you intend to pursue this feud against the mining companies, you cannot do it alone."

Alyas looked at him through heavy-lidded eyes. "What are you saying?"

"That if you want to challenge them, you need more men. There are only two of you. They can swat you any time they like. If you're going to survive, you must be more than just an inconvenience."

Alyas's eyes tracked Alondo as he rolled his carefully cleaned instruments back inside their silk case. Brivar could almost hear him thinking.

"People follow you, Alyas," Alondo said, looking up. "They always have. Perhaps it is time to put your efforts into building something. You need more people around you."

But Alyas's eyelids were already flickering, and Brivar wasn't sure he'd heard.

Alondo set down the cup and looked sadly at the sleeping man. "How else will you fight this war you seem determined to start?"

※

Only when both men were safely asleep did Alondo let Brivar out of the cupboard. As he uncurled cramping muscles, his master crouched beside him and helped him stand. In the blue-tinted Isyrium light, Alondo looked exhausted. He looked ancient.

Brivar turned away, uncomfortable at this glimpse of human

frailty, and his gaze was drawn to the bed on which the man Esar lay, pale and still. "Will he live?"

"Yholis willing," his master replied, his voice heavy and sad. "It would be a tragedy if he did not."

Brivar thought about what he had seen and heard and all the different things that might mean. He took a step towards the sleeping man in the chair, curiosity winning out over fear for the first time since Alyas had burst into the room, covered in blood. A thought occurred to him. "His leg is hurt, too."

Alondo glanced towards the chair. "Is it?"

Brivar nodded. "He was limping when you left the room."

"You saw that, little one? We'll make a surgeon of you yet, but not if you're too tired to keep your eyes open. Come, the sun will be up soon. It is time to get you to your bed since I'm afraid you can't sleep here tonight." He put a hand on Brivar's shoulder, the firm touch guiding him to the door.

Brivar hung back. "Aren't you going to check his leg?"

Alondo smiled. "If it's not bleeding or broken, it can keep for now. Better to let him sleep."

Still Brivar hesitated. The man had spoken of the king by his birth name, as a friend would, but he feared him, too, feared what he might do. "Who are they?"

A shadow crossed the Varistan's face. "A surgeon never speaks of his patients to others. That is the first rule of our profession, Brivar, and since you are my apprentice, they are your patients now, too."

It was so unexpected, so stunning, that he forgot his question. "I am?"

Alondo chuckled. "Yes, little one, I think you are. And you have your first confidence. Though I must ask you to curtail your nightly wanderings for a few days, and it may be best if you forget why. Can you do that?"

He nodded, overcome. Because just like that, his future had changed.

"You knew about the Lathai," Brivar said, staring at Alondo. "And the syndicates. You knew he'd been fighting them for years. When we came back—you knew, and you didn't tell me. What else did you know?"

You tried to help him, Alyas had said of his father. Had he been talking about the blades?

Yet he was not angry at Alondo's gentle deceit. Perhaps he was just too tired. That memory, that conversation—it was a raw, private thing. It had not been meant for his ears. But it explained so many things.

When the king had requested a representative of the temple to accompany his envoy to the former duke of Agrathon, Alondo had surprised everyone by sending his apprentice. Brivar had assumed it was because Sul-Barin was his cousin. Now, he suspected it was for an entirely different reason. Amid a sea of enemies, Alondo had been trying to send Alyas a friend.

"I didn't remember!" The words burst from him. "You told me to forget, and I did. I could have hated him like the rest of them." He had shut the memory away, desperate to prove himself worthy of becoming the Varistan's apprentice, and over the years it had faded to little more than snatched impressions, barely recalled.

"Could you?" Alondo asked. "I don't think so. I know you, and I knew you would see him for who he is."

Not that Alyas had made that easy. Had it not been for the circumstances that put Brivar within his orbit, he would have been kept at arm's length like the rest of the Lankaran embassy, and he might never have seen past his companions' prejudice to the man beneath.

Or would Alyas have understood what Alondo was trying to do?

"How much did you know?" he asked his master again. "Did you know about the Isyr? Did you know he would need me?"

Alondo shook his head, his face grave with regret. "If I had known that, I would have found a way to take them years ago. No, I knew only that in his last years his father had an unhealthy obsession with those blades. He would not be parted from them. But Gerrin's life had unravelled a long time ago. By then there was little left of the man I knew. It was a tragedy, for him and for Alyas." There was a pause as Alondo considered the near tragedy their skill had, perhaps, averted. "And they are so very alike."

Then he moved, gathering the surgical instruments for cleaning. What other memories he had would not be shared.

Brivar watched him, eerie echoes of that long ago night all around him. "What was it?" he asked. "What did he come back for?"

Alondo looked up, his face etched with exhaustion. Another echo. "That," he said, "is a question better asked of Alyas. Now, there are people waiting for you outside that door who have urgent need of news. Go and speak with them and then rest. This isn't over yet."

"Please," he said. "Just give them back."

– THE MANY SHADES OF MIDNIGHT

They had not moved Alyas from the surgery, even after he woke, and every time Brivar entered that room he felt the old memory wrap its folds around him, the shock and fear of the child he had been mingling with the terror he'd felt when Alondo had brought him here to find Alyas sprawled on the cot where Nicor-Heryd had left him.

Now, as he entered with the blades in his hands on the eve of their departure to Camling, it was particularly acute. Alyas was waiting for him, sitting in the chair where he'd sat while Alondo worked to save Esar's life. Nothing else about him was the same. There was no blood staining his shirt or dripping down his arm; his hair was shorter, less wild, the nervous energy of that night replaced by a careful stillness, as though if he moved too quickly he might break.

Alyas's eyes met Brivar's. Neither of them looked at the blades, though their presence filled the room. Brivar swallowed, adjusting his grip. He felt an intense sadness, a great welling up of grief that seemed to come from within. Was that the Isyr or just his own fear of what it might do?

Brivar held them out and felt that sadness reach towards Alyas, who actually flinched. Then he stood, one hand on the back of the chair because he was still not strong, and took them from Brivar.

"Thank you."

It felt wrong for Alyas to thank him for something Brivar feared would kill him, but Alyas had asked him to return the blades and he could not refuse. He looked away, uncomfortable, and his wandering gaze was caught by the cupboard in the corner of the room, the cupboard where he had hidden as a child, and he finally realised what had been bothering him about that memory.

"You didn't have them with you. I would have remembered sooner, but you didn't have them."

Alyas paused, his face a puzzled frown. He looked from Brivar to the cabinet that had captured his attention. "Ah, Alondo's mouse. I should have guessed."

Heat rose in Brivar's cheeks. "I wasn't spying on you. I was trying to sleep."

That almost made Alyas smile. Almost. "In a cupboard? I didn't realise the temple treated their apprentices so harshly."

"They don't. I was homesick. Alondo would let me sleep here, then you came…" He wasn't making sense. His flush deepened. "So I hid." His eyes strayed from Alyas to the windowsill and one of Alondo's little teapots, evidence of his master's frequent visits. For the Varistan, tea was the answer to all those ills his skills as a physician could not touch, and he wielded it like a scalpel.

Alyas followed his gaze. "Alondo knew you were there."

Brivar nodded. "And afterwards he made me his apprentice so I would have to keep your secret."

"I'm sure that wasn't the only reason."

There was the hint of a smile in Alyas's voice, but nothing else. Brivar didn't know what reaction he had expected, but it wasn't this utter disinterest, not from a man who guarded his privacy as savagely as Alyas. But everything about him was different now, movement replaced by stillness, sharp edges blunted, something too close to surrender where once he had been all biting defiance. And Brivar hated it. He liked even less that the blades were back in Alyas's hands.

"Where were they?"

"I left them with Ailuin. I could hardly bring them with me. We didn't want to be recognised." Then, answering the unspoken question, Alyas said, "It was easier then, to let them go. For a time. And Ailuin would make me sometimes. They were always quieter afterwards."

"And now?"

There was a drawn-out, difficult pause. "Now they are screaming."

It was not what Brivar had meant, but it was answer enough, in its way. He would never give them up again.

Alyas sat. Every movement was so careful. Brivar wished they weren't leaving the temple. It was too soon. Was it his imagination or did Alyas already look different with the blades back in his possession?

He cleared his throat. "The thing you came to find. What was it?"

There was another fraught pause. "Can't you guess?"

"No, I—" *Too many people have died for that already.* "Oh. It was Isyr, wasn't it? Lathai Isyr."

Alyas, his gaze distant, said, "A *xhidan*. Corado stole it. I promised to return it. The Lathai believe…" The words faltered, hitting something unbearable. He took a breath. "They believed the *xhiden* house the spirits of their dead. We thought he would give it to Raffa. I thought for a while that was why… But he didn't. He gave it to the syndicates and they protected him."

Corado. Brivar had known, from the moment the two men laid eyes on each other all those weeks ago, that there was history there. And he knew now why Alyas would not have wanted anyone to know they'd come back, or why.

"You're not angry?" he asked. It was so hard to tell *anything*.

"Why would I be angry?" There was genuine surprise in Alyas's voice. "What difference can it make now?"

Brivar thought back to that day on the riverbank. "You told me not to ask. That Esar didn't remember." He had been so sure that was a warning. Had he misunderstood?

Alyas looked away as though he too was remembering that night. "It was a difficult time. And Yholis knows, I've made enough mistakes in my life. Esar doesn't need to be reminded of that one."

Esar didn't want to come.

Because it had been a trap and he'd walked right into it. If not for Alondo's skill, Esar would surely have died. "It was the syndicates who tried to kill you?"

"Their first attempt, but not their last. We were in their way and that's what they do." The words were bitter, touching on grief too recent, too painful, about which he had never spoken.

"Because of the Lathai?" Brivar asked. The Lathai, who had, in the end, been murdered for what the mining companies thought they possessed, in spite of everything Alyas had done to protect them. Where were the spirits of their dead now? Where were the spirits of the men and women of the company who had remained in the mountains to protect them?

The moment teetered on the edge of a precipice, a yawning chasm of grief for friends lost that *needed* to be acknowledged. Then, just as he had every time before, Alyas stepped back from that edge.

"That," he agreed, "and maybe one or two other things. And before you ask," he said, catching Brivar with his mouth open, "Esar is much better at telling stories. Ask him about the temple in Lessing if you want all the ugly details. He's still angry with me and I'm sure he'd enjoy an opportunity to vent his feelings."

It was true. Esar's feelings had been on a knife edge for days, but for reasons that had everything to do with *now* and not whatever had happened in Lessing. Esar wouldn't just welcome an opportunity to vent, he needed it. Whether Brivar wanted to be on the receiving end was another matter. On the other hand, he was more than capable of recognising when he was being distracted. He asked, with suspicion, "Do I want to know?" He was, after all, an apprentice of Yholis. He had a duty to report all crimes against the temple.

Alyas, who knew this perfectly well, said, "What possible reason would I have to violate a house of Yholis?"

Which meant they *had* violated a house of Ithol. He should have guessed. To Alyas, the Ithol's acolytes and the mining companies were much the same and had been long before they'd locked Frey in their cells.

Alyas's thoughts must have been following a similar track. "If we had known, we would have done a lot worse." His amusement had vanished, replaced by the hard edge of anger.

If they'd known what the syndicates were really doing. What Ithol's disciples were helping them do. This too was dangerous ground, because it raised the spectre of what came next, and Brivar knew from Esar's building frustration that Alyas would not talk about that either.

"We know now," Brivar reminded him, as worried by this silence as he was by the other. "How to purify Isyrium safely." He had thought about almost nothing else since they had discovered the interaction of Isyrium and the na'quia plant that grew from it and seeded it in the soil when it died. The circle of life that had been disrupted with such deadly consequences by the syndicates. "We could even make Isyr again. If we're patient—"

"The world doesn't need more Isyr." The words were flat, unequivocal. For once, Alyas's expression was easy to read.

"But don't you see?" Brivar pressed. "If we end the mining, if we can stop this corruption, the land will be safe again, and so will the Isyr we make from it. I'm certain." *Almost* certain anyway. "We should at least try…"

Alyas was staring at him, the devastation of Isyr in every hollow of his face. "Is that a risk you're willing to take?"

"Yes," Brivar said with only a slight hesitation. He needed to know, to see his experiment through. The world needed them to see it through. Only knowledge, only true understanding, would stop them repeating the mistakes of the past. "We should…" But the words faltered and died as he realised what Alyas meant. "You don't think it will matter. You don't think the syndicates will accept it."

"Do you?"

He did not, not just like that. Because it meant taking only as much Isyrium as that precious circle of life could support, as the Lathai had done. It meant the syndicates would have to accept less—less money, less power, less influence. But when the alternative was losing everything, surely they would have no choice? Surely, rulers would force it on them?

"Raffa will never turn against them," Alyas said. "I'm not sure there's a distinction between them anymore. He'll hide from the truth, pretend it's not happening, they all will, because none of them, *none of them*, can conceive of sacrificing even a portion of their wealth and power, no matter what they stand to lose if they don't."

That was not at all what Brivar wanted to hear. "We have to try."

There was a long silence, the kind of silence that Brivar did not find remotely reassuring. Then voices sounded outside the door and the moment passed.

Esar entered, and it vanished, all of it. Every trace of uncertainty, of despair, gone. Like a door slamming closed, Alyas showed Esar what he wanted to see as he addressed the practical questions his brother brought him, all of which Esar could have resolved on his own and they both knew it. But Esar, in his own way, was also trying, and Brivar watched as they discussed the move to Camling until it was clear that Alyas was too tired to continue.

"Come on," Esar said, standing and giving Brivar a shove towards the door. He had seen the blades and he wasn't happy. "Pack your things. We leave tomorrow—if you're still coming?"

Brivar glanced back at Alyas, wanting to stay but unable to resist the insistent hand on his shoulder. He was about to be shouted at. "I'm still coming."

They walked down the corridor, Esar rigid with anger, the volatile emotions he had hidden from Alyas ready to boil over.

Since he wasn't any happier about it than Esar, Brivar said, "I didn't just give them back. He asked."

"He did *what*?"

For Esar, who had been trying so very hard to be patient with Alyas, that was the last straw. Brivar braced himself and let the storm break over him. Better that Esar rage at him than at his brother, who couldn't give up the blades now even if he wanted to. Brivar hated it, he didn't understand it, but there was nothing any of them could do other than take Alondo's advice and trust him.

Brivar wasn't reckless enough to say that at this moment, however, and when Esar's anger eventually wound down, he gambled that it was unlikely to ignite again so soon, and asked, as he had been prompted, "What happened in Lessing?"

The question stopped Esar in his tracks. "What? Why?"

"The temple in Lessing. Alyas said I should ask you."

"Ask me…" Esar frowned, his expression darkening. It was the wrong thing to say or the wrong time to say it, or both. "*Lessing*? Why? Why did he tell you to ask about that? Gods, Lessing was *worse*."

Brivar, horribly out of his depth, wished he'd never brought it up. Why had Alyas told him to ask? He must have known the reaction it would provoke.

"Why?" Esar asked again. "Why were you talking about Lessing?" His expression had changed, was changing. Brivar felt more and more like he'd been used to deliver a message and he had no idea what it was.

"It doesn't matter. I—" He caught Esar's look and said hurriedly, "I asked about the syndicates, about why they wanted to kill him."

Esar stared through him. He was thoughtful now, not angry. "Well then, Lessing would be up there."

"What happened?" Brivar prompted. "What did you do?"

"What did *we* do?" Esar shook his head, his expression caught between amusement and weary despair. "Oh no, that was all him. That was the first bloody temple."

Brivar took the tiny thing Esar offered him, a length of leather cord wound around something small and heavy. He held it up, letting the cord unravel, and it dropped into his palm. A small, imperfect circle of Isyr, silver-blue and beautiful. Irresistible.

Esar was watching him with a faint, sad smile. It was hardly compensation for what he had lost, but it mattered, and he knew it. "He made it for you."

Brivar hung the circle of Isyr round his neck. "I know."

– EPILOGUE,
THE MANY SHADES OF MIDNIGHT

THE AUNT

CASSANA

When she invited Alyas-Raine Sera to call on her, Cassana Gaemo had no idea of all the ways her life would change. Some of the changes were small, creeping up on her over the years, altering her view of the world and the people around her, opening her eyes to things, both good and bad, that she may never have noticed. Some were wonderful, happy changes. Others were terrifying, introducing her to a world filled with worry and fear. Fortunately, those occasions were few and far between.

And sometimes she didn't know how she felt about the way he changed her life.

"You want me to spy for you?" In the two years since their swim in the Gorlani lake, Cassana had, with one or two minor exceptions, resisted becoming entangled in the below-the-surface world in which her brother and Alyas moved. And, on the whole, she thought Alyas preferred it that way.

So when Melar invited her to go with him to Avarel for the summer, Cassana expected Alyas to object. When he didn't—when, in fact, he expressed a desire for her to go—she was suspicious.

He laughed. "Would I ask that of you?"

"Yes," she said bluntly. Because he would and he had—the one or two minor exceptions. And, in truth, she had no very great objection, it just felt different somehow. She felt exposed there, in the court of Avarel's king, the man who had done so much harm and caused so much hurt, but who, in the end, had given her so much, though he would never know it. Or she hoped he never would.

"Cassie," Alyas murmured, one hand trailing through the hair that was splayed on the pillow. The hair in which she had found her first greys only yesterday. She was thirty-eight years old. "I wouldn't ask it this time, I promise."

Because he understood what she could not to put into words, and that was why she loved him.

"Then why?"

She had not yet given her brother an answer; she hadn't decided yet what *she* wanted. Alyas and the company would be away somewhere, wherever their new contracts took them, and she would be alone in Sarenza as she always was. She didn't mind. Or, rather, she had grown used to the months of solitude. But as she got older, she worried more. What if he didn't come back? What if she never saw him again? It would happen one day, she was sure. That was the life he'd chosen, that she had chosen, too, when she chose him.

Melar, who was always perceptive of her moods, had made the offer in his typically irreverent manner. "Come with me into the den of the beast, Cass. We can entertain ourselves feeding him outlandish rumours about the thorn in his side."

And now, far from objecting, Alyas was telling her to go. "Why?" she asked again.

He was silent a moment, fingers teasing out the tangles in her hair. "Because there are people in Avarel I care about, and I would like to know they are well."

"The queen?"

She remembered the pretty young woman he had been meant to marry, remembered the way she had flirted with the king all night while he had been so wrapped up in his own pain that he never noticed. And she wondered if he knew.

"Mari, yes," he agreed, studying her face. "My sister." The emphasis was subtle, as though he wasn't sure she needed it. "And there are others of my family there. Melar knows who they are. I would welcome any news of them."

So she went, sharing the Flaeresian embassy with her brother and accompanying him to the official functions his duties required him to attend, which was how she found herself in the palace for the queen's birthday celebration.

Alyas need not be concerned for his sister, that was plain enough. Cassana watched Mari-Geled Herun hold court on this night that was all hers, the king by her side clearly besotted with his young wife, and found she could not stomach it. For this the pair of them had destroyed a man who had done them no wrong other than stand in their way through no choice of his own—who would have stood aside if only they had asked it of him.

She smiled and curtseyed to the queen when Melar introduced her, and Mari-Geled responded with the same empty formality, her attention already moving on to the handsome young man who was next in line. If Cassana had worried that rumours of her affair with Alyas had reached the Avarel court, the queen's indifference laid them to rest.

Until she stepped out onto the balcony of the ballroom, seeking an escape from the stifling heat and vacuous flattery. Was it as bad in Sarenza? Or did she just feel it more here because she knew the rot that lay beneath all the glittering beauty?

A woman was there before her, smoking a pipe in the warmth of the summer night, her other hand clasped around an ornate walking stick. She gave Cassana a friendly nod, making no attempt to disguise her interest. "Melar Gaemo's sister? I had hoped to meet you, Sayora."

Cassana studied her in turn and knew at once who she was looking at. Everything from the man's pipe to the unfashionably styled greying hair and practical clothes spoke of a defiance of convention that only belonged to one woman.

"Hailene-Sera," she said. "The honour is mine."

"Oh, I doubt that," replied Avarel's most famous spinster, "if my nephew has told you anything about me."

She froze, startled and wary. Hailene-Sera Ahn, sister to Alyas's long-dead mother, took a final puff of her pipe then tapped out the ash over the balcony. "Don't look so scared, girl. The kind of rumours that reach me never make it to the ears of that assembly of fools. And what if they did? Should you be ashamed?"

Cassana's chin came up. "Never."

Hailene nodded in approval. "Good. My nephew is worth more than all of them, even if he is the most infuriating man alive."

"I have never found him so," Cassana replied. Not anymore, anyway.

"That, my dear, is because he pulls in his claws with those he loves. Otherwise Esar would have killed him long since. I trust both my nephews are well?"

Cassana loved her for that. She had enough experience of Lankaran society to know that though Alyas regarded Esar as his brother, and Gerrin-Raine Sera had loved him like a son, he would never have been truly accepted at a gathering like this. And though she knew he didn't care, especially now, she still hurt for him.

"They are both well," she assured Hailene. "Should I pass on your regards?"

Hailene laughed. "Don't waste your breath, my dear. Alyas finds me as difficult as I find him. No doubt he considers our enforced separation one of the few boons of his exile."

There are other members of my family there. I would welcome any news of them.

"That's not true," Cassana said quietly and saw Hailene's head come up. "He would want to know you are well." Because there were no others of his family that she knew of. Only this aunt.

"Well," Hailene muttered, tapping again on her pipe to hide the way the words pleased her. "It was nice to meet you, my dear. Are you staying with your brother? Perhaps I will call on you before you leave."

And she clicked away with her stick before Cassana could think of anything to make her stay.

※

Cassana did not see Hailene-Sera again until the week before she left Avarel, though she looked for her at every party and court function and was surprised by how disappointed she was every time by her absence. So when Melar wandered in as she was supervising the packing of the guest suite and told her she had a visitor, she stopped what she was doing and hurried down to the salon.

Alyas's aunt was standing by the window, gazing out at the view—one of the best in Avarel, or so Melar told her. Certainly, it afforded an impressive aspect of the palace, which soared in all its glory above the trees crowding the edges of the embassy's grounds. But there was a set to Hailene-Sera's shoulders that suggested it was not the palace she was seeing from the window.

"I hoped to meet you again," Cassana said from the doorway. Not just for Alyas, but for her own sake.

Hailene turned from the window, her expression amused. "That is not something many people in this city have said to me. I make them uncomfortable."

It was, Cassana decided, a family trait. She had seen the way Alyas could, if he chose, reduce even the most self-assured person to a quivering wreck. The thought made her smile.

Then Hailene said, "Sit," as though she owned the house and Cassana was the guest. And such was her authority that Cassana did as she was told.

"Good." Hailene tapped over to the chair opposite and eased herself down. She looked up at Melar, who had followed his sister into the salon, his expression curious. He would know the identity of this visitor. "You may leave us, Ambassador. Nothing I have to say concerns Flaeres."

Melar raised an eyebrow to be so dismissed in his own home, but he went. Cassana knew he would press her for information later and she felt a flash of unease.

"Is that true?" she asked Hailene. Her love for Alyas had never yet been in opposition to her loyalty to her brother and she hoped it never would be.

"According to the current boundaries of our two nations. Would it bother you, then?"

"Yes," she replied, holding that brisk, pointed gaze.

Hailene nodded as though this confirmed what she had suspected, then she said, "You need not worry, because this is not a matter of nations. This is something much more important. So I must ask for your promise that you will not share it with your brother, as everyone knows he will whisper it into the pillow of his king and that I cannot allow."

"Why not?" She was not surprised Hailene knew of her brother's relationship with Diago. They did not flaunt it—after all, the king was married—but neither did they make any great attempt to conceal it. It was hardly unusual.

"Because kings cannot be trusted," Hailene retorted. "I should not have to tell you that. Now, your promise, or I will find some other way to reach Alyas."

Cassana felt her back stiffen. "I would like yours first," she said, "that my silence will do no harm to my brother or my country."

"My girl, I am not in the business of meddling in matters of state. I leave that to men like your brother who enjoy it far too much. Now, my spies have gone to a lot of trouble to confirm this news, and it is something that Alyas will want to hear. What he does with it is his business. Will you take it to him?"

Had he known, when he asked her to come here, that this might happen? Perhaps, she decided. Alyas's motivations were rarely simple. But if so, he had left the choice up to her. She made it now. "Yes."

Some of the tension went out of Hailene and she sank back into the cushioned armchair. "Thank you." But the moment lasted mere seconds before she was all business again, drawing a packet of papers from within the voluminous folds of her dress. "Modern fashions are so impractical," she told Cassana with a wink. "Where would you hide anything in those narrow skirts of yours?"

"I will bear that in mind," Cassana replied, hiding her smile as she took the packet from Hailene. "What are they?"

"Communications between the syndicates. Here, in Orleas, and in Hantara."

Cassana looked up, her heart thudding painfully, and saw Hailene watching her with those sharp eyes that were so like Alyas's. Alyas, who for reasons she had never fully understood, hated the mining companies with a fury that bordered on obsession.

"Yes," Hailene said, seeing Cassana's impulse to hand the papers back. "What's in there could be dangerous, but he will find out anyway. This way, he will know in advance and have time to decide how to respond. If he finds out later, the risk will be that much greater."

Because he *would* respond. Cassana took a deep breath, returning her attention to the oilskin-wrapped packet on her lap. "May I?" she asked, her hands on the string that bound it.

Hailene waved in assent and sat quietly as Cassana leafed through the correspondence. The only thing she understood was a map, appended to a coded letter—or at least she assumed it was coded, as it made little sense—that marked out an area of the Lankaran-Flaeresian border that chilled her to the bone.

She glanced at Hailene. "Do you know what these say?"

The old woman gave her a pitying look. "Girl, I have been doing this for longer than you have been alive. I trust that Alyas has broken the syndicate cyphers. If he hasn't, he doesn't deserve my help."

He had. These papers would not hide their secrets from him. Briefly, she flirted with the idea of dropping the packet in the river on her way home, but Hailene was right—Alyas would find out eventually and she could not protect him. If she tried and her actions caused more harm…

She carefully folded the papers back inside their protective wrapping and tied it tight, then set it on the seat beside her. Gathering her resolve, she looked Hailene in the eye. "Thank you. I will take them."

"Good girl." Hailene pushed to her feet and reached for her cane.

Cassana stood, ringing the bell for the steward, following ingrained habits even though this visit was like no social call she had ever experienced.

Hailene stopped by the door, turning to take Cassana's hand. "I know it is hard," she said, and her hand felt thin and frail and suddenly uncertain. "But he is what he is—and he's not wrong. Not about this."

Then the steward was there, shepherding the old woman out of the salon, and Melar was loitering in the corridor beyond, waiting to demand an accounting. Cassana closed the door on them all, staring across the room at the secrets with which she'd been entrusted, and tried not to weep.

They had a system of sorts, her and Alyas. He rarely knew where he would be month to month during the campaigning season, but there were places she could leave messages, if she had need, that would find their way to him. She left them now. He came.

She had been home a little over three weeks. He could not have been far away, or he had ridden hard. Both, she decided, watching him walk into her salon, tired but whole. Worried. She had never called him home before.

She made him rest and eat before she handed him Hailene's purloined correspondence, knowing full well that he would forget to do both if left to his own devices.

When, finally, she could put it off no longer, she pushed the packet across the table. He went still, watching her. "Hailene?"

She nodded. "Did you know?"

"That you would meet her? Yes. The old witch would want me to know she holds my secrets." There was fond amusement in the words, not dislike. "That she would use you as a courier, no. I trust her news is suitably important?"

Cassana kept her face neutral. "It concerns the syndicates."

Alyas saw what she tried to hide and made no move to take the packet. "You know what's in here?"

"No," she said, because she didn't *know*. She only guessed. "They used cypher."

"Cass…"

"I thought about not giving it to you," she admitted. "But I decided to trust you."

"Trust me?"

"Not to get yourself killed." Then, because she could bear it no longer, she snapped, "Just open the bloody thing."

He did, and she watched him read through the secrets Hailene's spies had gathered for him, trying to interpret the expressions that flashed across his face.

When he was done, he stood and came around the table, perching by her side. He handed her the letter with the map. "You saw this? You know where this is?"

She nodded. "The Lathai."

The Lathai, the tribe with which Alyas had forged the historic peace that so angered his king he had been stripped of everything he owned and cast out of Lankara. The tribe with which he had forged a friendship that would compel him, now, to act.

"The Lathai," he agreed. "The syndicates have designs on their territory. They will try to take it."

"And you will try to stop them?" It was what she'd feared, a war with the mining companies. Thousands against a few hundred.

"I won't try," he said, his voice hard. "I will." Then, seeing the fear on her face, he took her hands. "Cassie. There is nothing in here that I did not already know, nothing but the timing. And you must trust me when I tell you that I have good reasons for wanting to stop this."

She took back her hands, placing them in her lap. "But you won't tell me what those reasons are."

"They are not mine to tell. And knowing them would place you in danger, and *that* I will not do."

She would find out in time, of course, over the next ten years, as he dug in his resistance and the rumours swelled—that it was not just new territory for Isyrium mining that the syndicates wanted, but what else they thought the Lathai possessed. And when he was dying, she would find out the rest. But all that lay ahead. For now, all she knew was that he meant to pit himself against an enemy whose resources far outmatched his. For reasons he would not explain. Because he loved her.

There was a pause; she tried to keep the tears from her eyes.

He smoothed them away as they spilled down her cheeks.

"Cassie, look at me."

She took a breath, met his eyes.

"You said you would trust me, so trust me. We knew this day would come. We've had plans in place for years, should the syndicates decide to move. We are not unprepared, and now, thanks to Hailene, we have time to put those plans into action." He smiled, then played his trump card. "Even Esar agrees with me on this."

She couldn't help it; she smiled back. Esar's agreement, so rare, was no small thing.

"I'll ask him," she warned as he gathered up the scattered letters and bound them back inside the oilskin.

"Oh, I've no doubt." He tucked the letters inside his jacket and took her hand. "Come on, come to bed. I could sleep for a week."

He did not, in fact, sleep for a week, only two days, sleep of the kind only she could give him. Then he left, and a few days later, Esar presented himself at her house for interrogation. That in itself told her everything she needed to know, so she did not torture him, merely did what she had done for Alyas, and gave him food and a safe place to rest for the night in a life that afforded few such opportunities, and in the morning sent him on his way. After extracting an entirely unnecessary promise, because Esar would protect Alyas with the same instinct that saw him draw breath each day.

Then he went back to his lives and she to hers, and she did not see either of them again for many months. And when the news finally reached her that the syndicates had come, it was already weeks old and the danger long past, because it was Alyas who brought it. He also brought his own packet of news, which he placed by her bed.

"For Hailene, next time you see her. With my thanks."

THE FIRST TEMPLE

ESAR

"What do you see?"

Esar looked from Alyas to the magnificent brick edifice before them and said sourly, "Trouble."

Alyas exchanged a look with Frey that made Esar want to strangle him. "What else?"

He folded his arms and glared at the high walls of Lessing's Temple of Ithol. "Lots of trouble. Trouble we don't need. Why are you even considering this?"

The reason had appeared out of the rain the day before at the inn where they were staying in Hantara's capital, wringing his hands and oozing desperation. Esar had almost felt sorry for the man's distress until he'd explained what he wanted, which was for them to *break into the city's Temple of Ithol* and steal back a family heirloom he claimed the temple had stolen from him. Esar had nearly thrown him out right there and then. *No one* messed with the Temple of Ithol. Or, more specifically, with their inquisitors, who took a dim view of people stealing from the god, whatever they might claim about rightful ownership. He certainly hadn't expected Alyas to take the request seriously.

Alyas, however, appeared to be doing just that. "I like to help people."

Esar snorted. "You're bored, in other words. But this"—he jabbed a finger towards the temple—"is a terrible idea."

A hand squeezed his and Esar looked down into Frey's upturned face, her expression wheedling. "Come on, Esar. We're all bored. We haven't done anything fun in months."

"I'm not bored," he insisted. "In fact, I'm rather enjoying not having to fight anyone for once. And I have no desire to change that."

"You wouldn't, strictly speaking, be fighting anyone," Agazi observed. "We go in, steal whatever this is, and get out. Sounds simple to me."

"It would," Esar snapped. Agazi was from the southern Steppes, and despite their reverence for Yholis, Steppelanders had nothing but disdain for the more powerful and demanding of Ellasia's twin deities. Agazi would have no problem with robbing a temple of Ithol. He was also fiercely loyal to Alyas, so much so that Esar sometimes wondered just how ludicrous an idea his brother would have to come up with for Agazi to think twice about going along with it.

"What's wrong with you all? You don't fuck with the temple, you know that."

Alyas, his attention fixed on the comings and goings of Ithol's devotees, said, "We've done it before."

"That was different."

His brother's sharp gaze shifted to his face. "How so?"

Esar felt a swell of anger and for once it wasn't directed at Alyas. "Because they fucked with us first."

"Yes," Alyas agreed. "They did."

So, that was it. A sliver of a crack appeared in Esar's resolve and he stamped down on it hard. "This isn't about that wretched man, is it? This is about your father." He didn't say: *That was ten years ago. Forget it.* Because Yholis knew, he hadn't. But they had taken their revenge for that insult to the memory of Gerrin-Raine Sera and survived the fallout, just—the old wound in his side still ached sometimes—and as far as Esar was concerned, it was done.

Alyas looked back at the temple. There was a brittle silence.

Eventually, he said, "That wretched man—do you know who he is?"

"Beyond someone who could get us all killed? No, I don't. And I don't care. It doesn't change anything."

"Actually, it does. Didn't you see the ring he was wearing?"

Esar stared at him. It had been dark in their corner of the inn's common room, and late, and he hadn't been paying attention to the man's hands. Not when his own had been itching to throw him out onto the street and make sure he understood never to come back.

He sighed. "Go on then, tell me."

A trace of a smile crossed Alyas's face. He sensed the weakening resolve. "Do you remember the Selysian negotiations?"

"Vaguely," Esar hedged. "I was a little preoccupied." Because his foster father had just killed himself, his brother had walled himself away from the world in silent grief, and they had been sent to fight a pointless war against the Lathai. The ins and outs of Raffa's diplomatic endeavours at the time had largely passed him by. That Alyas remembered them was something of a surprise.

"Well then," his brother said with a wicked grin, "you'll remember the object of those negotiations, a certain marriage? One half of that marriage came to see us last night."

It took a moment. Then realisation struck. "Wait—you're telling me that man was *Kael Ito*? Sofia's husband?"

Alyas nodded, his eyes alive with amusement. "Sofia's husband. Raffa's brother-in-law and brother to the head of the Selysian Syndicate, to which organisation Raffa paid Sofia's not inconsiderable dowry, including the loan of a certain Isyr jewellery box."

Esar felt a laugh bubbling up. "Now that is a family heirloom."

Raffa's younger half-sister had married into the richest of Hantara's mining families, an alliance that had scandalised Avarel's noble houses, but which gave Lankara's king the backing of the Selysian Syndicate's vast wealth—and allowed him to get one over on his old rival, Hantara's ruling prince, Georgios Beor. The marriage bargain had included the loan, for as long as Sofia lived, of one of

Lankara's greatest Isyr treasures, the Empress Ivane casket. Rumour said the tiny, ornate box had been a gift from the Qidan empress to a Lankaran adventurer at the end of the Isyrium Wars. Esar had no idea how it had ended up in the royal treasury, but kings tended to take what they wanted. As they had cause to know.

Rumour also said Sofia was not in the best of health. The penalties for failing to restore the Ivane box to the crown of Lankara at the appropriate time were likely to be both punitive and unavoidable.

It would explain why Sofia's husband was desperate to get it back, if indeed that's who this man was. Because why would he risk coming to them? Alyas was not only one of the few people likely to recognise the Ivane box when he saw it, but he had also made his feelings about the syndicates plain. Too plain. His feelings towards Raffa were even less friendly.

"*If* you're right," Esar asked him, "why help Ito get it back?" Sofia's marriage had made Raffa and the Selysian Syndicate allies, at least theoretically. Helping preserve that alliance was not something he would have put on Alyas's list of priorities. His brother's innocent look confirmed his suspicions. "You're not getting it back for him, are you?"

"Of course not. You know who else really dislikes Raffa?"

"Besides us?"

"Besides us," Alyas agreed. "Someone right here in Lessing who would pay good money to drive a wedge between Raffa and the Selysians."

Georgios Beor, Prince of Hantara. Esar sighed. He could see where this was going. "And you get to poke all your enemies in the eye at once. How very satisfying for you. But did you not think that it might be a trap? *Another* trap. Why would Ito come to *you* for this?"

Agazi laughed. "Who else would break into a house of Ithol?"

"Are you trying to persuade me?" Esar snarled. "Because it's not working." He turned to Alyas. "It makes no sense to come to you, unless it's *you* they're after."

Alyas appeared unconcerned by the thought. "If he has been careless enough to let Ithol's grasping devotees get their hands on the Ivane box, he's not going to admit that to his brother. Would you?"

Esar had to agree that he would not. Mitka Ito had a reputation unpleasant enough that even they hadn't crossed it, though it appeared now that such restraint was merely the result of an absence of opportunity rather than the application of good sense.

"Besides, Agazi's right," Alyas added. "No one else would do it."

"Of course they wouldn't fucking do it, that's my point! Let's say you go along with this *and* you succeed, all you achieve is to make enemies of two of the most powerful factions in Ellasia." Bigger enemies. The syndicates were hardly anything else at this point.

"Only if they find out."

Esar wanted to ask how they could possibly not find out, but if reasoned argument was going to sway Alyas, they wouldn't be having this conversation in the first place.

"Fine." Never let it be said that he didn't know when he was beaten, and since Alyas was determined to do this, better that they did it together. There was always a chance he would come to his senses before things went too far.

Besides, the company *did* need something to do. They were on their way home from a boring stint in the Donea, working an uneventful guard duty for some lord whose name he had already forgotten. It was too late in the season for the realistic prospect of more work and Cassana would still be in Avarel with her brother as she was every summer, which meant an extended period of inaction. And quiet times were always dangerous.

As soon as the word left his mouth, Alyas was moving.

Esar grabbed his arm. "Where are you going?"

"Inside."

Esar gritted his teeth and took a deep, calming breath. "Now? You don't think that it might be an idea to think about it first?"

Alyas squirmed free of his restraining grip and stepped backwards into the busy street. "I'm just going to look around. I'll see you back at the inn."

When Esar finished cursing, Agazi laid a consoling hand on his shoulder. Esar shrugged it off. "You're going with him. Don't let him out of your sight, do you hear? And for the love of Yholis, don't let him do anything stupid."

※

"I told you not to let him out of your sight!" Esar fumed when Agazi returned to the inn two hours later, Alyas nowhere to be seen.

"You also said not to let him do anything stupid," Agazi said, unworried. "And I didn't."

Only Frey's hand on his arm stopped Esar from throttling the Steppelander. "Then where is he?"

Agazi shrugged, unrolling a parchment and pushing it across the table. "Said he had things to do. And to give you this."

"What is it?" He could see what it was, he just didn't like it. A sketch of the layout of the temple covered in his brother's precise notes. It dashed the last of Esar's hopes that Alyas would see sense.

His side twinged, the old wound reminding him that they trod carefully around the Temple of Ithol for good reason. There was the small matter of a stolen donation convoy ten years in the past. The temple almost certainly knew they were responsible. They may or may not have already tried to take their revenge, as the ache in his side attested—that point was still unclear. That Ithol's inquisitors hadn't pursued it further had nothing to do with forgiveness and everything to do with the temple's flimsy legal claim to the wealth the convoy had contained. That he and Alyas had taken it in the first place had everything to do with their violent disagreement with that claim. With both claimants, since technically Raffa was the other, thanks to his seizure of the Agrathon estates.

It had been an uneasy stalemate for years. If they did this now, they wouldn't just shatter that truce. It would be as good as a declaration of war against the temple and *it made no sense*.

Agazi was talking. Esar was in no mood to listen. He rolled up the parchment and shoved to his feet. "When he gets back, you see that he stays here until I've talked to him, understood?"

※

It was past midnight when Alyas returned, and he did not appear surprised to find Esar waiting in his room. He even endured Esar's temper with uncharacteristic patience. When it wound down, he threw a small package at his brother.

Esar caught it and eyed it with suspicion. "Is this what I think it is?"

He had used the intervening hours to think this through and had come to one conclusion: If Alyas intended to steal the Ivane box and avoid bringing down the temple's enmity on the company, they not only needed to *not be caught*, they also had to achieve it without the temple knowing they had been robbed.

"That depends on what you think it is," Alyas replied, dropping into a chair.

Esar unwrapped the little parcel, feeling the cool, smooth weight of metal on his palm. He swore. "Where did you get this?"

In the light of the Isyrium bulbs, the blue tones shone bright and clear. His breath caught, the allure of the Isyr taking him by the throat, despite everything.

Alyas, a slight smile tugging at his mouth, reached out and took the lump of metal from him, wrapping it back up in the leather cloth. "This is Lessing. You can get anything here."

"Not this you can't." Not just like that, in less than a day.

There was an illegal trade in Isyr, of course there was, but the underground market for northern steel was murkier, more dangerous and more specialised than most. It was harder to steal for one thing. Most Isyr heirlooms were locked away in vaults—or behind temple walls—and if you did manage to steal them, selling them presented its own challenge. They were too easy to trace back to their owners. Which meant they had to be melted down, as this had been, and reworked into new pieces. And that was a skill very few now possessed.

He didn't even want to think about how Alyas had managed to get hold of it so quickly.

"That was the easy part." Alyas unfolded a sheet of parchment. "Getting hold of this was much more difficult."

It was another sketch. Though 'sketch' didn't do it justice. In the centre of the page, surrounded by crabbed notes, was an illustration of the Empress Ivane casket, colours and details picked out by a skilled artist. Esar scanned the notes, what he could read of them, then the faded signature in the corner. Not any artist. *The* artist. *Eirik Hagan*. One of the most famous Isyr craftsmen who had ever lived and the man who had made the box.

He met Alyas's eyes with a sinking feeling. "Where did you get *this*?"

"Same place I got the Isyr. The Temple of Yholis. Their library is a treasure trove."

Esar dropped his head in his hands with a groan. "You robbed Yholis so we can rob Ithol? *Have you lost your bloody mind?*"

"I didn't steal it," Alyas protested, retrieving his prize. "I borrowed it."

"Do they know you borrowed it?"

"If I'd asked, they might have said no."

"Then you stole it. And I don't want to know about the rest. We'll have no friends left by the time this is over."

"If you're worried about the Isyr—"

"Yes, I'm worried about the Isyr."

"—they won't miss it. And *I* didn't steal it, I merely acquired it from someone who did. The Hantaran underground has been moving Isyr in and out of the temple for years."

How very reassuring. "And you know this how?"

"I asked Fazio." Alyas nudged the sketch towards Esar. "He's going to make it for us."

Esar considered this. Fazio Vanni was the most skilled metalworker in Lessing. They had used his services many times over the years, though usually for reasons considerably more legal. And if he knew where to source Isyr, then it stood to reason he must know how to work it. The other implications were best not thought about too closely.

But why make an Isyr replica of the Ivane box? Why steal the original and leave a fake that was just as valuable?

Alyas grinned. "This isn't for the box. This is Fazio's payment for making it. He would have refused otherwise."

"Sensible man," Esar grouched. If the substitution were discovered, Ithol's inquisitors would be thorough in seeking those involved, and if Alyas knew where to start looking, they would too. "But how will he make a convincing fake without Isyr?"

In answer, Alyas took another package from his jacket, smaller this time. Inside was a pendant shaped like a bird in flight, which flashed a cool blue in the lamplight.

"Do we have any money left?" Esar asked in despair as he took it. Even this tiny thing was worth a fortune.

"This is a sample," Alyas replied, unwrapping the nugget of Isyr again. "Now what do you think?"

Alone, with nothing to compare the pendant to, Esar would have sworn he was holding a piece of old Isyr. Side by side, the difference was subtle but unmistakable. Where the Isyr, even in its unworked state, seemed to glow from within, the pendant's brightness was diminished, the blue hues in the silvery metal flattened and dulled.

"Clever, isn't it?"

Esar couldn't quite keep the grin from his face. "How?"

"A small amount of Isyr in the alloy. Fazio didn't go into details." He yawned; it was late. "Will you go away now so I can sleep?"

Esar watched Alyas fold the Isyr back inside its protective cloth.

"You're taking this to Fazio tomorrow?"

Alyas nodded. "And I promise you can come with me."

"Fine." He stood. "I'll see you in the morning."

Esar didn't sleep well. Frey complained and kicked him out as soon as it was light, burrowing deep into the blankets and leaving Esar to stew over his fears alone until Agazi joined him. The Steppelander's blithe confidence only served to irritate him further, but then Agazi didn't know that a fortune in Isyr *stolen from the Temple of Yholis* was sitting just upstairs. Esar still couldn't quite believe that part.

It was the Isyr that prompted his cautious instruction to Agazi, who shot him a curious glance but nodded his agreement. Then, at Esar's pointed look, asked, "Can't I eat first?"

"Get something on the way." The inn's kitchens were only just coming to life and Alyas could show up at any moment.

Agazi grumbled his way out onto the street. Esar closed grainy eyes, listening to the bustle of morning activity. The common room began to fill up. Someone brought him food, hot, flaky Hantaran pastries filled with white cheese. Frey wandered down and ate them. He started to suspect Alyas had given him the slip despite his promise.

Frey shook her head, brushing away the last of the pastry crumbs. "Heard him in his room."

She left and Esar was still waiting. But when Alyas finally appeared, he looked even less well-rested than Esar and was in no mood to listen to his worries, stopping only long enough to catch his brother's attention before he was out of the door.

A frosty silence accompanied them to Fazio Vanni's workshop. Esar had long ago learned not to take such silences personally, let alone attempt to breach them, but it had been years since he'd been subjected to one this ferocious. Given the circumstances, he liked it even less than usual.

Their destination clung to the edges of the respectable quarter of Lessing, close enough for its location to be acceptable to wealthy patrons without being off-putting to Fazio's shadier customers, which, on this late summer morning, included them.

A sign with depictions of the shop's trade hung above the door, which jangled as they opened it. The lad on duty leapt off his stool and disappeared into the forge. Fazio appeared a few moments later, cleaning his hands on his leather apron as he pushed through the curtain that separated the shop from his workplace.

For a smith, he was small and wiry, but there was surprising strength in his arms. There had to be. He was a talented bladesmith as well as a silversmith, turning out beautiful, ornate silverware for wealthy clients and deadly blades for whoever could pay. And, it seemed, with a nice little side trade in Isyr, which Esar was still trying to wrap his head around.

Fazio's eyes lit on Alyas. "Shut the shop," he snapped to the boy. "Take yourself off. We're closed for the day. And don't come back tomorrow neither," he called after the lad's retreating back.

The door slammed closed. Fazio locked it and pulled down the blinds.

Esar said, "Why not just put up a sign, Fazio? Make sure everyone knows you're up to no good."

"Can't talk, can he?" Fazio retorted, eyes on Alyas. "Did you get it?"

There was a note in his voice that Esar didn't like. It was too eager, too possessive.

For an answer, Alyas put the leather-wrapped bundle on the counter. Fazio reached out; Alyas put his hand over it. With his other, he handed the silversmith the unfolded sketch of the Empress Ivane casket.

It took a few seconds for Fazio to shift his attention from the Isyr to the sketch. When he did, the avarice in his eyes transformed to admiration. He whistled. "Now that's a work of art. Really something." He took the parchment, flattening it on the counter. "You can tell that was made by a master. Tricky metal, Isyr."

"You'd know, Fazio," Esar said, his gaze wandering around the shop, absent any sign of that illegal activity.

The silversmith wasn't listening. He lit the lamp on the wall, moving the parchment into the light of the Isyrium bulb so the ink sparkled with hints of blue. He looked up at Alyas. "Where'd you get this?" He stabbed a finger down on the signature. "This is Hagan's work."

"Where do you get your Isyr?" Alyas countered, the first words Esar had heard him speak all morning. His tone was not friendly.

"Yeah, all right," Fazio muttered. "Good point. You see that? The way he cut out them roses? He'd have had to do this piercing before it cooled, and it cools fast. Can you imagine that kind of skill, eh? All that detail, so quick." He shook his head in genuine awe. "Good thing you don't want an Isyr copy. Take decades of skill to pull that off."

Alyas was unmoved by this display of artistic appreciation. "You've got two days."

Esar kept the surprise off his face. *Two days?*

Fazio's face split in a sly grin. "Someone had a bad night. Sleep with it under your pillow, did you?" His eyes slid sideways, towards the blades. "Thought you'd be used to it."

Esar frowned. "Used to what?"

Fazio cocked his head at Alyas, who said, "Can you do it or not?"

"Like that is it? Yes, I can do it. Won't be cheap, though."

Esar raised an eyebrow. Alyas merely picked up the Isyr and turned to leave.

Fazio moved like an eel to get between him and the door. He raised his hands in a placating gesture. "Not what I meant. Ithol's bollocks, you're tetchy this morning."

"What did you mean?" Alyas asked. His voice was hard, uncompromising. Fazio had chosen a bad day to fuck with him.

The smith saw it, backing down fast. "Gonna take longer than I thought, is all. Have to close up for a few days. More than two, anyway. Job like this…" He looked at Alyas. "A lot of skill there, takes time."

"Faz," said Esar, putting an arm around his shoulders. "You could shut up shop and retire on what we're paying you. So don't push it, eh?"

"Two days," Fazio agreed, wincing as the persuasive point of a knife pricked his ribs.

Esar patted him on the shoulder and withdrew the knife. It had been made in this very workshop and had dealt with worse villains than Fazio Vanni.

The package of Isyr reappeared. Fazio's hand snaked towards it.

This time, Alyas let him get his fingers on it before he said, "Only when you're done."

"What do you expect me to do?" the silversmith whined. "Paint it? You want this to fool people, I gotta have Isyr. I explained that yesterday."

Alyas closed his hand around the prize. "You'll think of something." He caught Esar's eye and indicated they were done.

Fazio, disgusted, muttered under his breath. Alyas, with more forbearance than he had shown all day, pretended not to hear. Esar just shook his head and followed his brother to the door.

"Not that way," Fazio snapped. "Out the back. If this goes wrong, the fewer people who've seen you the better. Folks round here don't know how to mind their own business."

Esar looked at Alyas, who shrugged and followed Fazio as he led them through the shop to the forge and the alley beyond.

"My offer's still open," the smith called as they reached the back door.

Esar turned. "What offer?"

Fazio's eyes darted from him to Alyas. "I'd pay a good price for them. Better for you, too."

Esar froze. *Yholis.* He was talking about the blades. Esar's hand strayed to his knife as he glanced at Alyas, whose back was rigid with anger. *Better for you.* "Is that a threat?"

"What? No. I just meant…"

Esar gave him a hard look. "You hiding a king's fortune in here, Faz?" He couldn't imagine what 'a good price' might be given the incalculable worth of that much Isyr, but it was certainly more than Fazio would ever see in his life.

The wiry craftsman shrugged, defensive. "Might be. Forget it then. Trying to do you a favour, is all."

"Well, don't," Esar said, pushing Alyas outside before Fazio could say anything else. He wasn't fast enough.

"Maybe sleep with it somewhere else tonight," the smith called after them as he slammed the door. "Bastard."

❦

The alley was filthy with waste from the businesses that backed onto it and had a stink that suggested some of it was human. Esar wrinkled his nose in disgust, hustling Alyas forward, ignoring the tension under his hand. If his brother's silence had been ferocious before, it was deadly now, and Esar was not going to let him get away with it.

"What was that?"

"What was what?"

"Don't do that," Esar growled. "You know what." Too many things about that conversation set him on edge. Fazio had offered to buy the blades and Alyas hadn't killed him even a little bit? And why would it be doing him a favour?

If the frigid silence was anything to go by, Alyas was regretting that act of mercy. With any luck he might regret the whole enterprise and they could go on home.

Sunlight flashed on steel. The alley darkened as the entrance was blocked by three men. Three men with weapons drawn.

"Shit." Esar reached for his hilt. Alyas had his blades in his hands. Esar caught him as he stepped forward. A glance behind revealed two more advancing on them from the rear. "Careful." They were outnumbered and trapped with little room to move. It was not the moment to react without thinking.

The man in the middle smiled. It was not a pleasant smile and revealed the broken teeth of a habitual brawler. "Hello, boys." He gestured to the men on either side, who took a cautious step forward. "Let's not make this more difficult than it needs to be. How about you drop your weapons and hand over the Isyr." His assessing glance landed on the blades in Alyas's hands. "*All* your Isyr."

Esar turned so his back was to the wall and he could see in both directions. "Don't," he hissed in warning, sensing the imminent movement. Alyas would have assessed their opponents within seconds, just like he had, and would have reached the same conclusion. But they were in a bad spot, and even an incompetent swordsman could kill you if they got lucky. Better to wait this out.

There was a flicker of movement behind their ambushers and someone dropped into the alley. Agazi put his fingers to his mouth and whistled, sharp and jarring.

The leader glanced round. It was enough.

Alyas was on him, the man disarmed and up against the wall with the blade of the Isyr sword at his throat before Esar had a chance to bless his forethought. Agazi sauntered forward, Aubron and Storn appearing behind him.

"Hello, boys," Agazi said with a grin. He was enjoying this. "I suggest you drop your weapons. You're not up to this."

"Or don't," said Alyas, whose attention had not wavered from the man he held at sword point. "And I'll kill this one then the rest of you."

The cold threat in his voice undid the last of their attackers' resolve, which had wavered as soon as they no longer held the upper hand. Metal clattered on the cobbles.

Esar caught Agazi's eye and nodded his thanks as Aubron gathered up the fallen weaponry, a collection of blades of far superior quality than their owners should have possessed.

He put a hand on Alyas's shoulder and hauled him back. The leader wriggled out from under his blade and edged to where the rest of his crew were huddled, all his swagger gone.

"Esar." Aubron held out the leader's sword. Its maker's mark was engraved just above the guard, a small F within a larger V, the same mark his knife bore. *Fazio Vanni.*

He swore. The underground trade in Isyr was almost as cutthroat as the legal trade in Isyrium. Who would have guessed?

"What is it?" Alyas had sheathed his sword but the dagger was still in his hand, and Esar hesitated before handing over the weapon and its damning mark.

Who else knew they had the Isyr? And the ambush had taken place outside Fazio's shop. The more Esar thought about it, the angrier he became, so he did not intervene when Alyas grabbed a handful of the leader's filthy tunic and slammed him into the equally filthy wall of the alley.

"Why?"

But Esar thought he could guess why. Fazio could have done the work and taken his payment, but he knew what it was he was meant to copy, and the unpleasantness of the consequences should that forgery be discovered were not difficult to imagine. Even so, he could have just refused. Alyas, for all that he could be stubborn and difficult when he was set on something, would not have forced him. Alas for greed.

Esar listened with only half an ear to the panicked explanations of the men they had disarmed. Until, that is, one of them started babbling about how Fazio had promised them a share of the blades. Melted down.

That tore it. Esar caught Agazi's eye and sighed. They had brought it on themselves, and at any other time he would have no objection to slitting their throats and having done with it. In their profession, leaving your enemies alive was not a recipe for a long life, but the last thing they needed right now was to call down official attention on their activities. And five bodies tended to be hard for authorities to ignore.

"Alyas," he said sharply. "Fazio." The smith was the one who had set up the ambush. There was no need to waste their time on this lot.

"Fazio," Alyas agreed, sheathing the dagger. The ripple of relief that ran through their captives was almost audible, and he hadn't even touched them. "Wait for me here." And he was gone.

Esar said a silent prayer to Yholis for Fazio's soul, which was more than he deserved, then gave their would-be ambushers a sharp kick. "Take my advice and fuck off before he gets back."

They did, with enthusiastic assistance from Aubron and Storn.

Agazi sidled over. "You think we should go in there?" *In there* being Fazio's workshop.

"Gods no." Fazio should have known better. Besides, no Fazio, no box, no breaking into the temple and bringing the wrath of Ithol's agents down on their heads. Esar wasn't going to do anything to preserve that plan.

Agazi looked at him askance. "Are you sure? He'll regret it."

And no one needed that. "Fine," he said with an exaggerated sigh and followed Agazi down the alley.

They met Alyas coming out of Fazio's workshop.

"Well?" Esar asked, looking him up and down and finding no immediate evidence of murder. Agazi pushed open the door and took a cautious look inside.

"He's going to need a while," Alyas replied.

Esar hurried after him. "To recover? What did you do?"

Alyas shot him an offended look, as if he had not gone in there intent on violence. "To make the box."

Esar stopped dead. *No.* "He just tried to have us killed!"

"And he won't do it again." Like the smith was a soldier caught napping on watch. Except a soldier caught napping on watch would be in a deal more trouble than Fazio was for *trying to have them killed*.

Agazi, catching Esar's eye, shook his head and shrugged. Fazio must really be whole and breathing.

Alyas reached the end of the alley and disappeared.

Esar kicked the wall in a burst of frustration. "What the fuck is going on?"

※

Alyas was in the corner of the common room with Frey and Keie when Esar made it back to the inn. His foot was aching and he thought he might have broken a toe, so he was in no mood to overlook the morning's weirdness.

"We need to talk," he said, coming to a stop by the table.

Alyas waved him to a chair as Frey, seeing his face, asked, "What's wrong?"

"What's wrong?" Esar demanded. "He just—" His gaze landed on the jug of wine on the table and the three cups. It wasn't that Alyas never drank these days, it was just that he did it rarely, and never casually. If he was drinking now, something was bothering him. And something had certainly been bothering him this morning.

Thought you'd be used to it. What the fuck had Fazio meant by that?

"What did he do?" Frey asked, looking between them.

Esar frowned at Alyas, suddenly aware of the way the morning had raked over old griefs. Reminded, uncomfortably, of those first bad years after Gerrin's death and Raffa's betrayal when Alyas's obsessive attachment to the blades had been a constant source of worry.

As he hesitated, unsure how to proceed, Alyas signalled the innkeeper to bring another cup for the wine. "Would you rather I'd killed him?"

Something loosened in Esar's chest. A serving girl placed the cup in front of him and poured the wine. "No," he admitted, taking a seat next to Frey. Because he wouldn't, not really. "But I would rather you give this up. What makes you think we can trust him? He already betrayed you once."

"We have an agreement."

"And most people would consider that agreement void after he tried to murder us."

Alyas brushed that aside as of no consequence. "Fazio did what he was always going to do, and better that he did it now than later."

Later, presumably, being while they were inside the temple. "What's to stop him doing that anyway?"

It was the most prudent course for the smith. He could claim duress for making the forgery and a pardon for informing on the conspirators, especially if it led to their capture. It wasn't foolproof as plans went, and not without risk—it assumed Ithol's inquisitors would care whether his participation was willing or not—but Fazio might well gamble it was better than staying silent and hoping for the best.

Alyas nodded across the table. "Because Keie will be with him the whole time and she will make it clear how unwise that would be."

Keie, enjoying herself, waggled her sharp little dagger and grinned.

Esar ignored this. "And between now and then?"

"Between now and then, we'll be watching him, and he knows it."

"Thought of everything, haven't you?" Esar said. It was annoying because it was true. "And if this all goes wrong? Fazio hangs with the rest of us?"

Alyas gave a careless shrug. "He can still claim duress, just more of it. And he did try to kill us, so I'm not sure I care. Besides, it won't go wrong."

"Because you've thought of everything?"

"Well, no," Alyas admitted. "That's not possible. You know that."

He did know. Even the best plans had an unavoidable tendency to unravel once set in motion. Which was why this was madness. "Then why, for Yholis's sake? Don't you remember what happened last time we did something like this?" His own memories were hazy at best. He had a vague recollection of waking up to Alondo's face and Alyas asleep in a chair, followed by days of semi-wakefulness that all blurred into one—and pain, he remembered that—followed, as soon as he was able, by an uncomfortable journey out of Avarel that was best forgotten altogether.

Alyas, who did not have a convenient gap in his memory, winced at the reminder.

Esar, not inclined to be sympathetic, drove his point home. "I do not want a rerun of that particular disaster, which, if you recall, I warned you against at the time." A thought struck him. "That's it, isn't it? This is about last time. Ithol's blood, Alyas. We survived. That means we won. You don't have to even the score."

"Of course we do," Alyas replied, his voice hard. "We have to tilt the score so far in our favour that they think twice before trying anything again."

Esar sighed and held up his hands in surrender. It was no use. Of all their quarrels with the syndicates—and Yholis knew, there were many—that was the one Alyas would never forgive. Were the situation reversed, he had to admit he might feel the same. Besides, on one level Alyas was right. Because at the core of it, all other quarrels aside, there were the Lathai and there was Isyr, and that was something worth defending. And the syndicates, already suspicious thanks to Corado, would keep pushing, keep testing them, until either they got what they wanted or the price became too high, even for them.

He took a long drink of his wine, thumping the empty cup on the table. "Then you'd better think of everything, because if this goes wrong, we'll be dead."

Alyas, his flash of temper vanished, refilled his cup with a laugh quirking his mouth. "You worry too much. I have a back-up plan."

"You do, do you?" Esar said sourly. "And what's that?"

Frey grinned at him, squeezing his knee under the table. "Me."

※

The arrival of Kael Ito, the source of all their troubles, interrupted the ensuing argument.

Alyas, who was facing the door, saw him first. "*Esar.*"

Esar turned. He swore. "How do you want to play this?" Whatever they planned, Kael Ito was a problem. Him Esar would happily have killed.

As Raffa's brother-in-law searched the crowded common room, Alyas nudged Frey, who got up from the table with Keie and disappeared into the throng of people by the bar.

"I'm relying on you to make your feelings plain," Alyas replied as Ito saw them and elbowed his way over. He was still wearing his desperate petitioner act, dressed to disguise his status—except for the ring that identified him. How stupid did these people think they were?

"Fine by me," Esar said, shoving his chair back. He caught Ito by the collar of his artfully stained shirt and spun him back around the way he'd come. "Fuck off out of here and don't come back."

Ito squirmed in his grasp, protesting and appealing to Alyas, who hadn't bothered to move.

"The answer's no, Kael," he said. "I suggest you take it up with Raffa. Or ask your brother for help."

Esar felt the fight go out of the man, his shoulders slumping in defeat. Mitka Ito had that effect on people, including his own brother.

"Please, if you know—"

"It's precisely because we know that we want no part of it," Esar snarled in his ear. He couldn't believe this man was married to a king's sister. "Now go away and get some other fools killed on your behalf."

Ito wasn't ready to give up. "I can pay. Whatever you want."

Alyas leant forward, reaching for the wine jug to disguise his sudden fury. "We don't want your money." The words were frigid with hatred. Raffa would come to them on his knees before ever they took syndicate gold. "Go home to your wife, Kael, and pray to Yholis she lives long enough for you to get back what you never should have lost."

"I didn't lose it! They stole it."

"Oh, I've no doubt," said Alyas. "They do that. The answer's still no."

Esar let go of Ito with a shove and he was immediately gathered into the rough embrace of those members of the company close enough to notice the scuffle and helped on his way out. Esar waited until he was sure the man was gone then sat back down, studying Alyas across the small table. "How I wish you meant that."

Alyas gave a quick, sharp smile that had no levity in it. "But I did, every word. I'm not helping him, and I will never take his money." He leant back, agile hands playing with his cup. "And he should go home to Sofia, poor woman."

Esar grunted. He hadn't known Raffa's half-sister well, but he wouldn't wish a man like that on anyone.

He refilled his wine, noting that the jug was more than half empty, and took a chance. "How did you know to ask Fazio?"

There was a fraught silence, then Alyas said, "That wasn't the first time he's offered to buy my father's blades."

Esar let out a long breath. Frey caught his eye from across the room and he shook his head. "And he's still alive?" He kept the words light, careful not to do or say anything that might break the rare confidence.

"I asked him first."

Of all the things Alyas could have said, *that* he would never have expected, and it shocked him into silence. For once, that seemed the right response. His eyes wandering away from Esar, Alyas said,

"It was years ago. Not long after… They reminded me too much, of him, of things…" He gave a small shrug. "It was years ago. I changed my mind, but he's never stopped asking."

Which explained why he had tolerated the smith's offers, since he couldn't do otherwise. But it explained precious little else. "What did he mean?" Esar asked. "What should you be used to?"

But the moment had passed. "Your guess is as good as mine," Alyas lied, rising to leave.

Esar caught his wrist. "Frey—"

"Will be in no danger, I promise. And you don't have to come if you don't want to."

"Fuck you," Esar snarled, offended. As if he would let Alyas go in alone. "But you must know this is a trap."

His brother laughed. "It wouldn't be fun if it was easy."

※

"This is *so* much fun," Esar muttered as they crouched in the shadow of the temple walls three days later.

Fazio, despite his protests, had produced the fake box, which Alyas had collected the night before along with the sketch he had stolen from the Temple of Yholis (now returned). Esar had to admit it was very good, but it wasn't perfect. Comparing Fazio's efforts with Hagan's drawing, the piercings about which the smith had rhapsodised were cruder, less delicate, but that's what you got when you rushed a man at his work. Was it good enough to fool the temple? Alyas seemed to think so, and since his plan relied on no one noticing the exchange, at least for a while, Esar hoped he was right. It was irrelevant anyway, as nothing would change his mind, not even the numerous guards currently making their lives difficult.

Frey and Agazi were already inside along with a handful of others, joining the crowd of petitioners seeking the favour of the god during the late summer festival of the harvest. At least now he knew why Alyas had been in such a hurry. The temple would be packed with Lessing's citizens for the duration of the festival, and its many devotions would keep Ithol's disciples occupied with an endless succession of ceremonies. That they had to go over the walls rather than through the gates like everyone else seemed an unnecessary obstacle. He suspected Alyas was having fun at his expense.

"This is stupid," he hissed as another chance came and went too quickly for them to take advantage of it.

"You're the one who thinks it's a trap," Alyas murmured.

"The point being that we shouldn't do it, not that we make it even more difficult."

"If it's a trap," Alyas explained, "and we go in the front gates, they'll know we're here."

As if there was no chance they could slip in with the crowd without being noticed. "Whereas if they see us scrambling over the walls, they'll think nothing of it."

Alyas shifted in the darkness. "If you're right and this is Ithol taking belated payback, we'll know soon enough, because they'll take us the moment we're inside. Why make it easy for them?"

Why go in at all if that was the case? But at least he was considering the possibility. "And if it's the syndicates?" It *was* the syndicates. They both knew it.

"If it's the Selysians, they'll wait until we've made the switch, since it's the box they're after."

"And if it's both?" It was the possibility Esar feared most, the temple and the syndicates working together to rid themselves of a man who had become a persistent problem.

"Then you'd better hope my back-up plan works. Listen. Are you ready?"

Laughter drifted on the summer breeze. The festival was a drunken affair, with feasting every night that extended into the small hours. Only the wealthiest and most important citizens of Lessing attended the actual feasts, but everyone else brought food and smuggled in alcohol and turned the courtyard into a festival of their own. Which was why there were extra guards. Which was why Esar wished they had gone in through the gates.

The laughter turned to shouts. The shouts got louder. The guards started to pay attention, calling out to each other. Someone went to intervene. The volume increased. A ripple of panic spread through the sentries on the walls.

Alyas tensed as one by one the guards abandoned their posts. The moment the rope appeared, he was moving, pulling himself up the high walls and disappearing over the top. One way or another, they'd had a lot of practice scaling walls over the years. Esar followed more slowly and joined Alyas and Agazi on the other side, the rope disappearing back where it had come from as Agazi grinned. Behind him, in the light of a thousand torches, a full-scale riot was in progress.

"What did you do?" Esar asked, impressed.

Agazi laughed. "Not a lot. Didn't need to." Agazi was of the opinion that everyone disliked Ithol if you could get them drunk enough to admit it.

"Where's Frey?"

"Here."

Esar turned. While he wasn't reconciled to Frey's involvement, he had to admit that the role Alyas had given her was unlikely to place her in any danger. He was also wise enough to know that continued objections would be a bad idea. Frey was set on this, and she did look good in the dress Alyas had bought her.

"They're all in the sanctuary," she told Alyas. "I asked around and it sounds like they stay there most of the night. Their guests are still in the hall. They'll probably stay there most of the night as well if the state of them is anything to go by. Ithol is generous with his wine cellar, at least."

Esar grunted. Made sense. Generosity designed to loosen the purse strings of donors.

"The Selysians?" Alyas asked Frey, handing Agazi a pair of knives. Esar did the same. No weapons were allowed on the temple grounds during the festival, so they had brought spares for those of the company already inside. That was one advantage of going over the walls and he did feel happier walking into a trap armed. Everything was good, plain steel. The Isyr blades were back at the inn under Storn's watchful eye. No point dangling temptation in front of Ellasia's most avaricious god.

"Not here," Frey replied.

Alyas paused, frowning. "You're sure?"

"I haven't seen them. But there might be some I don't know." Frey had spent the last couple of days watching the syndicate properties in Lessing so she would recognise their faces, and the evening with Lessing's elite as the guest of Prince Georgios Beor—who had proved as eager as Alyas had predicted to get his hands on the Ivane box—so she could keep an eye on them.

"What does it mean?" Esar asked. It was a syndicate trap and the syndicates… weren't here?

Alyas shook his head. "I don't know."

"You don't know or we should leave now while we still can?"

"We're not leaving without the box," Alyas said. "The vaults?"

"Guards, guards, and more guards," said Frey. "But the rest are out here dealing with this, so they can't call for help."

Alyas grinned in the darkness and Esar rolled his eyes. Whatever else he thought of this venture, his brother was having the time of his life, and it was hard to argue with that.

"Watch out," Agazi said, giving Esar a nudge to one side as a half-eaten loaf of bread came flying through the night. The chaos behind them was getting worse, convulsing through the entire courtyard. The guards would be busy for hours bringing it under control, but it was in danger of disturbing Ithol's devotees and the last thing they needed was anyone from the temple coming to investigate. Still, there wasn't anything to be done about it. Inciting a riot was a lot easier than stopping one and they had other things to do.

Alyas was watching the rioters with the kind of expression Esar didn't like.

"What are you thinking?"

"That this is too good to waste." To Agazi he said, "Do you think you can persuade them to take their party inside?"

Esar's heart sank. "Robbing the temple isn't enough for you? You've got to trash it, too?"

"Is there some reason we shouldn't?"

Too many, but since none of them would make a difference, Esar didn't waste his breath. "Fine. Sack the place. They can only kill us once."

Agazi disappeared. Alyas wasn't the only one enjoying himself, and Agazi was having fun indulging his Steppelander's dislike of Ithol. It wasn't long before the surge of the crowd took them to the gates of the inner complex, and Esar thought he spotted some faces he recognised at its head. The guards tried to rally. One was clubbed down by what looked like a haunch of ham.

Alyas winced. "Time to go."

They attached themselves to the straggling rear of the riot, dodging between the heaving, enthusiastic mass of brawlers and into the temple's central complex. Where predictable devastation was in full swing.

Esar looked around in despair as they picked their way across the inner courtyard. "If they catch us…"

"I think we can safely say it's not the temple that set this up," Alyas replied, pulling him back against the wall of the cloister as the crowd surged too close. "Where's Agazi? We need to move them on. They're no good to us here."

Ithol's great houses were grander and more elaborate than those of his sister Yholis, but they followed the same basic pattern. The outer grounds, where the riot had started, were open to all. Within the complex itself was a cloistered central courtyard, which the looters were currently dismantling, and beyond that was the great hall and the smaller, grander sanctuary. Both, from time to time, were accessible to worshippers, and tonight were full of all the kinds of people they wanted to avoid. What they were interested in was the smaller courtyard beyond both where the business of the temple was conducted. In temples of Yholis, that was the care of the sick. Here, it was a counting house.

That was where they needed the riot to end up. And it did, because someone planted the idea of looting the temple's treasure, and the largely poor, hungry crowd seized on this idea with the kind of enthusiasm that made Esar think there might be something to Agazi's theory after all.

But it also meant they had a new problem. Alyas tugged at his sleeve. "Come on. If they get into the vault, we'll have wasted our time." The box would disappear into someone's pocket who had no idea what it was and would likely never resurface.

Esar tightened his grip on Frey's hand. She was supposed to go back into the great hall to keep an eye on the Selysians, but they weren't there. Whatever that meant. Because this was a trap, and if the temple wasn't involved, that meant the nastiest man in Ellasia was out to get them, and Esar wanted to know where Frey was.

As they passed through the inner gates into the small courtyard, it was clear the guards had decided that rather than try to quell the riot, their best option was to barricade themselves inside and wait for the riot to quell itself. Alyas plucked a handful of lit Isyrium bulbs from their wall niches, hissing as the hot glass scorched his fingers, and tossed them through the nearest window to change their minds.

The result was a lot of frantic shouting but not much else. They were decorative bulbs, and tiny, and they had already been burning for hours. The small fires were quickly dealt with. Esar handed Alyas another armful, scorching his own fingers, and these followed the first, one by one. They didn't actually want to start a fire, just persuade those inside that they needed to come out. On the far side of the little courtyard, some of the rioters had adopted the same strategy, with rather less restraint.

The frantic shouts turned angry. Tossing the last bulb, Alyas pressed himself into the wall as the door slammed open and the temple guards changed tactics. Bunching together, they attempted to form a ring around the rioters, containing them in the centre of the courtyard, trying to protect both themselves and the wealth they were guarding. Their officer had kept his head and was struggling to maintain order with half his men cut off by the crowd, which was not interested in complying with his strategy.

Esar watched with professional interest until Alyas tapped him on the shoulder and made an impatient gesture. This was as good a distraction as they were going to get, and they needed to be in and out before either the looters or the temple guards got the upper hand.

The two guards blocking their way into Ithol's treasure house were quickly dealt with. Alyas peered down the empty hallway. "Ready?"

"Not really."

Alyas grinned and disappeared. Esar nudged an unconscious guard out of the way as he followed. With any luck, these two were the only ones left inside. He didn't particularly want to kill anyone tonight, but he wasn't going to be picky about it.

Frey made to follow; he stopped her. "Stay here with Agazi. Keep an eye out. And don't get arrested." They would be like rats in a trap now, and they needed Frey for their back-up plan if they found themselves in serious trouble.

Alyas ignored the rooms facing onto the courtyard, heading deeper into the building until they came to an iron door. A locked iron door. Esar faced back the way they had come as Alyas set to work on the lock. He had picked enough locks for Melar Gaemo over the years to have become quite proficient at it, and in this case, the lock was not the primary protection for what lay beyond. That was Ithol's inquisitors, whom no one in their right mind would provoke by robbing the temple.

The lock turned. Alyas pushed the door open. So far, far too easy.

Esar followed him inside and slammed the door behind them, plunging the room into darkness. He reached for a nearby table by feel and wedged it against the door. It wouldn't keep out determined looters for long, but it would serve to give them warning of company. Only then did he look around.

Alyas stood stock still in the centre of the temple's outer vault. The temple's windowless, lightless vault. And Esar could see him in the faint glow from the shelves that lined the long room.

Isyr.

So much Isyr. More wealth than he would see in a thousand lifetimes in this one room. In this one temple. In Lessing. They weren't even in one of Ellasia's great capitals. And this was the *outer vault*.

"Alyas?"

His brother was staring at the Isyr, unmoving, and they didn't have time for this. They needed to find the Ivane box and make their escape before they were caught. And Esar intended to leave the door open behind them. The looters were welcome to all of this. It made him sick just looking at it, hoarded to gloat over. What could Ithol do with so much Isyr? What could anyone?

"Alyas," he repeated, lighting a row of Isyrium bulbs.

Alyas turned. In the blue-tinted light, his face was stricken. And his eyes…

Esar felt a surge of alarm, his skin crawling. There was something about this place. He snapped his fingers. "Alyas!"

Finally, his brother focused on him. "Esar?" The way he said it was so unnerving that Esar almost dragged him out of there right then, box or no box, but they were here now. The point of no return had been passed some time ago.

He took Alyas by the shoulder and directed him to the shelves. "You take this side, I'll take the other. Let's find this bloody thing and get out of here." Out of this room that was making him unhappy for all kinds of reasons.

He waited only to ensure Alyas obeyed before starting his search, working quickly down the length of glittering treasures. The Empress Ivane casket was tiny, small enough to fit in a closed fist. A miniature, made as a gift by the emperor for his empress and given after his death as a token of her affection to a man who was rumoured to have been her lover. It had no useful purpose, but it was a thing of beauty, rare and precious. And it wasn't anywhere Esar could see.

A door opened into another room, and there was another beyond that. Yholis, please let them not have to search *every* room.

He glanced at his brother to find him once more frozen. Then he saw why. Alyas was staring at something in his hand, something small and piercingly bright in the Isyrium glow. The Empress Ivane casket.

"Thank Yholis," Esar breathed. "Let's get the fuck out of here."

He dragged the table away from the door. It nearly knocked him off its feet as it swung inwards and the question of where the Selysians were was answered in the worst possible way. They were here.

※

The vault that had felt vast before was now too cramped. Any room was too cramped when the syndicates were in it, but there really were too many of them here. Too many for the two of them.

"Well, well, Alyas-Raine Sera," said a tall man with a face that would have sent an artist into raptures. A nervous Kael Ito stood beside him, overshadowed in every possible way. "Except that's not your name anymore, is it? Kael said you wouldn't come. I knew you would. What do they call you these days?"

"Careful, Mitka," Alyas replied, all trace of distraction vanished. "Or we might get to what they call you."

Well, fuck. Mitka Ito, head of the Selysian Syndicate. The last man in Ellasia Esar wanted to meet.

The elder Ito laughed, wide blue eyes alight with anticipation. "But I like those names and I earned them. You lost yours, like you're going to lose that." He nodded to the box in Alyas's hand. "Hand it over before I practise my reputation on your brother. This is Esar Cantrell, I presume?"

Alyas smiled through his teeth. "You're as clever as they say." But he threw the box, a flash of brightness in the night. Esar had several sharp objects pointed at him, including Mitka Ito's infamous stiletto.

Ito caught it. He chuckled—the sound made the hairs on Esar's neck stand up—and threw it back without bothering to look at it.

"Not that one. Do you think we weren't watching you? Search him."

Alyas, arm extended to catch the box, tried to sidestep, but two of Ito's men grabbed him. One hit him, a vicious blow precisely placed, and Alyas folded to the ground, fingers scrabbling as he tried to breathe. The other kicked him in the face and Esar's control snapped.

It did neither of them any good. A fist caught Esar in the back, another on the side of the head. His vision exploded. When it returned, he was aware of his face on cold stone and movement above him. Ito's men were leaning over Alyas, who was looking straight at him, bloody fingers gripped tight around the box he had caught.

They made short, rough work of that search, and the Ivane box was in Ito's hands and Alyas hauled back to his feet while Esar was still struggling to make it to his knees.

Ito tossed the little box in the air and caught it, oblivious to Esar's agony at his feet. "We were going to wait for you outside, but you created such a devastating diversion that we couldn't risk missing you in the confusion. Thank you for this. It could have caused me a minor headache."

Alyas spat blood, wiping it away with his wrist. He leant unsteadily against the wall. "Glad we could be of service. Next time it'll cost you double."

Ito laughed, the little Isyr casket clenched in his fist. "Next time? Oh, I'm not letting you go. My colleagues will pay good money for you, even what's left when I'm finished. Put the fake back. I don't want Ithol's troublesome agents to know they've been robbed. *Now*," he added when Alyas didn't move fast enough.

Someone grabbed Esar by the shoulder, wrenching him upright. Too quickly. The world tilted and spun. He vaguely heard Alyas's protest and Mitka's laugh, but his vision was greying at the edges and nothing made sense. Movement, some of it his, his feet stumbling over each other. They must have been outside because he could feel a breeze on his face. Then nothing.

He lost hours. He didn't know how many. There were moments when he clawed almost awake. Once they were moving but he wasn't, and the bumping of a wagon over cobbles made his stomach revolt. He vomited. Someone cursed. The darkness returned. The second time, he was falling. Hands caught him; a voice spoke. He couldn't reply.

When Esar eventually peeled open sticky eyes, he was lying on damp stone, which was not in any way a good sign. He tried to move and groaned as pain spiked through his head. There was a shifting of movement and a blurry shape appeared at the edges of his vision. He wasn't alone on the floor. He blinked and the shape took on a more distinct outline. Alyas. The temple. *The fucking trap.*

He swore. Even that made his hurts more vigorous.

Something touched his face. A hand. He tried to swipe it away with his own, missed, and felt his wrist caught and laid back down.

"Stay still," Alyas advised, his voice rough around the edges. They had hit him, too. Esar remembered that. And the fact that it was entirely his own fault.

Mitka Ito. The Selysians. They were so fucked.

He tried to tell his brother exactly what he was going to do to him.

"Maybe save that for later," Alyas suggested. He sounded half amused, half worried. "When you can stand. Half your head is a bruise."

He knew. He could bloody well feel it. His whole face ached.

He swore again, the words slurring.

Alyas's blurry face hovered into view. He was frowning. "What's your name?"

"Fuck off," muttered Esar, draping an arm over his aching head. "What's yours?" And drifted off to the sound of Alyas's soft laughter.

When he next surfaced, the pain had subsided to a dull roar and he could see again, more or less.

The murmur of voices reverberated through his skull, making his stomach churn. He rolled onto his side and managed to brace himself on an elbow. Alyas was sitting on the ground leaning against the bars of what must be their cell, his eyes on Esar. There was dried blood on his temple and the left side of his face was discoloured with bruises, but the eyes studying Esar were clear.

Beside him, in the next cell, a filthy, ragged blond girl crouched with one hand on the bars that separated them, glaring at Esar with suspicion on her severe Qidan features.

"Who's this?" he mumbled, struggling into a sitting position. Yholis, but his head hurt.

The girl maintained an unfriendly silence. There were bruises on her face and ugly marks at her wrists. It was Alyas who said, "This is Della."

"Della," Esar murmured, closing his eyes as the thudding in his head reached a new pitch. He gave up trying to sit. "And what's a Qidan girl doing here?" There were enough northerners with the company that he could recognise Qidan blood when he saw it, and he didn't expect to see it in a syndicate cell in Hantara. Whoever this girl was, she didn't belong here. Neither did they.

Alyas said, "She stole from the wrong people."

"Lot of that going around," Esar muttered. "Where are we?"

"A syndicate safehouse, I assume. How's your head?"

"It hurts. How's yours?"

"Hurts," Alyas admitted. He said something to Della and she withdrew to the corner of her cell. "Are you all right?"

"No," Esar snapped. Because he wasn't. "Told you this was a trap." The worst kind of trap, so bad he didn't even want to think about it. He looked at the girl huddled in the corner. "You're very friendly."

"We've talked. You've been out for hours. I was worried." He would have been. People thought Esar was the protective one. They had no idea. Alyas just didn't show it in the same way.

Esar closed his eyes again.

Alyas said, "You threw up on Mitka's boots."

He snorted. It hurt. "Gods, we're so fucked." Because the thought was stabbing at him like the pain in his head.

The syndicates had wanted Alyas dead for years, ever since he had dedicated his life to making theirs difficult. Now they had him. And not just any syndicate, the Selysian bloody Syndicate, led by a man who so delighted in inflicting pain that the Temple of Yholis in Cadria was rumoured to have closed its doors to him. And Yholis denied her care to no one.

"Still," Alyas said. "It could be worse."

Esar glared at him. "How, exactly, could it be worse?"

A smile twitched Alyas's mouth. "They could have the Ivane box."

"They could—" Esar stared, his brain refusing to understand. "Oh, no. Ithol's fucking bollocks, tell me you didn't."

But Alyas was laughing too hard and couldn't answer, one arm wrapped around his bruised middle. "Gave it to him," he managed to gasp after a moment. "When he asked. He gave it back."

Because Mitka Ito'd had Esar at the point of his stiletto and Alyas, who would risk his own life without a second thought, got funny about risking Esar's.

And Ito, who thought he knew who he was dealing with and had quite sensibly been watching them, had assumed Alyas would give him the fake. Esar remembered the way it had glittered as Alyas threw it, but Ito hadn't even looked at it. He'd just thrown it back.

Now Esar was laughing, too, and it hurt. Gods, it hurt. And it wasn't even funny. Ito would realise sooner rather than later that the

Empress Ivane casket in his possession wasn't the real one, and he would not be happy.

"Then he can go and get it himself," Alyas said, once he stopped laughing. "I'm sure the temple will be happy to hand it over when he explains the situation." That thought set him off again and Esar didn't get anything sensible out of him for a while.

Eventually, in response to his increasingly irritated queries, Alyas said, "Frey saw them take us. They'll know where we are."

It was something, he supposed. Their back-up plan was safe, though it had been set up to get them out of a temple cell, not a syndicate one. And there was no getting away from the fact that their continuing existence depended on whether the company could pivot faster than Ito could identify the fake. "You should have told him."

Alyas said nothing. Esar looked at him. His face was set in a hard line. There was no way he would have told Ito his mistake. It wouldn't have saved them from this, but it might have saved them from the something worse Esar feared was coming.

"Next time I say it's a trap," he said with as much force as his aching head would permit, "I expect you to listen."

※

More time passed. Esar dozed while Alyas talked to Della, who had crept back to the bars. She was only half Qidan as it turned out, her father a Qidan Janath who'd met her mother in Lessing and taken her home with him. But the relationship had been short-lived, and though Qidans had a very different attitude to the rest of Ellasia when it came to personal relationships, they were famously unwelcoming of outsiders. Della might look Qidan to them, but in Qido she looked Hantaran. So she'd left, only to find no friendlier reception in Hantara, where Qido was an ever-present threat across the border.

Not that she volunteered any of this. Alyas teased it out of her over several hours, while Esar drifted, half an ear on their conversation, the other listening for the approach of Mitka Ito and his stiletto.

It took longer than he expected for Ito to come, but the man was an expert in torture. Perhaps he was giving them a chance to enjoy the anticipation.

When the door opened, Della was gone in a flash, retreating to the farthest corner of her small cell, thin, bruised arms hugging her knees. She had picked the pocket of a syndicate representative. For that, Mitka Ito had held her here for more than a month, or that was her best guess, and it was clear she had not been ignored. Esar felt a welcome burst of fury dull the edges of the terror.

They didn't get up. What was the point of giving an enemy the opportunity to knock you down?

Alyas, wrists crossed over his knees, said, "Hello, Mitka. I hope your latest acquisition is bringing you joy."

Ito regarded him without a flicker of expression, blue eyes cruel and bright in the perfection of his face. A beauty that would have made Yholis weep if the number of patients he sent her way hadn't done that already. "It will," he said. "Because I *am* going to enjoy this. Search them," he said to the men at his back. "No need to be gentle."

They weren't gentle; they were thorough. By the end of it, half their clothes were in a heap on the filthy floor with every seam slit and the rest were rags. Esar shivered. It was cold.

"Where is it?" Ito demanded of Alyas when the pile of discarded clothing was dropped at his feet.

Alyas, with the smile that made people want to hit him, said, "Back where you left it, Mitka. At the temple."

He was on his knees, hands tied behind his back. Esar was beside him in the same state. Ito crouched so his eyes were level with Alyas. "Don't lie to me."

Alyas's smile grew wider. He decorated it with his teeth. "I don't have to. I gave you the box when you asked for it. I put it back when you told me to. I can tell you exactly where it is if you like."

Ito hit him, an open-handed blow that rocked his head to the side and failed to dislodge the infuriating smile.

"It's on—"

Ito flicked a hand and it was the man behind who hit him this time. Alyas spat blood, but before he could provoke yet another blow, a hand in his hair yanked his head back.

Ito, still crouched at eye level, took his glittering little stiletto from its sheath. "Let me tell you what I'm going to do." His eyes were on Alyas, but he was speaking to Esar. "I would really like that box. So much so that I'm prepared to forego the pleasure of using your brother as my canvas. I'm just going to kill him. If you don't want me to do that, I suggest you tell me what he did with the box." He turned to Esar. "Quickly."

Fuck. Esar tried to speak, but panic and fury both were choking him. There was no contingency for *this*. Unless their back-up plan materialised *this moment*… His mind blanked. He couldn't think about it.

Ito stood, moving behind Alyas, jewelled fingers lacing themselves through his hair like a caress. They tightened. Alyas's chin came up, the needle point of the stiletto resting against the pulse in his throat.

Mitka Ito had his brother at knife point.

Ito, who learned quickly. And what he had learned was that Alyas was prepared to call his bluff.

Now he would find out whether Esar was willing to do the same, and Mitka Ito famously *did not bluff.*

"It's at the temple," Esar said, urgent with panic. "He was telling the truth. It's on the shelf in the temple vault where it came from, and you can get it yourself this time."

"You're lying."

"I'm not lying! Why would I lie? It's at the temple." The point of the knife drew blood. "Please! I swear it, it's at the temple."

Ito said nothing, merely put pressure on the blade; blood ran down Alyas's neck. Esar saw red.

"It's at the temple! It's at the fucking temple!" He lurched to the side, tugging desperately at the ropes at his wrists. "He gave you the real one! You think you're so fucking clever, you fuck—" He never saw what hit him, but he was on the ground, his mouth full of blood. "He gave it to you! Please. Please, don't." He would plead. If that's what Ito wanted, he would *beg*.

Ito's voice said, "But I will."

Someone grabbed at him. Esar kicked out with his legs, hit something. "It's at the temple, I swear it! It's at the fucking temple!" He repeated it over and over. He couldn't see Alyas anymore. Della was in the centre of her cell on her hands and knees, staring at him with eyes wide with terror.

Somewhere above there was a sharp movement. His vision splintered. He was screaming now, incoherent with rage and desperation. *Not like this!*

Hands yanked him back to his knees. He turned his face away, *refusing* to look. It was forced back. Alyas was staring at him, his face white with shock, blood at his neck. "Esar."

Ito's stiletto was back in its sheath.

The relief was so sharp and sudden he nearly collapsed. It didn't last.

Mitka's perfect beauty was marred by anger—a vicious, vengeful anger. "I think I'm so clever?" he said, voice as smooth as silk. "Oh no, I think that might be you." He flicked his hand up and Alyas was hauled from his knees to his feet. "It seems I will be practising my art, after all."

No! They shoved Alyas towards the door; Esar hurled himself after them on his knees, screaming his fury at Ito, at the whole fucking world, because *no, no, no, this was not happening!*

The door slammed shut. He was on his back, kicking at it. He kept kicking it until he thought his feet must break, his throat raw from screaming.

He stopped, exhausted. The silence was an assault. "Fuck!" The word was half curse, half sob.

"He won't kill him."

Esar turned his head. Della sat in the corner of her cell, knees up, hands in her lap. Her face was as white as Alyas's had been.

"He likes to play too much."

Esar closed his eyes; he felt sick. That's what he was afraid of.

His heart thudded in the silence, hard and painful. His chest hurt. Everything hurt, and it was nothing, *nothing*, compared to the visceral terror of that stiletto against Alyas's throat.

Della shuffled around her cell. "Is he honest, your brother?" she asked, closer now.

Esar opened his eyes and looked at her, crouched once more by the bars. He couldn't focus on the question. "What?"

"Is he?" she insisted.

He was too tired to think. "Why?"

She didn't answer, just stared at him, hostile and desperate. What had Alyas said to her?

Esar sighed, hands on his face, trying to breathe, to slow the rapid beat of his heart.

Is he honest? It was a difficult question. On the one hand, Alyas had a flexible approach to the truth, but his lies usually had a specific purpose, and as often as not that purpose was defensive. Alyas lied to him all the time, and mostly he let it go, because he knew why. On the other hand, if he said he'd do something, he meant it. Esar considered Della, who was waiting for an answer. "He keeps his promises." The words were hoarse, scraping over his lacerated throat.

She nodded to herself. "Said he'd get me out of here when you go."

Of course he had, and she was making sure he knew in case…

The door creaked. He was too exhausted to even raise his head.

It rattled; someone wrestled with the lock. A sharp voice called, "Esar!"

Frey. Oh, thank Yholis. They had come.

The door swung open. She was here, she was really here. Hantaran soldiers in palace livery pushed past her into the cells. Georgios Beor. Alyas's back-up plan. Gods, he was *crying*.

She saw him. Her face paled. He must look a sight, filthy with dried blood and vomit, his clothes hanging off him in shreds. But she wasn't looking at his clothes; her eyes were on his face.

"Esar?"

"Alyas? Ito took him—"

"We've got him," she said, dropping to her knees by his side. "We've got him. He's all right. Are you? He said…"

He didn't let her finish, just pulled her close, crushing her, hiding his face and the tears of furious relief.

She was still wearing the dress she had worn in the temple, dishevelled and dirty. Either the company had moved faster than he had given them credit for—he had no grip on how much time had passed—or Frey hadn't been back to the inn since they were taken. She was shaking too, tears of her own on his shoulder.

"I'm sorry we took so long. The prince, he needed an excuse to raid this place…"

He stopped listening; it didn't matter. They had come.

Esar leant into her. Relief had drained all the energy from him; his head was aching again. Frey brushed a hand over his temple. He hissed and pulled back.

Della was standing by the bars between their cells, staring at him. *Is he honest?* "She comes too," he told Beor's soldiers. "Check for others. We're not leaving anyone here."

He must sound as bad as he looked. "We know," Frey soothed, her hand hovering by his face, scared to touch him again. "Alyas said. She's coming with us, don't worry."

Frey helped him to his feet as the palace guards opened Della's cell. The girl was out so fast she was a blur, or maybe that was his vision. When Esar looked for her a few minutes later, she was nowhere to be seen. He couldn't blame her.

Beor's guards were crawling all over the mansion. As Esar emerged from the basement, it was to the opulence of any wealthy townhouse, as tasteless and uninteresting as any other, with no sign of its owner's predilections. Mitka kept the bloodstains below stairs.

Alyas was standing near the entrance with Agazi, who was winding a strip of bandage round a long cut on his forearm. He turned his head as Esar stepped into the hall and, for once, his face was stripped bare, dark eyes a mirror of Esar's. He pulled his arm from Agazi's grasp, the edge of the bandage fluttering loose, and in three mostly steady steps was in front of his brother. "I'm sorry. *I'm sorry.*"

Esar didn't know whether to hit him or hug him.

They were escorted to the palace where Georgios Beor, Prince of Hantara, was waiting to receive payment for fulfilling his part of the bargain Alyas had struck with him. Only they couldn't pay him, because the bloody box was still in the temple vaults.

Esar was too exhausted to care. This was Alyas's problem.

Fifty, grey-haired, and impatient, Beor watched them struggle in with a jaundiced eye and not a huge amount of sympathy. He knew as well as anyone that an extended stay with Mitka Ito meant they were unlikely to have what he had been promised. But he'd gotten them out anyway; he wasn't a monster. And he would bargain that act of mercy for future services at an extortionate rate, or Esar had never met him before.

"Thank you," Alyas said. It was unusually heartfelt.

The prince regarded him with irritation. "Well? Do I get anything other than your thanks?"

"I don't have it," Alyas admitted.

Beor's eyes narrowed. "I have been put to some inconvenience to secure your release—on your promise of it being worth my while. So far, that doesn't seem to be the case." There was a threat implicit in his words, though after the day they'd had it didn't have quite the impact Beor might have hoped.

"*I* don't have it," Alyas clarified, massaging his sore wrist. Mitka had made a start on his 'art', but Beor's intervention had arrived before he could do more than that one, precise cut. "That doesn't mean you won't."

Esar shot him a sharp look. "What are you talking about?" The box was in the temple vaults. Alyas had told him so. He had nearly fucking died because it was in the temple vaults.

A guard entered. Beor waved a hand to indicate he could approach, his eyes on Alyas as the guard murmured a message by his ear.

"It seems there's someone here to see you, Captain," the prince said. "Should I allow them in?"

"I think you should."

"What are you up to?" Esar hissed, turning to the door as the guard returned, heavy hand on the shoulder of the scrawny blond girl from the next-door cell. *Della*.

Oh, gods. Anger surged so violently he swayed on his feet. Alyas steadied him, frowning in concern. Esar shook him off.

"Who is this?" Beor demanded. Della was still dressed in the rags she had worn in the cell, her hair matted and filthy, making her Qidan face even paler.

"One of my company," Alyas replied. His eyes were on Della, who nodded.

"You don't look after you company very well," Beor observed. "What's she doing here?"

Alyas turned to Della, who took something from her pocket and tossed it to him.

"Delivering your payment." He shook out the little parcel of rags and held up the Empress Ivane casket. "See?"

Esar stared at it through a red haze, his throat so tight he could barely breathe. He bent over, hands on his knees, dizzy with rage. Frey touched his arm, frightened. "Esar?"

Alyas hadn't left the box at the temple. Fazio must have made two copies. That's why Alyas hadn't killed him. The smith's life in exchange for two bloody boxes. Ito's men had searched him, found one of the fakes, and stopped looking, because no one had known there were two. Alyas must have given the real one to Della while Esar was unconscious. And he hadn't said anything. Worse, he had let Esar believe the real one was still at the temple. He had let a man like Mitka Ito hold a fucking knife to his throat *knowing* what would happen if they didn't believe Esar's desperate denials. He had let Esar *beg* for his life and said *nothing*.

He was so angry he was shaking.

Beor's eyes fastened on the Isyr casket. He snapped his fingers and Alyas threw it to him. The prince caught the glittering little box in his gloved hand and nodded his thanks, his face aglow with satisfaction. "Pleasure doing business with you, Alyas. But maybe don't come back here for a while, hmm?"

They were never coming back here if Esar had his way.

And that was it. It was over. Beor snapped his fingers again and his guards hustled them towards the door. Frey took Della by the arm, leaning close to whisper in her ear as they walked out, and the girl tensed then shook her head. Frey laughed. Nothing made sense.

They emerged into bright sunlight on the steps of Lessing's palace to find Agazi waiting for them with Keie and a handful of men. Esar winced, shading his eyes, his vision still dancing with black spots that had nothing to do with the blow to his head.

Alyas was watching him with cautious concern. Esar glared at him as Frey tugged Della down the steps towards Keie. "Why didn't you tell me about Della?" He did his best to keep his voice level; he wasn't entirely successful.

Alyas, intent gaze on his face, said, "Because when they held the knife to my throat, you would have told them." He wasn't being glib. He was being honest. He had deliberately kept Esar in the dark, because he knew his brother would choose his life over a lump of metal, as any sane person would, and he had made sure that he couldn't. He had, in fact, gambled his life on the guess that Mitka would want to hurt him more than he wanted to kill him. Or maybe he simply didn't care.

And the irony of it was that if Ito had held the knife to Esar's throat, he would have had the box in his hand inside a minute.

"If they didn't believe me, what were you going to do then?" Of all the fucking stupid, pointless risks! Gods, he was furious. He was so furious he didn't know what to do with it. His hands were trembling.

Alyas was looking at him as he had looked at him in the cells, his expression an echo of that same shock. Yet still he had said nothing. He had let Ito take him and said nothing. Though by that point, it had already gone too far.

"I'm sorry," he said.

It wasn't enough. "Never again," Esar snarled. "Do you hear me? Never do that to me again." He drew in a painful breath and said what he never thought he would say. "Never again, or I'm leaving."

※

He meant it. He didn't speak to Alyas again that day. Although mostly that was because he was passed out and oblivious to everything until the following evening. He woke feeling not better but less awful. He was still angry but more capable of controlling it.

Frey approached cautiously. In response to Esar's question, she asked, "Are you still going to kill him?"

"Only if he asks for it."

She considered this. "In that case, he's downstairs. But could you forgive him? He really needs to sleep."

"No," he said. "But I'll talk to him."

He found Alyas in the darkest corner of the common room, in shadows so deep they hid the shadows on his face.

"Have you slept?" he asked. He knew how this went.

Alyas sat up. He shifted over so Esar could sit beside him on the bench. "Yes. Not much." Which could mean anything from a few minutes to a few hours and was exactly the kind of evasive half-truth that hid the things Alyas didn't want anyone to see.

"It's your own fault."

"I know."

The common room was full, mostly with the company. They'd been celebrating since they returned yesterday morning, and Esar envied them their uncomplicated victory. He wished the truth wasn't so tangled and murky and fraught.

That it wasn't so miserably predictable.

Esar was reminded of the last time Alyas had been so adamantly set on something that he wouldn't listen to reason—when he had tried to make peace between Lankara and Flaeres. That had been about freeing Raffa from syndicate influence. What was this if not the same? After all this time and everything Raffa had done, Alyas was still trying to get him out from under the syndicate yoke. Or if not him, Lankara.

And, like everything else about the last few days, that was just too bloody complicated for his aching head to handle.

He caught a flash of pale hair through the crowd. Storn, talking to Della.

"How did you know she'd come back?"

"I didn't. I made her an offer if she brought it back, but it was up to her." In other words, he had given the box to Della just so neither the syndicates nor the temple would have it. As far as Alyas was concerned, that would have been a perfectly acceptable outcome. If not for everything else that Esar refused to think about, he might have agreed.

"And Beor? You promised him the box in exchange for our release. If she hadn't come back, what then?"

Alyas shrugged. "What could he have done? He was hardly going to give us back. And he got to raid a syndicate safehouse, so he couldn't say he got nothing out of it."

"He could have turned us over to the temple."

"No, he couldn't. The temple doesn't know the box has been stolen, so how could Beor know? If he gave us to Ithol, he'd have to explain why, and then the temple inquisitors would be crawling all over him."

Esar shuddered. Prince of Hantara or not, Georgios Beor would be as anxious as the next person to avoid the attentions of Ithol's investigators. Alyas was right, he wouldn't have handed them to the temple.

But that didn't make him right about anything else. "I'm still angry with you."

"I know." Then, in a very different tone, "Would you really leave?"

Esar stared out at the rowdy common room with the ghost of that panic still souring his stomach. He had stayed through worse; he didn't even want to remember how much worse. He had stayed through the silences and the drinking and the grief and the… He had stayed through all of it and now it was behind them. Done. Then he recalled Alyas's unguarded face in the Isyr vault, a look in his eyes that was all too painfully familiar, and wondered whether any of it was done after all.

He wished Cassana were here. Cassana to whom Alyas opened up like he did for no one else—whose heart he had been prepared to break through sheer bloody-mindedness. That wasn't normal. It wasn't right.

None of it was right. None of it was done.

There were bruises on his feet from trying to kick down the door of their cell.

Is he honest? Della had asked, and Esar thought again of all the little lies he allowed Alyas to tell him because *he* wanted to believe everything was fine. Well, that stopped now, because he couldn't do it again. He refused to do it again.

"Yes," he said. "I would."

❧

Later, he went and found Della. She was with Frey and Keie, who had given her clean clothes and were trying to coax a smile onto her severe face.

She sat up as he approached.

"We need to talk."

Della nodded. She knew why he had come.

Frey was watching him, her expression worried. How much had Alyas told her? Judging by her face, the whole ugly thing.

Keie pulled up a stool, but Esar shook his head. What he had to say wouldn't take long. "He told you not to hand it over, didn't he? Whatever they did."

She nodded again. "I'm sorry—"

A raised hand stopped her. "You didn't know us. It's over and done. We're all still here. But if you're going to stay, you need to know how this works. You do what he says, when he says, and you don't hesitate. That's how we stay alive. Except sometimes you don't. That was one of those times. Do you understand?"

Frey said, "Esar."

He stopped her, too. "Do you understand?" he asked again. He had the promise he needed from Alyas. Now Della had to know how things stood. There were already too many in the company whose loyalty to Alyas meant blind obedience and they didn't need another, not until he proved he could keep that promise.

"I understand."

She did, he could see it. And she had already shown she could hold her nerve.

He assembled his face into a smile. "Good. Then welcome to our company, Della."

MIDNIGHT IN FLAERES

ESAR

The messenger from Alyas reached Esar when he was a day out from Sarenza and starting to think about home. The scout offered an apologetic shrug as he dashed that hope. "Says you're to go north to meet him. At Orsena."

"Orsena? What's he doing there?" Orsena was a dirt-poor plains town near the border with Qido. There was nothing there to interest them, just abandoned Isyrium mines, half-starved cattle, and people who hadn't left yet. More importantly, it was four days' ride cross-country when he could be back with the rest of the company in two, enjoying the last few weeks of quiet before the fighting season started and Ellasia's various powers began clamouring for their services.

The scout shrugged again. He had delivered his message and now all he was interested in was food and sleep. "Get some rest," Esar said with a tilt of his head towards where their small party was bedding down for the night. "Are you heading back or heading on?"

"On. Got messages for Viden, too."

"Lucky you," Esar muttered. "Wait—Agazi's with Alyas?"

The messenger tossed an affirmative over his shoulder as he headed to the fire and the smell of food, leaving Esar wondering what could be so pressing that Alyas would take Agazi with him.

He was still wondering about it when Frey appeared as he was heading to his tent. "I hear we're going to Orsena."

"You heard right. Alyas is there."

"Why? It's not like him to leave this close to syndie season."

It was true. The messenger had said Alyas had forty people with him, which meant the bulk of the company was back at their base in the Lathai mountains, but it was rare for both of them to be absent at the same time. Even rarer for both them and Agazi to be away, particularly at this time of year when the syndicates were apt to start testing their resolve, to see if they were still determined to keep the mining companies out of the mountains. And each year, they said yes. Yes, they were. Diago's summons must be urgent or exceptionally well paid to draw Alyas all the way out to the Qidan border.

But Esar didn't want to think about the syndicates now. If Alyas was in Orsena, he would have his reasons and they would find out when they got there.

He caught Frey round the waist, burying his face in her cloud of red hair. "I don't know. And right now, I don't care. Come to bed, woman. I'm tired, and we've got a long ride tomorrow."

※

Orsena, when they reached it, was a ghost town. More so than usual. The Isyrium mines had closed decades ago and the town had been in slow decline ever since, but Esar had been here two years back and there had been a few hundred people still clinging to a living. Now there was no one other than those Alyas had brought with him.

He met their sentries at the edge of town and was directed to what had once been the main inn on the square but was now abandoned like all the rest, even the furniture left behind. The only thing the fleeing townsfolk had taken was Isyrium. There wasn't a trace of it left in the town. All the bulbs were burnt out and the Isyrium fuel stores were empty. If they were here for any length of time, they would have to make warmth and light and everything else the old-fashioned way. At least they would have a roof over their heads, though, and beds. It was still early in the year and the nights were cold on the plains.

He saw the lean, dark-haired figure of his foster brother emerge from the inn and walk towards him. Alyas stopped by Esar's horse, shading his eyes as he looked up. "How did it go? Did you sort it?"

Esar nodded, dismounting. "There won't be any more trouble from that quarter."

"I hope Melar was suitably grateful." Alyas scanned the riders following Esar into camp, counting them in.

Someone called out a lewd remark about the usual nature of Gaemo's gratitude. "That's exactly what got him into this mess in the first place," Esar observed. "If Diago ever found out…"

Alyas shrugged, distracted. "I doubt he'd notice. He's got other things on his mind."

"Does that have anything to do with why you're out here?"

"It does. We're officially chasing monsters for the King of Flaeres."

"Ah, my favourite. What kind of monsters?"

Alyas was frowning. "Not the usual kind. There's something…" His eyes lost focus, and Esar saw his hand was gripping the hilt of the Isyr sword the way it sometimes did when he was lost in thought. Or disturbed by something.

"Is there a usual kind?" Esar asked. The plains of northern Flaeres were a superstitious place. Every time someone went missing or cattle were killed, there were whispers of something unnatural. It didn't matter how many times the culprit was discovered to be a wolf or a jealous neighbour, rumours of monsters were never far away. "Have you been drinking Agazi's moonshine?"

Alyas shuddered. "Never again," he said to the sound of the company's rippling laughter.

Esar grinned. It was good to be back.

※

Whatever had caused the townsfolk to up and leave had been sudden enough that the innkeeper had left not only the furniture but most of his liquor, as the company had discovered. They were too disciplined to get drunk on a contract, even if that contract was chasing monsters that almost certainly didn't exist, but they had nevertheless made a good dent in the inn's supplies. There was drunk and there was *almost* drunk, a subtle difference with which all professional soldiers were intimately acquainted.

As that careful drinking progressed into the night, Esar was prevailed upon to tell the tale of his recent adventure, which he did with plenty of help from those who had been with him. Except Frey, who was huddled with Della in the corner of the common room. They had their heads together and were deep in conversation.

Someone called out a question and Esar tore his attention from the women to the company's expectant faces. "Of course not," he replied. "Would we do something like that?" And the room erupted into laughter.

When he got to the part where he described how they had surprised the man who had been trying to blackmail his way out of *Gaemo's* blackmail, several of the company were laughing so hard they had tears streaming down their faces.

Then Agazi got out his flask of his evil, homemade Steppes liquor and passed it around. "Gods no," Alyas said when it reached him. He climbed to his feet. "I'm going to sleep. Don't expect any sympathy from me when you can't see in the morning."

Most of the rest refused as well. They wouldn't get any sympathy, they knew that from past experience, and no one had any desire to go out on patrol with the kind of hangover drinking Agazi's infamous moonshine would inevitably incur. That stuff was just wrong. But it was still a good few hours before the gathering broke up, and when Esar finally made it to a bed, Frey was already there.

She woke up when he climbed in, snuggling up against his warmth, and said drowsily, "He's not sleeping again, Della said."

Esar rolled over. "What did she say?"

"I already told you."

"What else?"

Frey yawned. "Ask her yourself. Or, better yet, ask him. We're not your spies."

"You are, though," he growled, tickling her.

She squealed and slapped his hand away. "Get off, Esar. I want to sleep."

He relented, wrapping an arm over her as she shifted to get comfortable. Then he lay with his eyes open for much longer than he was happy about. Alyas not sleeping usually presaged the taking on of some reckless contract or precipitous action of one kind or another—he was never at his most patient when he was tired, and the whole company knew it—and Esar began to have serious misgivings about this monster hunt.

Esar found Alyas in the morning. He was on the top floor of the abandoned inn, looking out of the window towards Qido.

"What's really going on?" Esar asked him. It was unlike Diago to pay the company's not inconsiderable fee to chase rumours, and unlike Alyas to consent. They'd had a profitable and mutually advantageous relationship with the King of Flaeres for many years, but Alyas had refused contracts from him before now.

Alyas turned from the window. His face was shadowed by the morning light at his back. Esar saw his hand was wrapped around the sword's hilt. "I don't know."

"What did Diago say? Where is everyone?"

"Everyone fled weeks ago. There are rumours out of Qido, and refugees. Bad enough, it seems, for the last of the people here to pack up and leave."

"These monsters?"

Alyas nodded. "They're not monsters, though. Not according to the rumours. They're as human as you and me, or they were. But they're changed."

Esar was liking this less and less. "Changed how?"

"Well, that's the question. Reports vary. We've been here a week and we've seen nothing. But…"

"But?"

Alyas shrugged, releasing the Isyr hilt. "I can feel something, Esar. There's something not right here. There's something not right *out there*."

He stepped back from the window. It occurred to Esar, watching him, that at no time since he'd arrived had he seen Alyas unarmed, and that was no longer as usual as it had been. There had been a time when you could only take the Isyr blades off him when he was asleep or otherwise out of his senses—or if you were Ailuin, and you had once extracted a promise from Alyas in exchange for forgoing your people's vengeance—but he had been wearing them less and less in recent years. If he wouldn't let them go now, something really was bothering him. As Alyas turned his head into the light Esar saw how tired he looked, shadows under his eyes so deep they looked like they had been carved there.

"Dreams again?" Esar asked. He called them dreams. It sounded better than nightmares and Alyas would be more inclined to admit to them. They had a deal since Lessing, but it had limits.

"Not unless I'm dreaming when I'm wide awake."

"You should try sleeping then."

Alyas shot him a quick, irritated look. "I knew I should have sent Della with you."

"Don't blame Della." It was all over his face. The quiet winter months were always difficult. Not enough to do, too much time to think. Which was why Esar had been surprised when Alyas had sent him to deal with Gaemo's little problem rather than going himself. Was this why? "What is it?"

"I don't know," Alyas snapped. "We should go."

"Go where?" Where did you start looking for monsters?

When he didn't get a reply, he sighed and followed his brother down the stairs to where the company was assembling in the common room, only slightly bleary-eyed. They responded with resignation to Alyas's sharp commands, abandoning their half-eaten breakfast with the air of men who had been here before, and grumbled their way to the stables and their horses.

Della threw Esar a look that said *see?* He made a face back at her. What did she expect him to do about it? Knock him out?

They spent the day hugging the Qidan border, looking for signs of something unnatural. Esar wasn't sure what that meant, but he was sure he didn't see anything that qualified. Alyas had split them into groups of ten, much larger than was necessary or efficient for this type of work. It was yet another sign he was nervous about what they might find, but other than a swathe of blackened ground from an early-season fire that they skirted from a distance, Esar couldn't see anything to justify that fear.

They met up again by the lonely, ruined barn that marked the northern edge of Orsena. Alyas was already there. He had stripped off his armour, draping it on a cluster of rocks that lined the road out of town, and he was watching the riders straggle in. Esar knew he was counting them. He always counted them, he just wasn't usually so obvious about it.

Esar dismounted and let Aubron take his horse back for him. Agazi was also there with a handful of others. The rest were already heading to the inn, dusty and tired and hungry.

"Anything?" he asked.

Agazi shook his head. "Nothing."

Alyas, hand on his hilt, said, "Nothing *yet*."

Agazi met Esar's eyes with resignation. He had been here a week and no doubt had spent most of that time in similarly fruitless searching. Still, Alyas's instincts were rarely wrong, sleep-deprived or not. Then he said, "Tomorrow we head into Qido." And Esar had to wonder whether the lack of sleep was getting to him after all.

This section of the border was hardly well-guarded—they could probably ride for a day or more before they met any patrols—but crossing into Qido uninvited rarely went well. It wasn't that they were unwelcome. Alyas's father, the old duke of Agrathon, had once performed a service for the emperor of Qido that had not been forgotten. That same emperor had made a point of extending his friendship to Alyas when his own king had stripped him of his names and title and exiled him from Lankara, although the precise nature of that friendship was something Esar didn't particularly want to put to the test, especially by bringing an armed company into Qidan territory. The emperor had views about such things. And they were here on behalf of Diago of Flaeres, and *he* would not be happy about Alyas provoking a diplomatic incident with his much larger and stronger neighbour.

"Is that wise?" he ventured.

"Wise? No," Alyas replied. "Necessary? Yes. Did you hear about Ado?"

"What about Ado?" Nothing ever happened in Ado. It was poorer even than the Flaeresian plains where they were currently wasting their time. The Qidans had plundered its natural wealth in Isyrium decades ago and left it and its people to rot as soon as the precious mineral had run out.

Alyas flexed fingers that had been gripping the Isyr hilt. "The other rumour," he said, "is that Qido has closed its border with Ado. No one in or out."

That was odd but it hardly justified an incursion into Qido from Flaeres. An unpaid, unauthorised incursion into Qido. "Has there been trouble?" He could imagine the Adoese were fed up with their treatment by the emperor and why else would Qido close the border?

"If there has, it's not our business," Agazi observed.

It was what Esar was thinking, but he was surprised to hear Agazi say it. If Agazi was openly questioning Alyas, it was not a good sign.

"Trouble *is* our business," Alyas retorted. "No one pays us to ride around doing nothing."

Except now, but Esar decided not to point that out. "And you're thinking there could be work in Qido? Or Ado?" Because the emperor had more than enough of his own men and Alyas knew it. And he couldn't believe Alyas would even contemplate going to Ado. The last thing they needed was to earn the displeasure of the most powerful ruler in Ellasia by taking the side of his enemies. They had always been careful about that.

Alyas frowned at him. "Of course not, but we need to know where trouble is coming from, and something *is* coming. So, tomorrow we go into Qido."

Esar exchanged a look with Agazi, who shrugged. The last group of riders came into view and Alyas went to meet them. Agazi watched him go, then said, "What's going on, Esar? I've never seen him so on edge. There's nothing out here. We've been all over this place for days."

"I have no idea," Esar replied, his eyes on Alyas.

"And now we're going into Qido? That won't go down well."

"Then don't tell anyone. We've done it before." Not while in the pay of a rival, however, no matter how insignificant Flaeres was when set against the might of the Qidan Empire.

"Della's right," Agazi muttered. "You should knock him out and then we can all go home."

Esar snorted, because Alyas with a raging headache would be so much more reasonable. "If there really is nothing here, he'll come around eventually. We'll be here a few more days and—"

Alyas had almost reached the first horseman when he stopped, turning. *Something* exploded from the rocks along the edge of the road where he stood. It happened so fast he didn't have time to draw a weapon, he just went down, a clawing, seething mass on top of him.

Esar was already running, Agazi half a pace behind. The riders were faster, sweeping alongside and hacking with swords and spears. Whatever the fuck it was, it reared up with a howl of rage, a spear embedded in its back, and Esar almost stopped in his tracks. It was *human*. Or it had been. The creature abandoned Alyas, leaping towards the horsemen as more of the monstrosities charged up the slope behind the rocks and onto the road. The horses shied, trying to bolt, their eyes rolling in terror.

Agazi dodged flailing hooves to skid to a halt beside Esar. "What the fuck are they?"

Alyas was still down. Esar hooked an arm under his shoulder and dragged him upright. He didn't stay there. Esar felt the weight hit his arm as Alyas's legs buckled, then Agazi was on his other side and together they were dragging him back. And Esar couldn't take his eyes off the chaotic melee around them to check if he was still alive.

The shouts had drawn the rest of the company. He could hear feet and hooves pounding behind them as they stumbled desperately back. The riders who had come to Alyas's aid were in danger of being overwhelmed, their mounts barely under control as the *things* kept coming.

Others reached them, forming a defensive screen between the creatures and Alyas. Esar caught Della's panicked look and turned his head. There was blood everywhere. Alyas hadn't been wearing his armour. There had been nothing between him and the creature's assault and his shirt was torn and soaked in blood.

"Go, go!" Aubron yelled and Esar realised he had frozen in place.

"Esar!" Agazi pointed at the abandoned building with his free hand and Esar unfroze. If they could reach it, it would give them some shelter. He adjusted his grip on Alyas and felt Agazi do the same, then they were running across the hard ground, dragging him between them. He was not taking any of his own weight.

The building was already occupied. Willing hands reached out to take Alyas from them and carry him inside and Esar followed to find Frey already crouched by his side, cutting off the ruined shirt.

"Fuck, fuck, fuck," she muttered as he dropped to his knees beside her. Blood was welling from a ragged wound across Alyas's left shoulder that had never been caused by a weapon. Esar felt sick as he realised what had made it.

"Clean that," he snapped, putting a hand against his brother's face and lacing his fingers through his hair. "Alyas!"

Nothing. He felt wetness against his fingers and withdrew his hand. There was blood on it.

"Get out of the way, Esar," Frey growled at him. Then she saw the blood. "Fuck," she said again and curled her own hand round Alyas's head, feeling for the damage.

There was a scream and a crash from outside. Esar turned towards it and someone took his place by Alyas's side. It was Della.

"Esar!" There was panic in Agazi's voice.

"Go, we've got him," Frey urged. There was panic in her voice too, but it was controlled. There was nothing he could do here. When Agazi called again, he rose from his knees and went to join him at the ruined doorway.

Crossbows were firing through what was left of the windows as fast as they could be loaded and the ground in front of the old house was littered with bodies. He recognised two of their own amid the unnatural corpses of whatever was attacking them. Their horses were dead too, pulled down by the weight of the frenzied attack, and now… He looked away, horror and disgust choking him.

As human as you and me, Alyas had said. *Changed.*

The things prowling the ground outside were certainly fucking changed. They were *blue* for a start, a blue so dark it was almost black, and it was not just their skin that had altered. They might once have been human, the ragged remains of clothing hanging from gaunt frames, but there was nothing human about them now that Esar could see. Their faces were contorted with hunger and fury and not one of them was upright. They were dropped on all fours, the blue-black hue rippling up muscles that were no longer quite right.

It was then that he realised that they weren't all human. He could see wolves among them, and prairie cats and other predators, but instead of turning on each other as they would in the wild, they were all utterly focused on one thing: the company sheltering in the building.

"I think we've found Diago's monsters," Agazi said. "Ithol's bollocks, look at that." He pointed to the ground where the attack had come from—the blackened, discoloured ground.

Esar stared at it in horror. "What the fuck is happening?" It was like a nightmare, the kind of nightmare that came after smoking one of Ailuin's pipes.

He recalled the scorched patch of grassland they had seen on their patrol—what he had thought was a scorched patch of grassland. Not a fire after all. It had been right there and he'd missed it, because he'd thought Alyas was worried about nothing.

Alyas with an ugly tear in his shoulder.

If just the touch of these things could do *that* to the earth, what would their teeth and claws do?

The crossbows stopped firing. The creatures had backed away, onto the road and out of reliable range, but the intensity of their attention had not wavered. In the distance, the scattered riders were regrouping. They did not approach. If they charged now, they risked driving the monsters straight at the crumbling building where the rest of the company was sheltering, but they were too far away to communicate with, and who was to say these creatures wouldn't understand shouted commands? They *were* human, even if they no longer looked or acted like it.

"Fuck," he swore. "This is bad."

It was very bad. The building was alone on the edge of town and it was a rickety refuge, missing its roof and most of its back and side walls. Surrounded and cut off in here, they would be dead the moment the crossbows ran out of bolts, and that wouldn't take long. No one had been expecting an attack.

Esar looked at Agazi and saw the same thought on his face. "We can't stay here." They needed somewhere that was easier to defend, somewhere like the inn, which also had food and weapons, a solid building where they could hole up until the creatures lost interest and went after easier prey. But the inn might as well have been in Lankara for all their chance of reaching it.

He risked a glance through the doorway, trying to measure the distance to the first of the houses. Perhaps fifty yards. They might make it. They would have to make it, because they couldn't stay where they were. Already the creatures were prowling closer, edging forward to either side. The crossbows took potshots at them, discouraging the advance. They couldn't afford to allow these things to get behind them—there was almost no cover at the rear of the building. They had to move *now*.

There was a snarl and a crossbow on his right released with a thud. A wolf dropped, a bolt in its chest. There was a moment of stillness, then they were coming, a wave of blue that exploded into motion and crashed towards them.

"Shit." Esar grabbed the spear that was thrust into his hand and braced it against the broken flagstones. The riders surged forward with a cry, hitting the back of the attack as its head smashed into the building and its defenders.

The crossbows spoke, a short, hard volley that sent a shudder through the front of the wave but didn't stop it, and then it was just terror and fury and the desperate thrust of blades.

Through the chaos, he saw the riders break off and pull back, losing sight of them as a huge man hurled himself onto the point of the spear. Esar shoved back with all his strength and the shaft was ripped from his hands as his attacker toppled over.

There was a scream as the man on his left was dragged through the ruined window. Esar lurched forward, snatching at his legs, but he was too late and only narrowly avoided the same fate as another of the creatures reached for him. He thrust forward with his dagger, taking it in the face, and it was replaced by another, and another.

He caught of flash of midnight blue and saw the creatures loping around the building. He screamed a warning. Alyas and Frey were back there!

Agazi was shouting too, and anyone who could was running to the back.

Something clamped onto his arm with bruising pressure. Teeth. He smashed a fist into the side of its head, shaking it loose, and thanked Yholis it had been human, not wolf, or those teeth would have gone straight through the thick leather of his sleeve.

More crossbows fired. One volley, then a second. Not from inside the building. The riders regrouped and charged again. The attack wavered. Another volley smashed into the creatures from the side as they tried to flank the defenders, and then they were backing off, snarling and spitting as they went.

"Esar!"

Dazed, he saw Aubron and a line of men across the road into town, crossbows levelled. He hadn't realised they were still out there.

"Get back!" he called. They were completely exposed. If these things turned on them, they would be overwhelmed.

But the creatures paid them no attention. It was like they didn't exist.

The riders were picking their way through the grasses on the far side of the road to join Aubron, equally ignored, despite the fact it was the crossbows and horsemen between them that had done the most damage. The focus of the assault was on the building.

"Esar!" Aubron called again, gesturing behind him. "Go! We'll cover you."

"Take Alyas," Agazi said, getting to his feet. "We'll follow. Go *now*."

There was no time to think about it. He could still feel the terror of those final few seconds. If Aubron hadn't been there, they would all be dead. "Frey!" he called as he stood. "We're moving. Get him up!"

Frey's face appeared. There was blood on her cheek. "What the fuck, Esar?"

"No choice. Can he walk?" It would be a lot harder if they had to carry him.

"This is a bad idea," Frey warned as he pushed past her and dropped down beside Alyas. "I've only just got the bleeding stopped."

"Staying here would be worse." Esar tapped Alyas's face, gently at first, then harder, and was rewarded by a flicker of brown eyes.

"There you are," Esar said. He grabbed Alyas under the arms and hauled him up. "Time to go."

Alyas's full weight hung from his shoulder for a few seconds, then he got his legs under him and the pressure eased.

"We're under attack," Esar told him. He had no idea what Alyas remembered and stuck to the pertinent details. "You're hurt. We need to move fast. Can you do that?"

There was a shifting of weight in his arms. "I'm fine."

"No, you're not." But he wasn't going to waste the confidence, already moving them both to the back of the building. "We're heading into the town," he told Frey. "Stay close to me."

She nodded, picking up her discarded spear as Agazi appeared. "We need to hurry."

Esar nodded, tightening his hold on Alyas, who felt worryingly unsteady. He didn't know if it was blood loss or the blow to his head. Probably both. Neither would be improved by what he was about to do. "Ready?"

Someone got a shoulder under Alyas's other arm and Esar looked over and saw Della. Her face was tight. If the plainspeople of Flaeres were superstitious, they had nothing on Qidans. She was badly shaken, but she had it together. It was her spear Esar had lost in the fight.

"Go," hissed Agazi, his attention on the prowling mass of blue at their front. Esar didn't need telling twice. With Frey a pace in front, he and Della got Alyas moving. He didn't seem to be entirely with them, his head lolling on Esar's shoulder, but his legs were working and that would have to do.

They crossed the rubble of the back door, others following on their heels, forming a protective ring around them. A growl rose from behind. The riders paced their horses forward.

Alyas raised his head. "Esar…"

Esar dragged him on, Della helping, but they hadn't gone more than a few steps before Alyas jerked away, almost falling. "They're coming."

Esar steadied him. "What?"

"They're coming. Now!"

A panicked shout confirmed it. Esar spun around to see the *things* surge around the building and hurtle towards them.

With one hand on Alyas's arm, Esar spun him around and shoved him back towards the shelter they had just left. "Run!"

Della and Frey skidded after them. As they tumbled behind the low wall, Aubron's men fired as fast as they could into the oncoming wave that *did not even look at them*.

Esar let someone take Alyas from him and turned to face the attack.

The crossbows had thinned it, leaving behind a swathe of dead and dying. The bolts stopped and the riders swept down, cutting between the creatures and the back of the building as the crossbows inside took up the attack in their wake. He could hear Agazi yelling and staggered from one wall to the next as he pushed his way through the tangle of legs to the front of the barn where yet more creatures were hurling themselves against the too-few defenders.

The riders thundered round the building, wheeling around to charge again. There were only seven now. One more had gone down. He couldn't see from this distance who it was, but he felt sick with rage.

The horsemen hit; the attack scattered. Esar slumped against the doorframe and saw a friend on the floor by his feet with his throat ripped out.

He closed his eyes, trying to breathe, and heard Frey yell, "Esar!"

New fear seized him. He pushed his way back to where Frey was crouched beside Alyas, one hand keeping him steady against the wall that was propping him up. She looked up as he knelt beside her.

Alyas, his eyes closed, said, "Fire."

A shadow fell over them. Agazi. "What did he say?"

"Fire," Alyas said again, opening his eyes. "Burn it down."

Esar exchanged a look with Agazi, who was already emptying the pouches at his waist. He withdrew two Isyrium bulbs. A flask of fuel would have been better, but smashed bulbs would do in a pinch. And this was a fucking pinch.

"Flasks at the inn," Alyas said. His eyes were slits of pain but he was evidently alert, for which Esar gave heartfelt thanks to Yholis.

"The inn is on the other side of town," Esar pointed out grimly. They would never make it.

Agazi disappeared. The roar of noise died down. A clatter of hooves sounded outside.

"Esar?"

He left Alyas and moved to the window. Storn reined in. A Qidan like Della, his pale hair was damp with sweat and streaked in mud from the road. "We'll take Alyas, get him away from here. But you need to hurry."

Esar hesitated. That last attack had demonstrated how badly they needed better shelter. Alyas would slow them down; he could barely walk. So far, the creatures' attention was concentrated on the building, ignoring those outside, but he didn't understand why. Instinctive caution made him reluctant to risk anyone's life on something he couldn't explain. If he sent Alyas out there and the creatures' focus changed, the riders were too few and too exposed to protect him.

Agazi reappeared. His arms were full of Isyrium bulbs scrounged from pockets and belt pouches, enough to burn this place down and have some to spare. Esar had never been so grateful to the Lathai and their generosity with Isyrium. It meant the company could afford to carry spare bulbs with them wherever they went.

Storn saw them and understanding flickered across his face. "Give him to us," he urged. They would have their hands full setting the fire and covering their retreat without carrying Alyas.

Esar nodded. They had enough Isyrium to guarantee a big blaze. It changed things. There wasn't a living thing that didn't fear fire. "Get him back to the inn," he said. "We'll join you there."

"Wait," Agazi called, passing a handful of bulbs through the window to Storn. He caught up with Esar. "Are you sure?"

"No." But all his options were bad. Esar reached Alyas, whose face was so pale it was almost white. There was blood on the bandages Frey had tied round his shoulder and rusty trails marking the outline of his ribs. "We need to get you out of here."

Alyas clasped his wrist, gripping tight. "No. You go."

Esar pried his fingers loose. "I'll pretend I didn't hear that."

Alyas wouldn't budge. "Focused on me." His words were slurring, but his meaning was clear.

Esar's eyes narrowed. Could that be it? They were predators and Alyas was covered in blood. There was no denying that *something* was holding the creatures' attention, and as soon as they had tried to move him, those things had attacked. But that didn't explain how Alyas had known they were coming, or how he had somehow known that Diago's monsters were more than rumours.

I can feel something, Esar.

"No," he said, fear making him snap. "No way." But he couldn't send him away with the riders either.

"Flasks at the inn," Alyas insisted.

And then Esar understood. Not a command to leave him behind, but to fetch the means to fight back. He felt a knot in his chest loosen as he said, "We don't need to. We have enough here."

"What are you waiting for then?"

It was a good point.

※

In the end, Esar did send Storn for Isyrium flasks—because 'just in case' seemed like a sensible precaution—but it was a gamble. As he watched the handful of riders leave unmolested, it looked like Alyas was right, but it left them more vulnerable for the time it would take the horsemen to return. While the creatures had learned to keep a wary distance from Aubron's men on the road, their attention remained on the ruined barn. With the departure of the riders, they were already edging closer.

Esar crouched by Agazi near the door, the sharp mineral tang of Isyrium making his eyes water. Crushed bulbs were strewn across the inside of the front wall. There were more at the back. When they moved, Aubron would crush the bulbs Storn had given him across the road, creating a line of fire that would give them time to retreat to the next building, and the one after that, until they made it to the inn. If need be, he would burn the whole fucking town. It was dead anyway. But their horses were at the inn. If they were getting out of this, it wasn't going to be on foot.

"They're back," Della called.

A moment later, he heard the pound of hooves as the riders swept into view. Several of them were carrying lit torches. Storn was taking no chances.

There was a hissing recoil from the creatures when they saw the flames, then they stalked forward, as if the fire was a signal to attack.

"We're going," Esar snapped, collecting his sword from the ground and waving at Storn.

Agazi repeated the order at a shout and the crossbows disappeared from the windows as the company pulled back to where the rest were waiting, ready to move.

Esar took Alyas from Della and Frey. He had his eyes open and looked steadier, but the bandages were redder than they had been and they badly needed to get him somewhere he could stay still.

But first they had to run.

The thud of crossbows from the road underlined the urgency. "Go, go, go!" Esar called, and they tumbled out of the building, Frey beside him. Behind them, one of the riders threw a lit torch through the front window just ahead of the blue wave.

Their shelter went up like a bonfire, the explosion of flame a wall of heat against their backs. Seconds later, the Isyrium ignited on the road, adding its fury to the blaze, and suddenly the air was full of sparks and smoke and screams of fury.

The fire bought them precious seconds, then the horsemen galloped past, each with one of Aubron's men behind their saddles. The horses stopped and wheeled round ahead of them, the crossbows came up, and Storn yelled, "Down!"

They dropped. The crossbows fired, thudding into the creatures that had skirted round the fire on the far side of the building.

An Isyrium flask arced overhead, then another. They scrambled to their feet. Alyas didn't. Esar hauled him up, ignoring the gasp of pain and the blood coating his fingers. They didn't have time for him to be gentle. "Don't fucking collapse on me," he snarled. "Move!"

Alyas moved, responding to the urgency in Esar's voice as the flasks ignited with a roar of blue flame.

They ran.

Esar looked back. He could see nothing except the fury of the fire, and now they faced a different kind of danger. Northern Flaeres was prairie country, and late summer and autumn often saw wildfires sweep across the grasslands. It was not yet spring, but if the fire reached the expanse of grass that bordered the town, if it took hold, the creatures wouldn't be the only things burned out. The wind was on their side for now, keeping the fire contained, but that could change at any time. Esar abandoned his plan to barricade the company behind the shelter of the inn until the attack died away. They needed to get out of here.

The Isyrium started to burn itself out. Behind the fading intensity of flame, he saw dark shapes massing.

Storn had seen them too. He kicked his horse alongside Esar, reaching down, and together they got Alyas up behind him.

"They'll follow him," he warned the Qidan.

But they were more than halfway to the inn now, close enough to risk sending Alyas ahead. Someone shouted a warning and more Isyrium flasks went flying, smashing into the dirt of Orsena's main street, and the flames roared up again. Something screamed, the sound transforming into an agonised wail.

Storn nodded and put heels to his horse, sending it leaping forward.

Aubron dropped back beside Esar, handing him a crossbow. He spanned it as they slowed to a walk, turning to face the fire. The last flasks had landed in the middle of a pack that had made it through the dying edges of the flames and grotesque shapes writhed in the blaze.

They backed up, the horses keeping pace with them, eyes scanning the street. Nothing moved beyond the heat shimmer of the retreating fire. It left behind blackened corpses and scorched ground.

"Are they gone?" Aubron asked.

Esar shook his head. He looked to the side, checking on Frey, assessing their surroundings. The houses were closer together now, too close to see what was happening behind them. Too close to set ablaze unless they wanted the whole town to burn. It would come to that, but they had to get out first.

They reached the inn. Storn was waiting, still mounted with Alyas behind him. Esar moved to his side, looking up into his brother's pale face as he called, "Get the horses."

It was an unnecessary order. While Agazi and Aubron organised a defensive line across the entrance to the square, the rest raced to the stables or disappeared into the inn, emerging with flasks and weapons. Esar fretted. The creatures were out there still, he was sure of it, hidden behind the houses. If they left, they would be pursued, but stay and they would be trapped, and they couldn't defend the inn *and* the stables. Which meant losing the horses. Which meant dying.

"Can you ride?" he asked Alyas. No horse could be asked to bear two adult riders for long, and when they went, they would go hard.

He saw Alyas think about it. Lives depended on an honest answer. "Not for long," he said at last.

Esar nodded. That was his assessment. "Ride with Della. Take my horse." Della was the lightest of them, his horse one of the strongest.

"Esar."

He recognised that tone. "What?"

"They'll come after us."

"I know."

"We can't let them."

Esar knew he wasn't going to like what was coming. "What do you want to do?"

"This is a terrible idea," Agazi muttered, his eyes on Alyas.

Esar agreed. "Do you have a better one?"

"What if he falls off?"

Esar didn't want to think about that. And Alyas had promised he wouldn't, that 'not for long' was long enough for this. "When have you seen him fall off a horse?"

"Come on, Esar, look at him," Agazi said, and Esar wanted to snap at him to stop saying what he was thinking.

Frey had strapped Alyas's left arm across his chest and someone had thought to fetch spare leathers from the inn, so the worst of the blood was hidden. He looked steady enough in the saddle, but he had done an awful lot of bleeding and Esar would never have agreed to this plan if they had another option. But they didn't, so here they were.

Storn pulled up beside him. Both he and his mount looked exhausted. They had been riding all day before this disaster even started. It was a reminder that they could not risk pursuit. All the horses were tired.

"Ready?" Esar asked.

"Ready," Storn agreed. He too glanced at Alyas and opened his mouth to ask whether this was a good idea.

"Don't," Esar snarled. "It's not. But we're doing it, so don't let him get killed."

A shout echoed across the square and Esar turned his head to see dark shapes appearing between the buildings at the end of the broad avenue. They were running out of time.

He kicked his horse to where Alyas waited. His right hand was twisted securely in the reins and his bright Isyr blades were at his hips. Esar had tried to take them—he couldn't use them with one arm out of action—but Alyas had not taken that well and they didn't have time to waste arguing about it, so he let it go.

"They're coming. Are you sure?"

Alyas gave him a lopsided smile. "Have you ever seen me fall off a horse?"

"A hundred times. Don't make today a hundred and one. *Promise me.*"

Alyas's head turned to the side. "Go," he said, and Esar heard Agazi yelling at him.

"Promise me!" he called after Alyas, who was already riding into the middle of the avenue and didn't answer.

Esar rode back to join Agazi and Frey, who was watching him with a knowing expression. He resisted the urge to look behind him as he followed them across Orsena's central square. It was not like the beautiful squares in Sarenza, paved in marble and surrounded by the palazzos of the city's wealthy citizens. And a good thing, too. You couldn't burn marble. Orsena's square was hard-packed mud lined with a jumble of wooden buildings. Once it had been an impressive sight for a border town, the colourful peeling paint evidence of former prosperity, back before the Isyrium had run out and the upkeep of the larger buildings had become too much for the town to bear. Now it was as sad and empty as the rest of the place.

On either side, Esar could see riders bunched at the entrances to the side streets, spears in hand. The only one left clear was the main street where Alyas waited, opposite where Esar and Agazi turned their horses to wait.

It wasn't a long wait. They came, out of every street and every alley, from behind every building, midnight blue shadows padding silently towards Alyas as though drawn by some invisible force, leaving behind them a trail of dark footsteps. And it was the eeriest, most terrifying thing Esar had ever seen.

"Yholis have mercy," Agazi muttered. "What the fuck are these things? Where did they come from?"

And what did they want with Alyas? Why him? It surely couldn't just be the blood.

Alyas sat there and let them come. They moved cautiously at first, wary of the company's crossbows and their fire, then more confidently, emboldened by his isolation and stillness, the human intelligence that should have warned them as absent as their lost humanity.

Storn shifted in the saddle, hands tight on his reins. "If he doesn't move soon…"

"He will," Esar said, scowling at Alyas's back as though he could make him move with the force of his glare.

He did move, but he left it to the very last moment, waiting until they had almost reached him, his horse stamping nervously under him. In the end, Esar wasn't sure if the horse bolted or Alyas finally gave it its head, but suddenly they exploded into motion, riding hard for the square.

They streamed after him, those midnight blue monstrosities. The wolves and other predators outstripped the once-human monsters, closing on the fleeing horse. Alyas, by luck or skill, had timed his move just right. They thundered through the square just ahead of the pack, and as it streamed into that enclosed space after him, the trap closed.

The creatures recoiled as the smell of Isyrium clogged the air, scattering from the broken flasks that smashed around their legs, but the weight of numbers coming behind prevented a retreat, as did the lowered spears bristling from the alleyways. As Alyas reached the far side of the square, the fire followed, exploding upwards with a roar that took sight and hearing.

Esar threw up his arm as heat scorched across his skin. "Back, back," he yelled, hoping the others were doing the same.

The fire reached the houses and the Isyrium-laced buildings went up like torches until the entire square was a fury of white-blue flame that nothing could survive. Fire followed them, nipping at their heels as they fled, hungry and out of control, leaping from one building to the next, devouring what was left of Orsena and the nightmare creatures it contained.

They didn't stop until they were clear of the last buildings. Riders were streaming out of Orsena from all directions, tossing the last of the flasks behind them as they went, until fire ringed the entire southern edge of the town. Nothing followed them, though they sat there and waited, watching the fury of the fire turn Orsena to ash, Esar praying silently that the wind did not pick up, that they had killed them all, that there were no more out there. He was particularly fervent about that final point as Frey pressed close to his side and slipped her hand into his.

They waited until the sun started to dip and they had to move or camp closer to the ruins of Orsena than would have been comfortable.

He let go of his grip on Frey's hand, shaking the company out of their silent vigil and turning to leave.

Agazi said urgently, "Esar."

He looked around just as *not for long* became *no longer* and Alyas slipped sideways. Agazi caught him before he hit the ground.

Esar swore. One hundred and one.

※

No one slept well that night. If not for bone-deep exhaustion, Esar was sure he would not have slept at all. Even Frey didn't fall asleep at once. He could feel her tension as she lay beside him, and she didn't object when he crushed her against his side. He could have lost her today, too.

He must have dropped off at some point because all too soon someone was shaking his shoulder and telling him to get up. It was only just getting light. He wanted to cover as much ground as possible today. They could rest when they reached Sarenza.

He found Alyas awake and propped up against someone's saddle. It had been too dark to do much for him last night other than replace the blood-soaked bandage, and Esar was pleased to see that the new one was reassuringly not red. He was otherwise as filthy and dishevelled as the rest of them. The blades were lying close by his side.

Esar stood looking down at his brother, reliving the panic he'd felt when he'd seen him go down, letting cautious relief take its place.

Alyas shifted, tilting his head back. His eyes stayed half-closed, sure sign of a headache. "Don't glare at me, Esar. It hurts. What happened?"

"Before or after you fell off your horse?"

"All of it. Yholis, will you sit? I can't see you up there."

Esar took pity on him, crouching down and surveying the visible damage. "You're a mess. What do you remember?"

"Not falling off my horse, obviously."

Esar snorted. "You never remember that." He filled in the events of that desperate fight, skirting over some of the details.

Alyas heard what he didn't say. "How many did we lose?"

Esar looked away. "Five." He named them.

Alyas was silent for a long time. Then he said, "Anyone else hurt?"

"Just you." It was a minor miracle they didn't have more wounded. "They went for you. Only you. Why?" And how had he known they were out there?

Silence again. It lasted so long that Esar nudged him with his foot.

"I don't know," Alyas said and Esar couldn't tell if it was a lie, part truth, or evasion. He had known *something*.

"What do you *think*?" Esar pressed. He was not letting this go—they had a fucking deal—and the sight of those creatures appearing from everywhere to go after Alyas would give him nightmares for some time to come. It already had. If there were more of them out there—and much as he hated it, that was more likely than not—they needed to understand what had made him a target. It could not just be him. That made no sense.

"I *think* I don't know," Alyas snapped. "It was a feeling. I can't explain it. We need to go to Sarenza, report to Diago."

Esar resisted the urge to snap back, to insist he try to explain. There wasn't time to waste arguing with him now and he really was a mess. Instead, he stood, holding out his hand and pulling Alyas carefully to his feet. He only wobbled a bit. "It's a long ride. Try not to fall off again."

They rode into Sarenza six days later, tired and irritable, necks aching from looking over their shoulders, shadows under their eyes from sleep interrupted by nightmares.

Alyas tasked Agazi with finding quarters while he and Esar went to the palace. It had taken longer than Esar liked to get here. Alyas still couldn't ride for long stretches, the constant exertion aggravating the wound in his shoulder and leaving him exhausted. He looked thin and ragged, but the rest of them weren't much better after six days in the saddle with little sleep, which made it less noticeable.

He should have noticed.

The officer on duty at the palace gates took one look at them and sent a man running to announce their arrival, a flurry of activity that Alyas watched in pensive silence. They were well known here; their presence didn't usually provoke frantic messages. Esar did not consider it a good sign.

Melar Gaemo appeared to greet them, Flaeres's current ambassador to Lankara and long-time favourite of King Diago, lately absent from his post because of a minor blackmail problem Esar had resolved for him.

"I thought you'd be back in Lankara by now," Alyas said as Gaemo emerged from the palace entrance and descended its broad steps.

"I'm heading back there tomorrow," Gaemo replied. He surveyed Alyas. "What happened to you?"

"We found Diago's monsters."

Gaemo's eyes narrowed. He nodded at the arm still in its sling.

"Did they do that?"

Alyas nodded and Esar *did not like* the expression that crossed Gaemo's face.

"We lost five," Alyas told him.

"Dead?"

"Yes, they're dead," Esar growled. "We didn't mislay them."

Alyas said, frowning, "What's going on, Melar?"

"You probably know more than us," Gaemo replied with a worried glance at Alyas. "Come. Diago wants to see you."

The king wanted to see them so much that he had dismissed his usual gaggle of attendants and was pacing his chambers awaiting their arrival. He was a tall, good-looking man in his late thirties, fond of horses, hunting, and his ambassador—who had paid them extra to ensure Diago never heard about his recent need of their assistance.

"Alyas, Esar," the king exclaimed as they entered, approaching with arms wide for a typically enthusiastic Flaeresian greeting. Then he saw the sling and he stopped. He didn't just stop. He took a step back, his expression changing from welcome to caution. If it wasn't so unlikely, Esar would have called it fear. "You're hurt."

Alyas glanced at the sling then back at the king's face. "Five of my men are dead."

Diago exchanged a weighted look with his ambassador. "You will be compensated, of course. When did it happen?"

Alyas gave him a brief account of the disaster in Orsena. When he finished, he said, "There have been more attacks." It wasn't a question.

Diago grimaced, his face rather pale. "I'm sorry. When I sent you out there, I didn't know what you would be facing. It's only since you left that we've learned more—and it's not good."

"We know *that*," Esar said with feeling. It couldn't be much worse.

"Indeed," Gaemo agreed. "But…"

"But?" Esar demanded, crossing his arms. There was something they weren't being told and that was a direct breach of the terms of their agreement with the king. They were never sent anywhere without knowing all the facts. If that had happened here, Alyas *should* be furious. They had lost five friends. He had nearly died. His lack of reaction was unsettling.

"But," Gaemo said carefully, a wary eye on Esar, "to our knowledge, there have been no survivors of these attacks. Except you."

His gaze shifted to Alyas, who returned it without a flicker of expression. "So we were lucky."

"We weren't lucky," Esar growled, feeling he could be furious enough for the both of them if necessary. "We're good. That's why you sent us."

Gaemo held Alyas's gaze a moment longer before he looked away. Though their priorities had diverged over the years, though Gaemo's time in Lankara had changed him—his time as Diago's spy had changed him—this was the first time Esar wasn't sure they could trust him, and he didn't like it. "Of course. Your services will be much in demand. Perhaps even by your own king."

Esar snorted. "Raffa would rather cut off his own arm than call us home. That's never happening."

Gaemo gave a thin smile, but his eyes were worried. "Even so, when word of this spreads, rulers will be clamouring for aid." He shared a significant look with his king. "Flaeres would be glad to extend your current contract. We—"

Alyas shook his head. "We're going home. My people need rest."

Gaemo, with a frustrated glance at Esar, said, "Alyas—"

"No, we're going home."

"Of course," Diago agreed, too quickly. It was Gaemo who pushed, saying to Esar, "After that? What will you do?"

Esar frowned at the king and his ambassador. Something cold and hard settled in his stomach, that echoed the fear he had felt when he'd first seen the wound on Alyas's shoulder and realised what had made it. *When?* Diago had asked. Not 'what?' Not 'how?' "Why are you asking me?"

Gaemo held up his hands. "As I said—"

Alyas cut him off. "If you have need, you can send word."

He *was* angry, Esar realised. But even Esar, who was just as angry, could see that what Gaemo was proposing made sense. If this thing, whatever it was, was coming from the north, they would be needed here. Flaeres and neighbouring Hantara were the gateway to the rest of Ellasia. And Alyas would be close to Cassana, which could only be a good thing however you looked at it. But Alyas would not be moved. They were going home.

Gaemo might have continued to argue if Diago hadn't stopped him. The king seemed relieved, and Esar wanted to shake it out of him, whatever it was he wasn't saying. But he knew from experience that threatening kings rarely ended well.

"The compensation for your men?" Diago asked.

"Give it to the Temple of Yholis," Alyas said, already walking away, beckoning Esar with a tilt of his head.

Gaemo took a step after him. "Alyas. My sister…"

Alyas stopped dead, his back rigid. "I will tell her."

Gaemo looked like he wanted to say more. Alyas didn't give him a chance. "Esar."

With a last glare, Esar followed him. No one tried to stop them, but eyes watched their progress as they emerged from the palace and crossed the courtyard. He was quite sure, suddenly, that they wouldn't be back.

Storm was waiting outside, engaged in a staring contest with the guards on the palace gates who were eyeing his Qidan braids and visible weapons with suspicion. Flaeres and Qido were uncomfortable neighbours.

Storm straightened when he saw them, tossing a last wordless challenge at the Flaeresian guards. "City's packed. People coming in from the villages. Some bad rumours flying around. We've found rooms at the Falcon, but it cost four times what it should, Agazi says."

Esar grunted. Figured. The reality of those creatures was bad enough. He hated to think what rumour made of them. He was deliberately not thinking about what it all meant. "What now?" he asked Alyas. Cassana would expect him to stay for at least a few days—and he badly needed to rest before they made the journey home—but his words to Diago implied they would not be hanging around.

Alyas confirmed this. "We go home. Tomorrow."

Esar exchanged a look with Storn. "We just leave?" Yholis knew, he wanted nothing more than to be safely back at their camp, but there was trouble coming, trouble that wouldn't stop at the mountains. And they were all exhausted. Alyas wasn't wrong about that.

Alyas, however, appeared not to hear.

Storn was frowning, his face worried.

"Cassana?" Esar ventured. If anyone could persuade Alyas to rest, it was Cassana.

"I will tell her," Alyas said. "Then we go."

"Why?" They could recover here as well as anywhere. It didn't make sense.

With a last look at the palace, Alyas turned his back and began to walk. "Because we have things to do, and I don't have much time."

THE LAST TIME

CASSANA

The last time Cassana Gaemo saw Alyas-Raine Sera was a year before he died. Because she did not count the final time. She could not think of that husked-out shell of a man in the temple as Alyas, as her Alyas. He had been half-dead already, barely there, and she'd held his hand for the three days it took him to die and hated him again for leaving her.

She knew what he had done, everyone did. His name was a curse, a cypher for all the suffering and hardship that followed in the wake of the syndicates' fall. Diago blamed him for her brother's death. He had raged about it for days when news first reached them, but even though he'd known Alyas was in Sarenza, even though it had been Diago himself who'd told her, he did not lift a finger against him. There was no point. There was nothing Diago could do to him that he had not done to himself, and worse. And she thought, perhaps, that the king had understood what no one else seemed to—that what Alyas had done had been *necessary*.

But she would not think about that. No, the last time she saw him was the year before, and it was not a good memory, just a better one. He had come to her in Sarenza, straight from the palace, his arm in a sling and his face hollowed out by pain and exhaustion. And something she had never seen before. Fear.

"Cassana," he said, and it was like the first time. A breath of pain. He *needed* her then as he had never needed her before, needed the peace only she could give him, but this was different, deeper. He was so distressed that she sent a messenger to find Esar, to tell him where his brother was, because she knew how much Esar worried, and if he had any idea what kind of state Alyas was in, he would be frantic.

She also sent a message to the temple, because there was red blood on his clothes.

It wasn't a good memory, but it was still better than the other.

They had come from Orsena on the Qidan border. She had seen him three weeks before, on his way out. He had been fine. Distracted, on edge, but fine. He wasn't fine now as he told her what had happened, what he could remember of it, while her eyes strayed to the blood stains and she tried to make him eat. But he just sat there with his head in his hands, white-knuckled fists pressed to his temples. "I can't keep them out anymore," he said. "They are screaming, *screaming*, at me."

A cold weight settled in her chest. *They.* His father's blades. The voices in the steel.

She knew what the blades did to him. She was alone in that. Not even Esar knew what they cost him. *Especially* not Esar. She took them from him and placed them on her dresser, and he let her. Then she took him to her bed and did her best to soothe that fear, to take it from him, but gently, because he was so tired and hurt, the ugly wound in his shoulder still oozing blood.

It worried her, that wound, already a week old but so raw. Once he was asleep, she cut away the stained bandage and wrapped it in a clean one. Her surgeon would look at it in the morning. After that, she climbed into the bed beside him, the bed that was so cold and empty when he was gone, feeling the sharp outline of bone that stirred fear deep in her chest—when had he become so thin?—and gave him the comfort of her presence that guarded against dreams.

When the insipid light of dawn woke her hours later, the bed was once again cold and empty, but he had not gone far. He was sitting in a chair by the dresser, staring at the blades. The bandage she had put on the night before was spotted with red.

"Alyas?"

He turned his head. "Cassana." The fear was gone from his eyes. In its place was sheer exhaustion, as though he didn't have the energy to be afraid anymore.

The silver-blue of Isyr glinted in the morning light, and she slipped from the bed and covered it with a cloth. Then she took him by the hand and coaxed him back into the bed where he drifted into an uneasy sleep.

Her surgeon arrived, an elderly man who had served her family for decades. He clicked his tongue when he saw the wound and Alyas turned his face away, answering the old man's questions without looking at him.

The surgeon was as gentle as he could be, but he had to take out the old stitches and put in new ones, and by the end of it, Alyas was as pale as the sheets on which he lay. Then the surgeon asked her to leave the room, and she knew then that she would lose him, that he was dying, and something in her that he had set alight died down to ashes.

Esar arrived while the surgeon was still with Alyas and she was sitting frozen in her salon, the day moving around her as her world stood still. She had not thought about Gaden in years, but she thought about him now. It had been just like this, and she didn't know if she could bear it again. She could not.

Esar was speaking. She looked up. His words were meaningless; she didn't understand anything. He frowned. "Cass?"

"Esar."

He drew up a chair, sat before her, concerned eyes studying her face. "What's wrong, Cass? Where's Alyas?"

And that's when it hit her. He didn't know. How could he not know?

Her surgeon appeared and she stood, Esar rising with her, taking in the green of Yholis's disciples with dawning realisation.

The surgeon did not seem surprised to see Esar there, merely asked his name, and she realised Alyas had known Esar would come and had given his permission for the surgeon to speak to them, to tell them what he could not tell them himself.

He did not try to soften it. He was not an unkind man, but he had been doing this for more years than she had lived and knew there was nothing that could soften such news, that however he phrased it, the outcome was the same. The man they both loved was dying.

Esar took the news badly, his face twisting in anger. "No, he was fine. Yesterday, he was *fine.*"

Cassana thought of the state Alyas had been in when he had come to her and did not understand how Esar, who knew him so well, could have missed it. But sometimes she thought Alyas kept his guard up with Esar more than any other person. That he would, at all costs, protect him. It was why he had never told his brother of the toll the blades took on him, of the nightmares they gave him, or what they made him think and feel. Not even the promise made after Lessing could change that. Alyas would protect Esar as long as he could, but this… this was something he couldn't shield him from. Not anymore.

The surgeon regarded Esar with sympathy. "He has not been fine for some days, I suspect. From the little we have learned of this disease, you can expect it to be quick."

She saw Esar's face close down, his wilful *refusal* to hear.

"What? What will be quick?"

Cassana sat, pulling him with her. She pressed a hand to his cheek, forcing him to look at her. "Esar." She could not keep the tears from her voice. He heard them, flinching away from her touch. It hit him then. She saw the pain go sharp and deep and would have done anything, *anything*, to take that look from his face, because it was on hers too.

The surgeon was not an unkind man, but a kinder man would have recognised their need to absorb that news before he gave them worse. He was oblivious to the moment, delivering information in his steady, emotionless voice. "I can only guess, but I would say anywhere from a few days to a few weeks."

Days? The breath went out of her. She had expected months, like Gaden, and she was already bracing herself to face that. But days? *No.*

The surgeon was talking. Neither she nor Esar heard what he said. There was nothing he could say that she wanted to hear.

With parting instructions to call for him as they needed, her surgeon left. They stood looking at each other, caught together in the moment, then Esar spun away, marching out into the hallway and taking the stairs two at a time, calling out to Alyas.

"I'm here. You don't have to shout," he replied, appearing from her room. He sounded so normal, so contained, not at all like the man who had appeared on her doorstep the night before, hurting and desperate. He had dressed, the layers of clothing hiding the way his flesh had shrunk tight around muscle and bone, but the daylight exposed the pallor of his face and nothing could hide the shadows that had taken up permanent residence under his eyes.

Still, the energy and normality stopped Esar in his tracks. Alyas rested a hand on his shoulder as he passed. "I need to talk to Cass. Wait for me outside?"

"Stay," she pleaded when they were alone, but she knew already that he would not, that he would not force her to watch him die, as she had watched her husband die. Nor could he simply sit still and wait. He would be moving, doing, *fighting*, until he couldn't. If she made him stay with her, it would kill him as surely as this wound.

"Cassie." His fingers were twined in her hair, and his face…

"Don't," she said. Her cheeks were wet with tears; they wouldn't stop. "Please."

His hand tightened in her hair. "Cass, you've given me everything. This isn't over. I don't give up."

I don't give up.

But that's exactly what he did, in the end. When even the comfort she could give him wasn't enough. When there was nothing in the world that could make him able to live with what he'd done.

I don't give up.

It was a promise he couldn't keep and he knew it, they both did, but he meant it anyway, because otherwise this was the end and neither of them could bear that.

She let him go. She let him pretend he was fine, that he would be back; it was the least she could do. And she watched him walk to where Esar waited. Slowly, because he was tired, and he would not want to face Esar's denial and grief any more than he had wanted to face hers.

Cassana was too far away to hear what they said to each other, but she saw Esar shake his head, anger in every line of him. Alyas put a hand on his shoulder and they stood like that for an age, until Esar wrapped a hand round his brother's neck and pulled him closer, their foreheads touching.

Alyas broke the contact first. Whatever he said, it made Esar splutter with laughter or anger, probably both, and before he could recover, Alyas was walking.

She wanted to run after him, to beg him to stay. To break down and *plead*. But to do that would be to shatter the illusion of this moment, and she could not do that to him or to Esar.

Neither could she turn away.

He looked back, once, before he passed through her gates. Back to the window where she waited. He could not see her from that distance, not with the morning sun hitting the glass, but he would know she was there. He did nothing, just paused, looking back. Then, Esar's hand on his shoulder, he turned and walked out of her life.

That was the last time she saw the man she loved. Because she did not count the final time. She would not think about it, or the year he lived after he'd left her that morning, or what he had done. Instead, she held tight to the memory of the young man in her garden at midnight, laughing as she scolded him, and even though she had hated him then, she had always loved his laugh.

She took the letter with its small package that he gave her before he died, but she could not bring herself to send it, giving it instead to the temple. She had been angry that he was here, like this, alone. The temple could send it on. Then she waited. And sure enough, two months later, Esar appeared at her door.

They looked at each other across her empty salon, the two people who had loved him best, and her anger left her in rush.

Esar had come fearing he would have to break the news, and she had been prepared to hate him for leaving his brother to die alone. But then he came, and she saw that he was just as devastated, that he had lost just as much, and that, like her, he did not yet know how to live with it.

They were sitting on the floor. She didn't remember how it happened, only that her eyes were red and sore and his were no better, and that something poisonous had been cleansed from her.

"Did you know?" she asked him. "Did you know what he would do?"

Esar shook his head. "I should have. I should have realised. Because of Lessing."

Lessing, where Alyas had shown he was prepared to throw his life away to thwart the syndicates, even over so small a thing as the Ivane box. But after Lessing, he and Esar had reached an understanding. After that disaster, Alyas had made his brother a promise, and Esar would have trusted that promise, because when Alyas said he'd do something—or not do something—he meant it.

Some things, though, turned all promises to ash. She tried to imagine what it must have cost him to betray Esar's trust like that, to use that promise to hide his intentions, and found she could not. It hurt too much.

Because Esar would have forgiven him the moment he walked away.

She was crying again, and so was he. And it didn't help, it didn't make it *better*, but it eased some of the unbearable pressure in her chest.

They talked; they remembered; they cried some more. Then Esar said, "I'm sorry about Melar."

Cassana nodded and turned away, because it hurt.

Alyas had written to her, and while he'd still been able to, they had talked. She knew about the boy from the temple, the apprentice surgeon who'd saved his life not once but twice and had wormed his way into Alyas's heart. It was his name she had given to the temple for the letter, the letter with its tiny, precious gift of hope.

She knew about Mari's choice; she knew about the syndicates.

She knew about Melar.

She had burned that letter. Not from anger, though she had been angry. But because his pain and exhaustion and despair had ached through every word, and she had been too far away. It was the four hundred all over again, except this time they were his company, his people, his friends, and Melar and Diago had let them die. Maybe they couldn't have saved them, but they hadn't even tried. And it had broken something in him. She had felt the jagged pieces in that letter. So she'd burned it and remembered instead that night in her garden before everything had changed. Before it changed them.

"He made his choice," she said now. For Melar, it would have been the only choice. Diago. Flaeres. First and always. Who was she to say it was the wrong one? He too had been true to himself, and he had always been clear about what he was fighting for. "But I loved him."

The tears came again, this time for the brother she had lost. The brother who, in many ways, she had started to lose the day Raffa-Herun ripped the peace treaty to shreds. It was a bitter lesson and Melar had taken it to heart. The more deeply entangled he'd become in the murkier side of statecraft, the more that frivolous, irreverent façade she'd cherished had become just that: a façade. Under it had been something much harder and more ruthless that she had not recognised and hadn't wanted to. A necessary hardening, she supposed, for the world he'd inhabited, but one that saddened her.

And in the end, Melar and Diago had made the fatal mistake of standing by and allowing the syndicates to destroy the people Alyas had spent his life protecting. If not for her, Alyas would have killed Melar himself. Because of her, her brother's death was one more burden of guilt.

"What will you do?" she asked Esar eventually, when she had no more tears left to shed.

"What can I do?" he asked bitterly. "I have to keep going. Alyas made sure of that. And I have Frey and our daughter." A small smile broke through when he spoke of them. Alyas had told her about that, too. "What will you do?"

She already knew that, the practical, anyway. Diago had extended his protection, a place in his household, honouring his debt to her brother, and she had accepted, though the thought of a life at court after all she had endured, whatever that might look like in the years ahead, was almost too much to bear. But she was alone now in a world that was dark and threatening and uncertain. She was not brave enough to face that on her own. The house was already packed. She had only been waiting for Esar before she left it forever.

That was how she would survive; she had no idea how she would live.

Esar seemed relieved, as though it was something he had worried about. He would have worried about it. That was the man he was, and she held part of Alyas in her heart, so Esar would worry and want to help. Then he said, "He didn't keep anything. He sold it all or gave it away to... do what he did."

Of course he had. She had thought of him once that he would do whatever it took to get what he wanted, and then been ashamed because what he'd wanted was to save lives. This was the same, only so much bigger.

"But there is one thing he wanted for you."

"What?"

From the hallway came the *tap tap* of a cane. Cassana climbed to her feet, looking to Esar in confusion.

"Me."

Hailene-Sera Ahn stood in the doorway to her salon, older, frailer, determined. There were tears in her eyes. "Can you forgive me?" she asked Cassana. "I gave him what he needed and I knew he couldn't survive it. But someone had to do it, and there was no one else."

She'd thought she had no more tears to shed. She was wrong. Then, after a while, she found Hailene a chair and Esar made some tea, and she asked, "Why have you come?" The journey from Avarel to Sarenza was long and arduous—dangerous, as all journeys were now—and Hailene was not young. *She* was not young. In four months, she would be fifty. Alyas had been forty-four.

Hailene-Sera sipped her tea. "Because my nephew always did think he knew best, and he thought this would be best for both of us."

"I don't understand."

"My dear," said Alyas's aunt. "I am old, I won't live forever, and when I die, I have no one to inherit what I have built."

Cassana set down her cup, looking from Hailene to Esar. "You want to give it to me?" Alyas had asked his aunt for this? She had no need of Hailene's wealth. No one would in what was coming. "That is generous, but I don't need—"

"I'm not talking about my money, girl," Hailene said with a spark of the asperity Cassana remembered so well. "Though you can have that, too. I'm talking about something much more valuable."

"Aunt Hailene has the most extensive network of spies in the whole of Ellasia," Esar murmured, blowing on his hot tea to cool it. "It would put Melar's to shame."

"Yes, and we need them more than ever. Someone needs to ensure that we see this through. Esar can't do it alone. Come live with me.

Help me, and I will put all my secrets into your hands."

It was too much. She couldn't take it in. She couldn't do this. "I—"

Hailene reached out to take her hand. "Don't tell me you can't," she said. "You already have. How many times have you carried news for me or for him?"

Cassana shook her head. "It's not the same. I don't know how…"

"That's what I'll teach you," Hailene assured her, then she blinked, tears in her eyes. "Cassana, he knew you would be alone, that you would be lost. He wanted you to have a purpose, a reason to live. Let me give you one. Help make this future worth his sacrifice."

And what, in the end, could she say to that?

CHARACTERS

Agazi – member of the company.
Ailuin – chief of the Lathai tribe.
Alondo – Lankaran, Varistan of the Temple of Yholis in Avarel.
Alyas-Raine Sera – Lankaran, formerly Duke of Agrathon, exiled by King Raffa-Herun Geled, foster brother of Esar Cantrell.
Aubron – member of the company.
Brivar – Lankaran, apprentice surgeon at the Temple of Yholis in Avarel.
Cassana Gaemo – Flaeresian, sister of Melar Gaemo.
Corado – Lankaran, captain in the King's Guard.
Della – member of the company.
Diago – King of Flaeres.
Eldruin – Lathai, son of Ailuin.
Elenia – Lankaran, Varisten of the Temple of Yholis in Avarel.
Esar Cantrell – Lankaran, foster brother of Alyas-Raine Sera.
Fazio Vanni – Hantaran, silversmith in Lessing.
Frey – member of the company.
Hailene-Sera Ahn – Lankaran, Alyas's aunt.
Georgios Beor – Prince of Hantara.
Gerrin-Raine Sera – father of Alyas, foster father of Esar.
Gorlanis – Flaeresian, friends of Cassana.
Kael Ito – Hantaran, brother of Mitka Ito, head of the Selysian Syndicate.
Keie – member of the company.

Mari-Geled Herun – Queen of Lankara, formerly betrothed to Alyas-Raine Sera, grew up with Alyas and Esar.
Melar Gaemo – Flaeresian, ambassador to Lankara, brother of Cassana.
Mitka Ito – Hantaran, head of the Selysian Syndicate, brother of Kael.
Nicor-Heryd Zand – Lankaran, a captain in the King's Guard.
Raffa-Herun Geled – King of Lankara.
Sofia – Lankaran, half-sister to Raffa, married to Kael Ito.
Storn – member of the company.

GLOSSARY

Avarel – capital of Lankara.
Cadria – regional capital in western Lankara.
Donea, The – country bordered by Qido to the north, Flaeres and Hantara to the east and south.
Ellasia – name of the continent.
Flaeres – country in central Ellasia, bordering Qido, Lankara, and Hantara.
Hantara – country in central Ellasia, bordering Qido, Lankara, and Flaeres.
Isyrium – mineral used in every aspect of daily life, mined extensively by the syndicates.
Isyr (sometimes called northern steel) – extremely hard, valuable metal made from a highly purified form of Isyrium. It has not been possible to make Isyr since pure Isyrium ran out a century ago.
Ithol – one of Ellasia's twin deities, god of sun and storms, the harvest, craft, wealth, war and death.
Lankara – country in central Ellasia, bordered by Hantara and Flaeres to the north, the Steppes to the south.

Lathai – tribe that inhabits the mountains that form the northern border between Lankara and Flaeres.

Lessing – capital of Hantara.

Northern steel – another name for Isyr, a reference to the fact it was first discovered in Qido

Orleas – city in north-eastern Lankara.

Orsena – abandoned mining town in Flaeres on the border with Qido

Sarenza – capital of Flaeres.

Selysians – mining syndicate that operates in Hantara and western Lankara.

Steppes – the southern area of the Ellasian continent, ruled by various tribes.

Syndicates – regional federations of mining companies that formed after the Isyrium Wars, now powerful organisations that control the economy of the continent.

Qido – empire in northern Ellasia.

Varistan – title of male head of a temple of Ithol or Yholis. Rule of each temple is split equally between a Varistan and Varisten.

Varisten – title of female head of a temple of Ithol or Yholis.

Xhidan – (plural *xhiden*) – Lathai amulets given to members of the tribe in infancy according to their characteristics; believed to house their spirits after death. Some are made from Isyr.

Yholis – sister of Ithol, one of Ellasia's twin deities, goddess of spring, healing, fertility, and rebirth.

THANK YOU FOR READING

If you enjoyed this book and would like to stay up to date with future releases, writing news, and the occasional free story, please sign up to my newsletter.

andeira.net/newsletter

Finally, please consider leaving a review or even just telling your friends if you enjoyed this book—word of mouth and reviews are vital for authors and help us keep writing.

CREDITS

EDITOR
Sarah Chorn
bookwormblues.net

BETA READER
Rowena Andrews
beneathathousandskies.com

PROOFREADER
Isabelle Wagner
theshaggyshepherd.wordpress.com

COVER DESIGN
Mibl Art
miblart.com

ACKNOWLEDGEMENTS

When I finished *The Many Shades of Midnight*, I knew I would never write a sequel. I had told the story I wanted to tell, the story I *needed* to tell, and it was complete. But I wasn't done with the characters, and they weren't done with me, because they had so many stories still to tell. This book is a collection of some of those stories. Who knows, maybe there will be more one day?

That these stories are published at all, rather than just sitting on my computer, is thanks to all the people who read *The Many Shades of Midnight* and let me know they enjoyed it. So thank you to all my readers and reviewers and everyone who has supported me in any way. Your kind words and enthusiasm have been like oxygen.

More specifically, thank you to those who worked on these stories with me—my beta reader Rowena Andrews, editor Sarah Chorn, and proofreader Isabelle Wagner. I couldn't do it without you. And thanks also to Nick Procter for your behind-the-scenes support, and to Angela Boord, who never asked to be the recipient of my publishing questions but who answered them with patience and generosity.

Finally, thank you to everyone who has supported these books, shouted about them, or helped with this launch, in particular Rowena, Jamedi, Nathan, Nick, Krina, Michelle, Davie, Charlie, Isabelle, and Kevin. Your support means the world.

ALSO BY CM DEBELL

THE LONG DREAM
Silver Mage
Silver Dawn

TALES OF ISYR
The Many Shades of Midnight
In Midnight's Shadow

www.andeira.net

Printed in Great Britain
by Amazon